The
MAN WHO LOVED
JANE AUSTEN

The
MAN WHO LOVED
JANE AUSTEN

SALLY SMITH O'ROURKE

KENSINGTON BOOKS
http://www.kensingtonbooks.com

KENSINGTON BOOKS are published by

Kensington Publishing Corp.
850 Third Avenue
New York, NY 10022

All Kensington titles, imprints and distributed lines are available at special quantity discounts for bulk purchases for sales promotion, premiums, fund-raising, educational or institutional use.

Special book excerpts or customized printings can also be created to fit specific needs. For details, write or phone the office of the Kensington Special Sales Manager: Kensington Publishing Corp., 850 Third Avenue, New York, NY 10022. Attn. Special Sales Department. Phone: 1-800-221-2647.

Kensington and the K logo Reg. U.S. Pat. & TM Off.

ISBN 0-7582-1037-X

First Kensington Trade Paperback Printing: April 2006
10 9 8 7 6 5 4 3 2

Printed in the United States of America

For Jane Austen,
Jennifer Ehle and Colin Firth

But most of all for Michael, our Da,
My love, my friend, my soul mate.
This is our dream, the ultimate valentine,
As you said, it came out of the love
we had for each other
and will live in my heart forever . . .

Acknowledgments

With grateful appreciaton to
Daphne Maddison and Margaret Royle.
It was their unstinting enthusiasm that inspired
us to complete our journey through time.

A special acknowledgment and thanks to
Andy Stevenson and Mauricio Palacios
for their unparalled kindness during a very difficult
time in my life and for their help in preparing the book.

With love and appreciation to the Reno family—
Kate, Fred, Freddie, Kathleen, Jennifer,
Caroline, Shannon, Sarah, Shannon^2
and Mary Beth—who embraced me as one of
their own when I needed embracing most.
And love, too, to the newest members of the clan:
Chris, Hannah, Jimmy, Larry, Dan, Ryan and Blake.

And, of course, to "our" daughters,
Kyle and Kelly, whose love, support and
children—Nick, Sean, Alicia, Trey, and Ryan—
make my life a joy.

Time is too slow for those who wait,
Too swift for those who fear,
Too long for those who grieve,
Too short for those who rejoice,
But for those who love,
time is eternity.

—Henry Van Dyke

Foreword

The Man Who Loved Jane Austen is the embodiment of a dream. It is a fantasy viewed through the mists of time, in which Darcy, the enigmatic hero of *Pride and Prejudice,* is finally unmasked and Jane, the woman who created him, reveals the secret of her own true love.

But make no mistake, this is just a dream. Our dream, Mike's and mine. Not Jane Austen's. And though we have doubtless taken unconscionable liberties with the life and times of that illustrious author, we would like to think that Jane, of all people, would understand. And, at discovering herself playing the coveted role of the romantic heroine, even reward us with a smile.

This book is presented in three volumes, just as Jane Austen's books were published. During the Regency era, books were made by hand, and so for ease of creation and publication Jane Austen's books were issued in three separate volumes. We have included the three volumes of our fantasy, *The Man Who Loved Jane Austen,* in this one book.

Prologue

The slender young woman hurrying along a lonely woodland path beyond the village of Chawton this night seemed
heedless of the falling moisture that sprinkled her hair and
dampened the shoulders of her light cloak.

It had rained in the afternoon, a hard spring shower that
had passed over the wood in no more than ten minutes. And
though the downpour hadn't lasted long enough to muddy
the path that Jane now followed, the leaves of the overhanging trees were still shedding droplets that glittered like jewels
in the cold moonlight.

As she moved through the silent wood Jane imagined the
scandal that would erupt should a neighbor happen upon her
in this lonely place. For she was a respectable young woman
by any standard, the unmarried daughter of a clergyman with
aristocratic family connections, and youngest sister to the
owner of the great country house on which the village de-
pended. Which circumstance rendered her midnight foray all
the stranger. For Jane had never before dared nor even considered an adventure such as the one on which she was now
embarked.

Yet here she was, gliding wraithlike through the dark forest, en route to a clandestine meeting with a man—a mysterious and possibly dangerous man—whom she had known for scarcely five days. She prayed that he would be at the appointed spot, as he had promised. And she felt her heart thundering in her breast at the mere thought of what she had committed to share with him this night. She who had long since abandoned all hope of ever finding love.

She was thirty-four years old—an unremarkable spinster who lived an unremarkable life in a house provided by her devoted brother and shared with her elder sister and their aged mother. And, until fewer than twenty-four hours ago, she had never known a lover's caress.

But last night that had changed. Now Jane wanted nothing more than to be again with the man. For he had reawakened her girlhood dreams of love and romance, all the lovely dreams she had so carefully preserved on countless sheets of neatly inscribed vellum that she kept hidden away in the deepest recesses of her closet.

Of course, she fully realized, going to meet him like this was madness. But then, she reminded herself, madness had been the hallmark of their brief but intense relationship, a relationship that had been doomed from the start. For she could not go with him and he could not stay.

And if they were found out, she knew to a certainty, scandal and disgrace would be her only reward.

But love knows not reason. And Jane did not care what consequences might ensue. For, in her mind, the risks she was taking to meet with her new-found lover tonight were as nothing compared to the dread she felt, of slipping into her old age without ever having tasted love.

After a few more minutes she came to the edge of the woods, which bounded a broad meadow. Covered now in swirls of mist frosted by the light of a near-full moon, the grassy field had taken on an otherworldly look, like one of the fairy-tale landscapes she was forever imagining in her dreams. At the end of the path she hovered like a frightened deer, huddling in a pool of darkness beneath the dripping trees, until he should appear.

Presently, she heard the drumming of muffled hoofbeats from the far side of the meadow. Willing her joyously thudding heart to be still, Jane boldly detached herself from the sheltering shadows and advanced into the open, anxious not to waste a precious moment of the brief time they would have together.

Slowly a horseman emerged from the mist. Spying her moving through the grass, he altered the course of his great black steed to intercept her. Within seconds he reined to a halt beside her. His face was obscured beneath the brim of the tall hat he wore, and she ran forward to meet him as he dismounted. "I prayed you would come," she laughed, prepared to throw herself into his arms.

But instead of the joyous response she was anticipating, the rider nervously swept the tall hat from his head. The moonlight struck his plain, sun-reddened features and she saw to her mortification that he was not the one for whom she had so anxiously waited, but an awkward young servant named Simmons.

"Sorry, miss," the nervous messenger stammered, "the gentleman went away in a great hurry after the troops came. He had asked me to come and tell you if he could not get here himself tonight."

Jane felt herself flushing beneath the servant's questioning gaze. Her bitter disappointment at the broken rendezvous was overlaid by a sudden pang of fear. For young Simmons was a groom from her brother's stables, and she wondered how much he knew . . . or would tell.

"Oh . . . I see," she said, forcing her voice to remain calm, and wondering what motive the servant must be imagining had brought her to the lonely meadow at this ungodly hour. "Thank you, Simmons."

His unlined, honest features betraying no hint that he

thought the situation odd or particularly scandalous, Simmons fumbled in the pocket of his greatcoat and produced a folded letter sealed with wax. "This is for you, miss," he stammered, bowing slightly and extending the letter to her.

"From him?" Abandoning all pretense of calm, Jane eagerly accepted the envelope and attempted to read the address in the dim light.

"No, miss. It's the letter *you* sent to him," Simmons replied. And in his voice Jane heard something that sounded like sympathy as he hurried to explain. "The gentleman had already gone before it could be gotten to him."

Simmons paused then, as if considering his next words carefully. "There was such a row up at the manor house," he finally continued. "Well, I thought you'd want to have your letter back . . ."

Jane tucked the letter into the folds of her cloak and looked up at him, realizing that in the groom she had found an ally who would not betray her indiscretion. "Thank you, Simmons," she said again. "That was very thoughtful of you."

She hesitated awkwardly, aware that such loyalty should be rewarded. "I am afraid I have no money with me at the moment—" she began. But before she could suggest that she would have something for him on the morrow Simmons cut her off with a wave of one big, work-hardened hand.

"Don't you worry, miss," the young groom assured her with dignity, "I didn't come here for money. The gentleman was very good to me while he was here." Then his broad features creased in a smile and in a gentler tone he asked, "Shall I see you home now, miss?"

"Thank you, no," Jane replied, the little catch in her voice promising that tears would very soon follow. "It is only a short walk. You have been very good."

Simmons bowed again, then, taking a step backward he put on his tall hat and climbed back onto the black horse. Once mounted he looked down at Jane and leaned closer so she could hear. "I never met no one like him," he said softly. "He's the *best* gentleman I ever knew."

Jane nodded in silent agreement, feeling the hot tears welling up in her eyes and wondering what magic her mysterious lover had wrought to engender such regard on the part of this simple country lad. For it had suddenly occurred to her that Simmons was also at risk, both for having slipped away from her brother's manor at this late hour, as well as for having allowed himself to become an instrument in her conspiracy.

She had no time for further reflection, for the black horse was stamping its hooves, impatient now to be back in its warm stable. "Do you think the gentleman will ever come back, miss?" Simmons's voice was a barely audible whisper above the snorting of the animal.

Jane slowly shook her head. "I fear he may not be able, Simmons," she replied. "You had better go now, before you are missed."

The servant straightened, touched the brim of his hat, then wheeled the horse around and rode away across the meadow. Jane watched him until he was once more swallowed up in the mist.

A bright tear ran down her cheek as she looked up at the lowering moon. "So this is how it is to end?" she asked the cloud-streaked sky.

Turning to the wood, she ran into the trees and back along the moonlit path the way she had come. Soon the dark outlines of a large stone house appeared through the trees. Warm light was shining from an upper window, and Jane knew that Cassandra had awakened and discovered her gone.

Making her way across the broad lawn at the rear of the house, Jane quietly let herself in through a low wooden door. Inside the kitchen the glow of embers in the fireplace provided the only light. Moving as quietly as possible across the flagged stone floor, Jane removed her cloak and hung it near the fireplace to dry. She took a candle in a copper holder from the mantel and lit it with a broom straw. Then, pausing just long enough to brush away her tears, she left the kitchen and walked through a dark hallway to the center of the house.

She had just reached the foot of the wide central staircase when she heard a footstep and saw the glimmering of another candle on the landing above.

"Jane, is that you?" Cassandra, her heavy plaits of golden hair falling about the shoulders of her nightgown, stood peering down into the dark stairwell, her soft features filled with concern.

"Yes, Cass, I am just coming up." Fixing a cheerful smile on her lips, Jane hurried upstairs. She reached the upper landing to find her older sister regarding her with frank amazement.

"Surely you have not been out again at this hour," Cassandra asked. "It is well past midnight."

"I felt like walking in the moonlight," Jane replied, brushing past the astonished Cass and making quickly for the door to her room.

"The moonlight?" Cassandra, who could always tell when Jane was lying, moved to block her way, forcing Jane to look directly into her steady gray eyes. "Jane, what have you been up to?"

Jane shrugged, attempting to inject a carefree note into her voice. "I have heard it said that Lord Byron highly commends the moonlight, when he is courting the muse," she replied brightly.

"And I have heard that the wicked young lord goes abroad at night only to court ladies of dubious reputation," Cassandra retorted. "What *have* you been doing, sister?"

Once again Jane felt her tears threatening to burst forth. She shook her head stubbornly. "I have done nothing either very dubious or very wicked," she replied. And in her mind's eye she glimpsed the handsome features of the man she had gone to meet. "I was not given an opportunity," she murmured with regret.

Cassandra's mouth fell open. But before she could find adequate words to express her shock, Jane kissed her on the cheek and pushed past her. "Good night, Cass," she whispered as she reached the door to her room.

Cassandra's lined features softened and she regarded her younger sister with concern. "Dearest Jane, you know you can confide in me," she said softly. "Please tell me what has happened?"

"Oh, Cass, I am not yet certain," Jane replied, feeling the salty wetness beginning to sting her cheeks. "Perhaps my foolish heart has been broken at last." She sniffled and managed a little smile. "I shall have to reflect on it and let you know in the morning."

Then without another word she entered her bedroom and firmly shut the door behind her, leaving Cassandra alone in the hallway to wonder.

Lit only by her single candle, the large, cheerful room that Jane loved so well by day was now a warren of leaping shadows. They danced impishly across the flowered wallpaper and pooled deep in the corners behind the bed as she walked to her mirrored vanity by the fireplace. Placing the candle on the table, Jane sat and began slowly taking down her elaborately curled hair, allowing the shining dark tresses to fall loose.

When she was done, she regarded her dim reflection in the mirror, raising one pale hand to touch the silvery-looking glass with her fingertips. "Only one of us is real," she said quietly to that other Jane who sat gazing at her from the glass, "the other is but an illusion. The question is, which am I?"

Removing the undelivered letter from her gown, she placed it on the dressing table before her and stared down at the address she had so neatly written there a lifetime ago. She was startled from her reverie by an insistent knocking at the door.

"Jane, do let me in," Cassandra entreated. "I will not sleep a wink until you have told me what has happened."

"What *has* happened?" Jane repeated in a voice so soft that only she could hear. "That, dear sister, is one thing that I will never tell you."

She scooped up the letter as Cassandra knocked again. "Jane!" she called, demanding now to be let in.

"Just a moment, Cass." With a heavy sigh Jane pushed back from the vanity, bowing to the inevitability of admitting her sister. Ever since they were small children Cass had always been the one who had soothed her hurts and given her the courage to go on. That would never change, certainly not now that *he* was gone.

Picking up the letter, she looked quickly around the dimly lit room. "And what *am* I to do with this?" she wondered aloud. For she could not reveal its contents, even to Cass, nor did she dare destroy it because of the secret it contained.

Jane caught her own worried reflection looking back at her from the shimmering depths of the mirror as Cass's knocking grew louder.

Volume One

Chapter 1

New York City
Present day

"Oh, now I do like this!" Eliza Knight exclaimed, though there was no one within earshot.

She brushed a thick layer of dust from the mirror of the scarred little vanity table and peered into the silvery glass. The sudden appearance of her own reflection startled her and she paused for a moment to regard the hazy image. The familiar face looking back at her was, she thought, if not exactly beautiful, then slightly exotic, with its high cheekbones, straight if somewhat narrow nose and full lips. Her dark eyes were, she confirmed, still her best feature, though she also liked her glossy black hair, despite the longish, flyaway cut she'd let her hairdresser talk her into a couple of weeks before.

Grimacing at the hair, Eliza stepped back to take a better look at the old-fashioned rosewood dressing table. In the hour or so that she had been poking through the clutter of the shabby West Side antiques warehouse that was allegedly open only to the "Trade," the vanity was the only thing that had caught her eye. She had spied it just moments earlier, crammed between an art deco floor lamp and a Jetsons pink

1950s Formica coffee table, and had immediately felt herself drawn to it.

Taking her eyes from the dulled mirror, Eliza scanned the rows of dusty merchandise stretching in every direction like a bad Cubist painting. She finally spotted Jerry Shelburn three aisles away. He appeared to be taking stock of an ancient gasoline pump with a cracked glass top.

"Jerry," she called excitedly, "I want your opinion. Come over here and take a look at this!"

Jerry had gotten them admitted to the wholesaler's warehouse through one of his clients, who ran a small freight-forwarding business. Now he smiled good-naturedly and waved back. He carefully replaced the brass nozzle on the gas pump before starting toward her, the round lenses of his wire-framed glasses glittering like little moons beneath the cold fluorescents of the overhead fixtures.

Eliza sighed inwardly as she watched him picking his way through the maze of old furniture, noting the extraordinary care he took not to soil his Old Navy khakis and spotless cotton pullover. They had met two years earlier, through an artist friend of hers, when Eliza had been looking for someone to manage the small investment portfolio her father had left her. Jerry had turned out to be an excellent manager, increasing the value of her stocks by nearly thirty percent in the first year and then shrewdly using the capital to secure the down payment on the condo that also served as her studio, thus eliminating more than half the taxes she'd been paying as a renter.

Somehow while all of that was going on they had started dating and then, occasionally, sleeping together. It was marginally comfortable and definitely low maintenance on both sides. There had been a few times in recent months when she had felt as though the relationship was either going to progress into something more serious or end altogether, and had to admit that it wouldn't really bother her that much if it did end. Feeling slightly mercenary, she consoled herself with the thought that at least her net worth had never been higher.

Turning her attention back to the vanity table, Eliza dragged it out into the aisle and slowly ran her strong artist's hands over the marred top. Despite its numerous scratches, the old wood felt comfortably warm to her touch. The slightly formal, squared-off design vaguely reminded her of a Georgian piece she'd seen in one of her antique guidebooks, and she wondered how old it really was.

"So, what rare treasure have you uncovered?"

Eliza raised her eyes to the mirror and saw Jerry adjusting his glasses to peer over her shoulder.

"Look," she said, stepping away to afford him a clear view of the vanity, "isn't it adorable?"

"I thought you were looking for a floor lamp," he said, barely glancing at the table.

"I was," Eliza replied peevishly, "but I really like this. It's kind of charming, don't you think?"

"Hmmm . . ." Frowning as if he'd just been served a piece of tainted fish, Jerry leaned over and examined a tiny pink sticker that Eliza hadn't noticed adhering to the side of the vanity. "At six hundred dollars it's not *that* charming," he sniffed. "Besides, the mirror's a mess." Jerry straightened and gave her a patronizing wink. "As your investment counselor, I heartily recommend going with a lamp."

Chapter 2

Fresh from a scalding shower, swaddled in her threadbare, old terry robe with her hair wrapped in a towel, Eliza stepped barefoot into her bedroom and regarded the prized vanity, which looked right at home among the mismatched collection of antique furniture filling the room.

"I really want your honest opinion now," she said, turning to look at the figure sprawled carelessly across the colorful patchwork quilt covering her Victorian-era four-poster bed. "Do you think I made an awful mistake?"

Wickham, an overweight gray tabby with a severe personality disorder, spread his considerable jaws wide and yawned to demonstrate his complete indifference to her question.

Not to be so easily deterred, Eliza scooped up the cat in her arms and crossed to the corner by the window, where Jerry had somewhat sullenly deposited the antique dressing table two hours earlier. The hazed rectangular mirror stood on the floor beside the table, leaning against the wall. After admiring the newly acquired pieces for a moment Eliza sank cross-legged onto the carpet before them, cradling the squirming cat in her lap.

"I think the whole problem with Jerry and our relationship," she explained to Wickham, "can be summed up in this table. Because when I look at it I see something warm and beautiful. But all Jerry sees is a piece of used furniture. You're a creature of discerning taste. What do you see, Wickham?"

Eliza smiled and scratched the special spot between Wickham's ears. The cat's yellow eyes rolled back in his head and he stiffened and moaned in ecstasy.

"My point exactly!" Eliza gloated. "Because, unlike you and me, Jerry has no soul, just a bottom line." She released her grip on Wickham, who leaped out of her lap and settled himself comfortably on the carpet.

"It really is a lovely piece," she said, gently reaching to stroke the satiny finish of an unscarred table leg. It needed major cleaning and some linseed oil but she was pretty sure that it was very old.

As Eliza carefully removed the single drawer from the table, setting it on the floor before her, she noticed that it was lined with now-faded pink wallpaper that still retained a floral pattern. Ignoring the liner, she turned the drawer around and examined the outside corners, which had been fitted together without nails.

The slightly irregular dovetails holding the sides of the drawer together meant they were obviously cut by hand, reinforcing her belief that the table was old, crafted before the age of machine-made, mass-produced furniture.

Eliza smiled ruefully, for though she was entirely correct about the dovetails, she had also exhausted virtually the entire store of knowledge she remembered from the NYU evening extension class she'd taken two years earlier on appraising antique furniture.

Nevertheless, she turned the drawer over to inspect the bottom, vaguely recalling something about being sure the wood colors matched or didn't match or something. The pink liner fluttered to the floor, coming to rest upside down on the carpet.

Interested at last, Wickham swatted at the crumbling paper. Eliza shooed him away and then stared in surprise at the liner. For adhering to its underside was another strip of yellowing paper densely covered in cramped black type.

"Look, Wickham, it's a piece of . . . old newspaper!" she exclaimed, squinting to read the oddly shaped and embellished letters. "Listen to this," she breathed, tracing with her index finger a heavier line of print bannered across the top of the sheet: "THE HAMPSHIRE CHRONICLE, 7 APRIL, 1810 . . . My God, that was almost two hundred years ago!"

Her attention now riveted by the partial sheet of ancient newsprint, Eliza carefully lifted it onto the top of the vanity and spent the next few minutes curiously poring over several tightly packed columns of ads for "Gentlemen's best quality silk cravats," "beneficial beef extracts," "drayage and forwarding" (whatever they might be), and a host of other mysterious products with names like Gerlich's Female Potion, calibrated boiling thermometers and India rubber goods.

When finally her eyes tired of squinting at the strange, old-fashioned print she gave the sturdy little table another cursory inspection. Then she knelt beside the mirror and stood it upright, noticing again with some dismay that the silvered surface was, as Jerry had pointed out in the warehouse, badly worn.

Cheerfully dismissing the hazing as enhancing the overall charm of the piece, she experimentally tilted the mirror toward her and was distressed to see that the wood backing on one side was pulling away from the frame. "Oh, great! The backing seems to be warped," she murmured to the cat. "Now give me some support here, Wickham, I'd hate to have to admit that Jerry might have been right after all."

Wickham stretched and meowed.

"Thanks," Eliza grinned. "I needed that."

She pulled the mirror to her and turned it around to get a better look at the damaged backing. To her relief, though, the visible gap appeared to be no more than six inches long. "Well, it's not as bad as I thought," she said. "I think it only needs to be reglued." With her fingernail she experimentally lifted the edge of the backing from the mirror frame in an attempt to determine how far the separation extended. As she did so, something fell out of the mirror and landed on the carpet with a soft plop.

Attracted by the sudden motion, Wickham leaped onto the fallen object and hissed menacingly. Eliza pushed him away and stared at the thing in surprise. She slowly leaned the mirror back against the wall, then reached down and lifted the fallen object into the light.

She remained frozen on her knees for several seconds, gazing at her hand while she tried to reconstruct what had just happened. For she was holding a slim packet of thick, sepia-toned paper tied together like a Christmas package with a crisscross of bright green ribbon.

"Good Lord," she whispered, letting her eyes dart back to the mirror and glimpsing her own puzzled expression.

Something swatted against her hand and she looked down to see Wickham resolutely batting at the end of the bright ribbon. Snatching her hand away from him, she got to her feet and examined the packet more closely. Held together by the broad ribbon, she saw, were two rectangles of folded paper. The one on top was smaller than the other and had been written across in reddish brown ink, the words obscured by the ribbon covering them.

"Letters!" she exclaimed.

Eliza turned the packet over and saw that the larger of the two letters had been sealed with a blob of shiny red material that she guessed must be sealing wax, though it looked like no other wax she had ever seen, having more the consistency of brittle plastic. Intrigued, she carefully untied the ribbon securing the packet, so that she could read the address on the top envelope.

"'Miss Jane Austen, Chawton Cottage' . . . *Jane Austen!*"

Stunned by the name of the famous nineteenth-century author, Eliza paused and took a deep breath before she could read the remainder of the address on the letter. Jane Austen! Again she had to pause as her eyes raced ahead of her trembling lips. "'Jane Austen ~ Mr. Fitzwilliam Darcy, Chawton Great House,'" she squeaked.

Eliza stood there on her bedroom carpet for several more seconds, silently reading and rereading the words inscribed neatly across the front of the smaller envelope.

The thoughts racing through Eliza's head at that moment were somewhat difficult to define. For although she would not have classified herself as a voracious reader, she was well-enough read, her tastes running largely to popular fiction with a smattering of respectable old favorites, ranging from the works of Agatha Christie and Damon Runyon to a few major poets and several classical novelists.

And, like many women, one of Eliza's very favorite novels, numbered among half a dozen well-worn books occupying the small shelf beneath her bedside table, was *Pride and Prejudice*, Jane Austen's timeless story of Miss Elizabeth Bennet's uncompromising quest for a perfect love.

Which is only to say that Eliza Knight knew precisely who Jane Austen was, and she certainly knew who Fitzwilliam Darcy, the purported recipient of the letter she now held in her hand, was, or at least who he was supposed to be.

With the letters in her hand she went to the bed and sat down. Gazing at the window, her reflection surrounded by a moonlit halo, Eliza's imagination swirled with what ifs and could it bes. She smiled to herself. Jerry would be laughing and berating her for such romantic notions and, in truth, as wildly romantic as the idea was, it was ludicrous, patently absurd; because the relationship suggested by the enigmatic address on the letter was flatly impossible. Darcy was, after all, a fictitious character, wasn't he?

Looking down at Wickham, who had followed her to the bed, she said, "Well, there's only one way to find out: read the letters."

In spite of her well-founded skepticism as to the authenticity of the letters, Eliza felt her heart trip-hammer in her chest and her hands tremble as she opened the larger of the two letters: the one that was addressed to Jane Austen from Fitzwilliam Darcy with the broad, scrawled pen strokes of a man's hand. She read aloud:

12 May, 1810

Dearest Jane,
    The Captain has found me out. I am being forced to go into hiding immediately. But if I am able, I shall still be waiting at the same spot tonight. Then you will know everything you wish to know.

F. Darcy

Eliza paused to consider the meaning of those few sparse sentences. And when she began to read it over again there was a slight quaver in her voice. For this was not at all what she had expected. Though, on momentary reflection, she was not quite sure exactly what she had expected to find in Darcy's letter—some flowery romantic tribute, perhaps, or a poetic declaration of undying love to a lady fair. How odd . . . being found out, going into hiding. What did that mean? Maybe the other letter was Austen's reply and so held the answers.

Slipping the first letter behind the other in her hand, she examined it with awe. The lovely feminine handwriting flowed across the page and, turning it over in her hands, she saw that the sealing wax was still intact, a fanciful letter *A* impressed into it. This one had never been read, maybe never sent. Why? Tracing the curves of the seal with the tip of her finger she curiously experienced a tingling sensation that shot like a jolt of electricity through her body.

"Wickham, can you imagine what it would mean if the letter really was written by Jane Austen?" She looked at the cat, who was unconcernedly applying his long pink tongue to one of his wickedly clawed front paws. Eliza sighed, "No, of course you can't, you poor thing, you have no forehead."

Looking at the letter she turned it over and over again in her hands. If it was genuine and she opened it, she would forever be known as the stupid artist who ruined a historic document.

Before she burned her bridges, Eliza decided she needed to try and find out something about the fictitious Mr. Darcy. Maybe the Internet would give her the answers she sought.

Chapter 3

In sharp contrast to Eliza's bedroom—which, with its eclectic collection of old wooden furniture, framed prints and warm fabric accents, could only be described as cozy—the living room of her small condo (actually the workroom and studio where she created her art and operated her Internet gallery) was all twenty-first-century business.

In front of the large window that allowed her to look directly into the wheelhouses of passing freighters on the East River were arrayed her white IKEA computer desk and drawing board, and beside them the wide steel filing cabinets, airbrush, paints and other equipment necessary to her work.

Hanging on the otherwise bare walls were several meticulous illustrations of the idyllic, flower-filled country landscapes and other natural and whimsical subjects in which she specialized.

With the envelopes in her hand and her bare feet tucked into a pair of warm sheepskin moccasins, Eliza crossed the polished hardwood floor of her studio and seated herself on the tall chrome-and-leather stool at her drawing board. Taking care first to cover the painting of a woodland cottage to which she'd been adding a mistily airbrushed backdrop of thickly forested mountains, she laid the two envelopes on the board side by side and switched on her halogen work light.

Outside the moon caressed the surface of the river with a ribbon of silver light and while her rational mind believed firmly that the letters were some kind of elaborate hoax, she couldn't stop the flights of fancy inspired by the implausible correspondence. Shaking off the romantic thoughts as silly schoolgirl fantasies, Eliza shooed Wickham out of the desk chair and sat down in front of her computer console. Signing onto the Internet, she called up a popular search engine and typed in "Jane Austen."

The computer whirred softly for several seconds before the screen was filled with the information she requested. Eliza stared at her monitor in disbelief; there were over a million and a half Web sites. Looking over at the cat now perched on the high stool, she sighed, "I thought this was going to be easy." Looking back at the monitor she found an array of Web sites pertaining to the author. Scrolling down through the list, Eliza discovered to her amazement that there were sites devoted to Jane Austen's life, her birthplace, the times in which she lived, each of her books and all the movies and television shows that had ever been made from the books. There were even more Web sites devoted to the actors in the movies and television shows made from the books. In addition to those, there were hundreds of fan sites, history sites, sites for scholarly discussions of Jane Austen's work, and sites devoted to the many sequels to Jane Austen books, written in the style of the author by latter-day imitators.

There were Japanese Jane Austen Web sites, Australian Web sites, Norwegian sites, discussion sites about Jane Austen's letters, her family, her friends . . . the list went on and on.

Eliza scrolled until her finger ached and her eyes grew bleary, and yet she realized that she hadn't even made a dent in the endless list. "Where do I start?" she groaned to Wickham.

After several more minutes of scrolling she sat back, rubbed her eyes and blinked at the screen again. The title and description of one Web site in particular suddenly caught her eye.

"Austenticity.com," she read, liking the sound of it. "'Everything you ever wanted to know about Jane Austen.' Now that sounds promising," she told the cat.

Wickham rubbed against Eliza's arm as she clicked onto the site. A burst of romantic theme music suddenly poured from the computer's speakers and a title popped up onto the screen:

AUSTENTICITY.COM PRESENTS
Jane Austen's
PRIDE AND PREJUDICE

The title faded away as a scene from the BBC/A&E television miniseries *Pride and Prejudice* began to play on the computer screen. In the scene, Elizabeth Bennet and Mr. Darcy were alone in a sitting room.

Eliza found her lips moving in silent accompaniment to the actor playing Darcy as he recited one of her favorite lines from P&P: "You must allow me to tell you how ardently I admire and love you . . ."

Her face reddening, Eliza abruptly broke off the monologue and turned down the sound, smiling at the casual ease with which she had been captivated.

"Darcy, you seductive devil!" She grinned at the now-silent actor still mouthing his lines. "I dearly love your first proposal to Elizabeth Bennet," she told him. "But right now I need some hard information about the real *you*! If there *was* a real you."

She stopped the film clip by clicking onto the information menu at the top of her computer screen. Another screen immediately popped up, featuring a rather dour portrait of the author herself beneath a new title:

AUSTENTICITY.COM
THE EVERYTHING AUSTEN SITE

CAN'T GET ENOUGH JANE AUSTEN?

Dying to know what she ate and wore, what books she read, songs she sang? Post your question on our message boards.

One of our Austen experts is sure to have the answer you seek.

"Austen experts! Now that's more like it," Eliza said, reading the message. She examined the several topics on the message boards, selected one titled "Jane's Life & Times" and started to type.

POST MESSAGE:

Was Darcy from *Pride and Prejudice* a *real* person? Please reply by e-mail to: SMARTIST@galleri.com

Smiling to herself, she sent the message.

"There!" she told Wickham. "With any luck, somebody will have the solution to our little mystery right at their fingertips."

The cat rolled his yellow eyes up at her, as if to say, Don't kid yourself.

Eliza shrugged and closed out the Austenticity Web site. "Okay," she grudgingly conceded, peering once more at the daunting list of other Internet sites. "I'll look at a few more, but I'm not going to keep doing this all night."

More than an hour later a thoroughly exhausted Eliza sat propped among the pillows piled against the elaborately carved figurals decorating the headboard of her bed.

As she leafed idly through her copy of *Pride and Prejudice* her imagination was filled with the possibilities presented by the two mysterious letters. Out of the corner of her eye she could see the little vanity table by the window, she wondered who had placed the letters behind the mirror, and for what possible purpose.

Wickham was comfortably dozing on the pillows beside her as she finally put her book aside and switched off the bedside lamp. Moonlight filled the room, casting soft reflections in the hazed mirror of the vanity table. Eliza gazed sleepily at the golden orb outside her window and snuggled down next to the cat.

"You must allow me to tell you how ardently I admire and love you . . ." she murmured dreamily. "Oh God, Wickham, that is *so* romantic! Could there have been a flesh-and-blood Darcy who actually spoke those words to Jane Austen *before* she wrote them?"

Wickham's deep-throated purr rumbled up from somewhere inside, indicating that he was already fast asleep.

Eliza's exploration of the Internet had provided her with no more clues to the existence of a real-life Fitzwilliam Darcy than the letters had. However, she had discovered that most scholars believed Jane Austen peopled her novels with characters from her own life. Sighing deeply she wondered about the man who had inspired one of the most romantic characters ever written.

If Darcy had been a real person, she wondered, were they in love, how did they meet, why didn't they marry? Reminding herself that Darcy's note was not a love letter, she questioned the identity of the captain and what he had found out about Darcy. Eliza sleepily entwined her fingers in the warm ruff of fur around Wickham's neck.

She tried to imagine herself in the arms of a passionate, ardent lover. The fantasy was interrupted by an extremely unsatisfying image of Jerry, sitting across from her at a deli restaurant table, eating a naked green salad and reeling off stock quotations between mouthfuls.

The uneasy laugh that followed the image reminded her of the neatly constructed boundaries she had so carefully erected around her passions and as a consequence, her life; Jerry was most definitely one of the boundaries. Now she wondered why she put such limitations on herself. But, of course, that was easy; it was safe, no risks.

Drifting off, she dreamt of a man who would ardently admire and love her.

In a misty valley far from the city a great country estate lay basking peacefully in the light of the same moon that shone through Eliza Knight's bedroom window.

Set in a gentle landscape of rolling hills and surrounded by deep, silent woods, the graceful architecture of the huge house that was both the jewel and the centerpiece of the estate was accentuated by the soft wash of moonlight that touched its soaring columns and silvered the slender balconies gracing its majestic facade.

At this late hour the idyllic old structure stood almost entirely dark from within, the mullioned panes of its many windows glittering silently beneath the glowing light of the heavens.

All but one.

From a single window on the lower floor at the front of the stately mansion—and no other name could adequately describe the Great House—there came a steady blue flicker of artificial illumination that was too strong to be confused with the external light of either the stars or moon.

The window was one of several that extended from the richly carpeted floor nearly to the high, elaborately decorated ceiling of a large and luxuriously appointed study, the darkly paneled walls of which were lined with shelves of priceless, leather-bound books and historic journals and hung with ancestral portraits and ancient battle flags.

The blue glow showing at the window came from a computer terminal set atop a massive desk that had been hewn at least a century earlier of native hardwoods harvested from the extensive forests surrounding the house.

Behind the desk in the darkened room a shadowy figure sat in a well-worn leather chair, gazing raptly at the screen of the computer.

He had been sitting there for some time, contemplating the simple question that Eliza Knight had placed on the Austenticity.com message board.

MESSAGE:

Was Darcy from *Pride and Prejudice* a *real* person?
Please reply by e-mail to: SMARTIST@galleri.com

He felt his pulse quickening as he read and reread those few lines of insubstantial type.

For perhaps a thousand nights he had scanned the Internet in search of messages precisely like this one. He searched because there were answers he had to find, truths he must discover. And the vast worldwide electronic web of the Internet was one of the many possible avenues he was compelled to explore.

Though his exhausting quest had seldom produced anything worthwhile, once, two years earlier, his vigilance on the Internet had been rewarded. And so he had expanded his nightly hunt to a dozen or more web sites in hopes of making another find.

For the most part he confined his online search to scholarly sites devoted to literature and history, and to a number of special-interest boards having to do with the buying and selling of rare documents. But he also kept a steady watch on popular entertainment web sites, including occasionally silly ones like Austenticity.com, whose fan members were generally more interested in film and television productions of Jane Austen's books than in either the author or the books themselves.

Whether serious or frivolous, he visited his Internet listening posts with a singular sense of dedication that he feared at times bordered on the obsessive. But then, as he frequently reminded himself, he was obsessed, though perhaps enchanted was a better word.

He read the brief message again: *Was Darcy from* Pride and Prejudice *a real person?*

Though that very question had been debated for almost two hundred years by biographers and academics alike, experience told him it was not the sort of thing one would expect to find on a popular public web site. The phrasing was too precise, the writer neither speculating nor framing the question, as was typically seen on message boards about some passage from P&P, but rather making a very direct query . . . A query, he felt, that could have been prompted by some discovery.

Though he could not define his reasons beyond those vague feelings, the very strangeness of the message struck him as a potential clue to the answer that he himself was seeking. And any clue, no matter how vague or insubstantial, had to be tracked to its source.

He sat gazing at Eliza's question on the screen for a while longer before he at last pulled his keyboard to him and began to type out a carefully worded reply.

Chapter 4

The following morning Eliza rose early. She quickly shooed Wickham out of the warm nest he'd created for himself among the pillows and made up the bed, looking forward to the day ahead.

Since she had no meetings scheduled for the day, she was planning on taking care of a few routine business matters and then seriously delving into the possible origins of the two mysterious letters. The prospect of discovering the truth about the old letters was exciting and she could hardly wait to get started.

Smiling at her reflection in the hazed mirror, which she had affixed to the top of the antique dressing table the night before, Eliza brushed her long black hair, allowing the loose curls to fall gracefully over her shoulders, then she dressed casually in slacks and a silk blouse and went out to the kitchen.

As she passed through the living room she glanced over at her computer console, noting with satisfaction that the powerful machine was already humming busily on its own as it performed an automatic upload of two replacement paintings to the online gallery that displayed and sold her work.

Eliza was particularly proud of the Internet art gallery she had created less than a year ago. Galleri.com had freed her almost entirely of the tedious and costly dealings with art dealers that had formerly consumed large percentages of both her time and her income.

With the new online gallery in operation, customers could now view her whimsical creations on their own computers and order their favorite prints, stationery or original paintings directly from her, via a secured credit card shopping cart. And whenever Eliza sold one of her original paintings— and she had just sold two the previous week—new pictures were uploaded into the gallery to replace them, which was what was happening now.

In the kitchen she attended to Wickham's perpetually empty food bowl, then made herself a couple of pieces of whole wheat toast and brewed fresh coffee. She intended to breakfast while she checked the gallery web site, to be sure the replacement paintings had uploaded without a problem, and then to check her e-mail and shopping cart for any new orders or customer queries.

She was just walking back into the living room, balancing a small tray in her hand, when the computer chimed, indicating that the upload cycle was complete.

Before Eliza had reached her desk the computer chimed again and an electronic rendition of the 1950s pop hit "Please Mr. Postman" blasted from the speakers, signaling that her overnight e-mail was waiting to be read. Anxious to be done with the task so she could get started researching the old letters, she settled herself before the computer, buttered a wedge of toast and took a bite, then opened the e-mail folder.

Although she had not forgotten about her message board posting of late the night before, Eliza was anticipating only the usual list of morning mail and Internet updates. So the sender's address on the first piece of e-mail on the overnight list caused her to catch her breath. She stared at it for several seconds before clicking her mouse.

The e-mail popped instantly onto her screen.

Dear SMARTIST,
    A very strange question, "Was Darcy from
Pride and Prejudice real?" I happen to be firmly
of the opinion that he was. But then I am slightly
prejudiced. Why are *you* interested?
                    FDARCY@PemberleyFarms.com

Eliza read the strange note with growing consternation.
She had genuinely hoped to find someone on the Austenticity
site who would take seriously her question about Darcy, thus
perhaps providing some indication of the genuineness of her
letters, or at least a direction in which she might pursue her
planned research.

Now, she reflected, as she raised the cup of scalding coffee
to her lips, posting the message had obviously been a big mistake. And she was convinced that she had unwittingly tapped
into some previously unsuspected lunatic fringe of Jane Austen
fandom.

Wickham suddenly jumped up into her lap, nearly upset-
ting her coffee and further aggravating her ill-tempered view
of the ludicrous message. "Look, Wickham!" she said, grab-
bing the unruly feline by the scruff of his fat neck and direct-
ing his attention to the screen. "It's a cute little e-mail from
Darcy himself, at Pemberley, no less."

Wickham meowed and struggled to free himself, but Eliza
held him firmly in her grip.

"Pemberley was the name of the fictional Darcy's fabulous
estate in *Pride and Prejudice*," she informed the wriggling
cat. "Ridiculous, huh?" She looked down at the furry head in
her lap and rubbed his ears, then released him. He leaped out
of her lap and hit the floor with a heavy thump as she leaned
over her keyboard and began to type.

Dear "Darcy,"
    I posted my question for a reason, not to indulge

your fantasy. Please keep your crackpot opinions
to yourself.

SMARTIST@galleri.com

Grinning with satisfaction at having properly told the idiot
off, Eliza stabbed the key to send the e-mail. Then she shut
down the computer and leaned back to finish her toast and
coffee in peace.

Wickham had found his way up onto the drawing board
while she had been typing and was sprawled out enjoying the
morning sunlight. Together they watched a rusting Japanese
container ship navigating past the window.

"I can't get over that weirdo on the Internet," she said, exchanging waves with half a dozen grinning crewmen perched
on the ship's bridge railings. "But then I guess the world is
full of weirdos." She reached out to stroke Wickham's fur
and smiled as she shook her head.

"Darcy at Pemberley!" she sighed. "I'll bet he wanders
around with a walking stick and a top hat."

Getting to her feet, Eliza cleared the breakfast tray and
carried it back into the kitchen. "All I can say, Wickham,"
she called back into the other room, "is that it's a good thing
you insisted I keep looking last night until I found a place
where I could do some *serious* research."

Chapter 5

When Eliza was twelve, her seventh-grade English teacher had brought her whole class into the city from their distant Long Island suburb to visit the New York Public Library on Fifth Avenue in Manhattan.

She had not been back inside the wonderful old building since that day.

Now she alighted from a taxi and looked up at the famous stone lions guarding the main entrance. Above the huge doors a blue silk banner edged in gold fluttered gaily in the breeze. Across it, in elegant script letters a foot tall, was emblazoned the title: THE WORLD OF JANE AUSTEN, A WOMAN OF TWO CENTURIES.

Eliza smiled. For on the Web the night before she had accidentally discovered a notice for the special exhibit. And though she was not entirely certain that a display of the famed English author's books would be all that helpful in her research, she had reasoned that the library exhibit would at least provide her with a good starting point.

So, clutching her shoulder bag to her side, she climbed the broad steps and entered the library, not exactly certain what she would find within.

From the echoing lobby she followed a series of neatly labeled blue-and-gold placards past the cathedral-like vault of the main reading room and down an echoing, marble-floored corridor that had not been on the seventh-grade tour.

To her great surprise, as she neared the far end of the corridor Eliza heard the sounds of lively music coming from the large, high-ceilinged exhibit room that turned out to be her destination. Her surprise was compounded as she peered into the huge space and saw that it was crowded with visitors.

In the fashion of latter-day museum extravaganzas, the library exhibit room had been converted into a multimedia entertainment setup that surrounded the Jane Austen books and other artifacts on display with moving kaleidoscopes of light, color and sound.

Stepping into the large, airy room, Eliza found herself nodding in artistic approval of a mood-setting wall-sized projection. The video appeared to have been filmed from a carriage rolling along a leafy drive toward the great English manor house the author had employed as the setting for her novel *Mansfield Park*. Adding to the charming pastoral effect created by the unfolding scenery on the wall, an accompanying surround sound soundtrack featured the music of a string quartet, backed by the sounds of hoofbeats, snorting horses and the crunch of steel-clad wheels on gravel.

Turning away from the thematic eye candy, Eliza saw that the room was alive with video, each display of rare or notable editions of Jane Austen novels accompanied by superb, digital-quality monitors playing scenes from film or television adaptations of the works.

Elsewhere, a few personal articles thought to have belonged to the famed author were enhanced by other video presentations that featured running commentaries by distinguished British authors and actors.

"I am all astonishment!" Eliza smilingly murmured to no one in particular.

She worked her way slowly through the exhibit hall, looking at everything, but noting with growing disappointment that none of it appeared to be particularly helpful in determining whether her letters were authentic.

Then, unexpectedly, she happened on a small display case containing an original letter written in 1801 by Jane Austen to her sister, Cassandra.

"Fabulous!" she exclaimed, feeling she was at last getting somewhere.

Opening the top of her shoulder bag a few inches, Eliza carefully compared the handwritten address on the sealed letter she had found in the vanity mirror to the Austen letter displayed behind half an inch of bulletproof plastic.

Although the library's letter was larger than the one in Eliza's purse and the paper entirely different, the neat, unremarkable handwriting on both appeared similar to her untrained eye. However, she also saw at a glance that even a clumsy forger could probably have achieved the superficial resemblance between the two documents.

At least to the extent needed to fool her.

Stymied.

At that moment Eliza was struck by the painfully obvious realization that only an expert was going to be able to authenticate the letters that she had found. And while it may seem odd that she had not immediately thought about the need for laboratory testing and forensic comparisons of the old documents when she first discovered them, the simple truth was that Eliza's mind didn't function that way.

She was a dreamer and a fantasizer, and so it was the romance of the letters, not their physical characteristics, that had caught hold of her imagination.

Still, she admitted, coming down to the library and actually seeing the carefully preserved letter in the exhibit had served its purpose. For she had been made suddenly aware that she was totally out of her depth in even attempting to seriously research the authenticity of her letters.

"Fine!" she exclaimed a little too loudly, even for the noisy exhibit room. "Where do I find an expert in this damn place?"

Eliza snapped her bag shut in frustration. The sharp sound of the metal clasp closing echoed through the big room like a gunshot and she looked up guiltily just in time to see a middle-aged security guard with a ponderous belly turning in her direction to look for the source of the sudden noise.

"Whoops!" Another mistake. Eliza immediately stepped away from the display case and made for the far end of the exhibit hall, forcing herself to maintain a leisurely pace, despite her racing pulse.

For it had also just occurred to her that bringing a letter from Jane Austen into a heavily guarded exhibit of priceless Jane Austen artifacts had probably not been the smartest move she had ever made.

"Stupid!" she berated herself under her breath. "Stupid, stupid, stupid!"

Reaching the far end of the long room, Eliza found temporary refuge amid a freestanding display of mannequins dressed in clothing representative of the fashions popular during the era when Jane Austen was published.

Safely concealed along a winding pathway peopled with costumed dummies, which had been artfully positioned among various props and pieces of painted scenery to suggest that they were in a park, a drawing room or some other location, she chanced a look around and was relieved to see that she had not been followed.

Her momentary fear of being caught in the ludicrous position of having smuggled her own property into the library quickly faded and she began to look with a designer's interest at the clothing display, proceeding slowly along the path from item to item.

Grinning inwardly because she was almost certain she recognized some of the Regency-era costumes in the display from recent film versions of P&P and *Emma*, Eliza stepped closer to examine an elaborately embroidered and extremely low-cut gown of bright rust-colored velvet. A small metal stand beside the mannequin held a descriptive placard. Eliza read aloud from the card:

> *"A young woman of the Regency period would have felt both comfortable and fashionable wearing this exquisite gown to a grand winter ball."*

"Ha!" she snorted derisively. "Fashionable maybe . . . comfortable, no!"

"Really! And why is that?"

Startled, Eliza spun around to see a man in a well-cut dark suit regarding her with obvious curiosity. Narrowing her flashing dark eyes with the wariness of a born New Yorker, she quickly assessed the tall stranger. Athletic but not from working out at the gym. By the deeply tanned features she judged him to be an outdoor type, a cyclist maybe, or a mountain climber—and not bad-looking either, she thought. He was rather good-looking in fact.

The stranger arched his eyebrows, still waiting for her reply to his question.

"Well look at this ridiculous gown!" she said, covering her embarrassment at having been caught sizing him up by turning back to the hideous orangish dress.

"In the first place, it's extremely ugly," she declared. "And, secondly, it's cut so low that the poor woman would have risked pneumonia every time she wore it, at least if what I've heard about English winters is true."

Her handsome interrogator nodded agreeably. "It's very true," he said in a soft voice tinged with a slight Southern drawl. "And not only are English winters cold, there was no central heating in the early 1800s."

He wrinkled his brow thoughtfully and moved around for another perspective on the terrible dress. "On the other hand," he observed, gazing pointedly at the revealing bodice, "twenty years earlier, aristocratic French women wore gowns that exposed their breasts almost entirely."

He grinned at her, then quickly added, "All in the name of dame fashion, of course."

Eliza found herself grinning back at him, and at the same time she noticed his eyes were sea green in color and sparkled when he smiled.

"Well, the French!" she laughed. "What can I say?"

Her laugh reminded him of crystal glasses ringing together in a toast.

"However," she continued, jerking an unladylike thumb at the offensive gown, "I can't imagine Jane Austen having worn something like that."

Eliza paused thoughtfully, searching for an apt comparison with which to illustrate her opinion. "That dress reminds me of those see-through designer numbers that celebrities are always showing up in at the Oscars," she explained after a moment of contemplation. "You know the kind I mean, supposedly the height of fashion, but completely impractical and just plain silly."

The stranger considered that and she saw in his eyes that he was conceding the point before he spoke. "I have to agree with you," he finally admitted. "Jane was *not* a silly person. She'd never have worn a gown like that."

He then turned to indicate a male mannequin just across the aisle from where they stood. This one was dressed in a splendid uniform of dark blue spangled with gold braid, and had a gleaming silver saber belted to its side.

"This naval officer's uniform of the period is probably far more accurate in terms of clothing that someone who knew Jane might have worn," he observed. "Her brother, Sir Francis Austen, became admiral of the British Fleet, you know."

Eliza stepped across the narrow aisle to look at the uniform. "I didn't know that," she admitted. "In fact, I'd always had the impression that her family was relatively poor."

"The Austens weren't rich," he explained, "but they were very well connected, with many wealthy and aristocratic friends. And, in time," he continued, "the family did ultimately become rather prosperous. Another of Jane's brothers was adopted by wealthy relatives and inherited a very large estate, and Henry, the youngest, became a prominent banker."

The stranger paused while Eliza absorbed all of that, then he pointed toward the end of the winding path. "If you want a glimpse of how the Austens really lived," he offered, "come down and look into the next exhibit room."

Without waiting to see if she would follow, the tall man turned and walked off in the direction he had indicated. Eliza stood there for a moment, watching him go. She briefly considered remaining where she was, just so he wouldn't think she was hanging on to him, then she shrugged and hurried to catch up.

Stepping out of the clothing display she found him standing by an open doorway that had been roped off so visitors could look through but not enter.

Eliza stepped up beside the stranger and looked into the dimly lit room beyond. "Oh," she breathed, "it's wonderful!" She was looking into a comfortable room in what she assumed was a Regency-period English country house. The furnishings and decorations were exquisitely inviting, right down to a richly colored needlepoint settee, a fine piano and a roaring fireplace.

"This is a reproduction of Jane's music room at the house in Hampshire, as described in a biography written by one of her brothers," Eliza's anonymous guide informed her. "She is said to have written the final drafts of several of her novels there," he continued.

Standing at the velvet rope, Eliza was only half-aware of the descriptive lecture she was receiving, her head tilted to one side as she gazed longingly into the cozy space. The tall man took a step back to allow her the privacy of the moment. He watched as her hair fell over her shoulder hiding her face, the flickering light of the artificial candles playing among the highlights of her dark hair. A raven-haired beauty; he blushed at the overly romantic thought and turned his eyes away.

Dreamily she sighed, "I feel as though I belong in there." Only half-jokingly she queried, "You don't suppose they'd let me move in?"

He chuckled and shook his head. "I seriously doubt that Dr. Klein would go along with that," he replied. "I read somewhere that she borrowed most of these furnishings from the British Museum."

Eliza tore her eyes from the delights of the room long enough to glance over at him. "Dr. Klein?" she asked.

He nodded. "Thelma Klein, head of the Rare Document section here at the city library. She's the one who put this exhibit together. She's also reputed to be a leading Austen authority," he said somewhat sarcastically.

This new bit of information definitely piqued Eliza's interest. Turning away from the charming exhibit, she fixed the stranger in her gaze and asked, "Do you happen to know this Dr. Klein?"

Strangely, she thought, the question seemed to make him uneasy. "No . . . not personally," he confessed, abruptly raising his arm to consult a gold watch.

"Well *you* seem to know an awful lot about Jane," she persisted. "You wouldn't happen to be an authority on her yourself?" she asked hopefully.

"An authority?" The stranger frowned and glanced over Eliza's shoulder into the music room, then he slowly shook his head. "No, just a confirmed fan," he said. "But I have read several of Dr. Klein's articles, so when I came into the City today I couldn't resist dropping by to see her exhibit."

He smiled again and gestured toward the busy hall behind them. "I must admit it's very well done, don't you think?"

Eliza smiled slyly. "Well," she conceded, "except for the ball gown . . ."

"Yes," he laughed, "except for that."

He looked down at his watch again. "Well, I'm late for a meeting . . ." And without further ceremony he turned and walked away.

"It was nice talking with you," Eliza called out.

Without looking back he raised a hand in farewell. "Yes. Enjoy the rest of the exhibit," he said.

Eliza stood and watched as his straight, athletic figure was swallowed up in the crowd at the far end of the exhibit hall. She hadn't wanted him to leave. Why hadn't she said something to stop him? Sighing deeply, she scoffed at herself; she'd waited for him to ask for her phone number or something and when he hadn't she did . . . nothing. No risk in nothing.

She shook her head, casting a final backward glance at Jane's cozy little music room and set off in search of Thelma Klein.

Chapter 6

"I'd like to see Dr. Klein in Rare Documents." Eliza stood at the circular information desk in the main lobby, addressing a long-haired, gum-chewing security guard who appeared to be hearing impaired. "Hello! I'm talking to you," she called, though he was sitting not more than three feet away. "I said I want to *see* Dr. Thelma Klein."

The guard finally glanced up from his *Spawn* comic book, clearly annoyed at the interruption. "I heard you," he said. "But Dr. Klein doesn't see anybody without an appointment." He gave Eliza a taunting smirk. "You got one?"

"No, I don't," Eliza replied evenly. "So I'd like to *make* an appointment."

"Klein *never* makes appointments," the guard gleefully reported. Then, pointedly dismissing her, he returned his gaze to a full-page illustration of an implausible buglike creature attempting to ravish an equally implausible Amazon babe in a strategically tattered bikini.

Moments later he noticed that Eliza was still standing at the counter, scanning the lobby. "Anything else I can do?" he asked over the top of the magazine.

Biting her tongue to prevent herself from telling the little creep precisely what he could do with his comic book, Eliza shook her head. "No thanks," she said sweetly as she walked away. "You've been ever so helpful."

Slowly circling the lobby, she stopped to consult a wall directory near the front entrance and learned that the Rare Document section was located on the third floor. She spotted a staircase nearby and casually walked over to it, only to discover that a velvet rope blocked the stairs. To one side of the steps a small plastic sign informed her that the stairway was reserved exclusively for library administration and research personnel.

Sneaking a quick look back at the information desk where the guard was once again wholly engrossed in his garishly illustrated tale of bug rape, Eliza unclipped the brass hook on the rope, stepped into the forbidden zone and vanished up the stairs.

A metal fire door on the third floor opened onto a darkly paneled corridor of offices with old-fashioned frosted-glass doors and tall overhead transoms. Each door had a department title and the name of an individual neatly lettered in bold black type on the glass.

Eliza walked down the deserted corridor, reading the signs on doors marked ANTHROPOLOGICAL STUDIES, POETRY, LITERATURE-MEDIEVAL, LITERATURE-AMERICAN, ADMINISTRATION, PERSONNEL, FOREIGN LANGUAGE, SPECIAL COLLECTIONS and LITERATURE/POETRY-ANCIENT NEAR EAST. She was beginning to worry that she was going to run out of corridor before she found what she wanted when she spotted the words RARE DOCUMENTS/FORENSICS LAB—T. KLEIN, PHD, DIRECTOR stenciled onto a door set in a recessed alcove.

Taking a deep breath, Eliza raised her fist and knocked twice on the wooden frame with feigned confidence.

Nothing happened.

After waiting for several seconds she knocked again. When there was still no answer she looked around to be sure the corridor was still empty. Then she placed her ear against the door. From the other side she thought she could make out the low murmur of voices.

Straightening, Eliza placed her hand on the worn brass

knob and turned it. The door was unlocked, so she pushed it open halfway and peeked into a long, narrow room cluttered with computers, benches filled with complex mazes of bubbling, horror-movie-type lab equipment and several large pieces of unrecognizable electronic machinery. At the far end of the room three or four white-coated techs were leaning over their equipment or peering into microscopes, oblivious to her presence.

After considering her options for a moment, Eliza decided that walking into the lab unannounced was probably not a good idea. Perhaps if she waited in the corridor someone would come along who could help her find Dr. Klein.

Her mind set on this new plan of action, she backed out into the corridor, stealthily pulling the door shut behind her. She squealed as her backside bumped into something unyielding and a booming voice oddly reminiscent of carriage wheels rolling over crushed gravel boomed in her ear.

"What the hell are you doing up here? This is a restricted area. No visitors!"

Her face reddening, Eliza whirled about and found herself face-to-face with an imposing, iron-haired, middle-aged woman built like an oil drum. The woman was blocking the entrance to the alcove with her thick body and glaring at her quarry like a hungry cat that's just discovered a parakeet in its litter box. The corners of her razor-thin mouth were turned down almost to her jowls and she was in the process of raising a cell phone in one stubby hand, doubtless to call Security.

Realizing that she was trapped, Eliza quickly scrutinized the woman, assessing the chances of bowling her over and making a run for it. Then her eyes fell on the plastic library ID badge clipped to the lapel of the woman's shapeless gray suit and Eliza breathed a sigh of relief.

"Dr. Klein," she said, smiling as brightly as possible under the awkward circumstances. "My name is Eliza Knight and you're *just* the person I wanted to see—"

Thelma Klein slowly lowered the cell phone and rolled her

slightly bulging blue eyes ceilingward. "Oh God, not another one!" she groaned, stepping out of the alcove and pointing back toward the stairway. "You'll have to make an appointment."

"You don't *make* appointments," Eliza countered, standing her ground. "Which means you won't *actually* see me."

That prompted a thin smile from the portly researcher. "Very good!" she said grumpily. "You're a regular genius! Good-bye now." She started to move forward, intent on entering the lab, but now it was Eliza who blocked the way.

"I have some documents that I think you'll find very interesting—" she began.

Thelma Klein raised a chubby hand to stop her explanation. "Wait! Don't tell me," she said sarcastically, "let me guess. You went to an estate sale and bought a genuine copy of the Declaration of Independence. Now you just want my lab to authenticate it so you can sell it for a million bucks. Is that it?"

"No! That is *not* it!" Eliza responded, injecting an equal measure of venom into her tone. She fumbled in her purse for the letters and thrust them at the other woman. "I discovered these letters last night and I thought they might be important. I learned about your Jane Austen exhibit and I came here hoping you could give me some advice." Eliza softened her tone slightly as she added, "I've already tried researching the Internet."

Thelma Klein grimaced and wagged her big head in disapproval. "The Internet," she growled. "What made you think you could learn anything from that soulless monstrosity dedicated to reducing the power and majesty of the written word to moronic babbling? I *hate* the damn Internet!"

Leaning forward until their noses were almost touching, the big woman lowered her basso voice yet another octave. "You want some advice from me?" she rumbled. "Go home to your computer and smash it with a sledgehammer, while you still have some semblance of a brain left."

Before Eliza could think of an adequate response to *that*, Thelma emitted a deep sigh of defeat and held out her hand. "Okay," she said, "let me see the letters!"

Eliza silently handed them over. From a hidden recess somewhere in the massive bosom of her jacket the researcher produced a pair of dainty reading glasses with lobster-pink frames and squinted at the letters.

"At first I thought maybe they were some kind of joke," Eliza explained breathlessly. "But then I couldn't figure out why anyone would go to the trouble. There was a scrap of old newspaper with them, dated 1810 . . ."

Without taking her eyes from the letters Klein swatted at the air in front of her, the way one wards off a pesky mosquito. "Newspapers," she snorted. "That's the oldest trick in the book, honey. Every two-bit junk dealer knows an old newspaper will make the suckers think the stuff with it is old. Now kindly shut up and let me read this."

Eliza fell silent as the researcher, still reading, pushed past her and opened the door to the lab. The younger woman started to follow but Thelma suddenly turned and blocked the doorway. "Come back tomorrow afternoon, late," she ordered.

A protest rose in Eliza's throat but Thelma cut her off with a reassuring smile that completely transformed the older woman's forbidding visage. "Don't worry," she said warmly, "your letters will be safe with me. I'm going to have to run a lot of tests," she explained, "and it's going to take time. But you have my word I won't let these letters out of my sight."

Thelma Klein's smile broadened. "Now, if you'll just wait here a minute," she said, "I'll have my secretary make color copies of the letters for you and I'll sign a receipt confirming that they're your property and that you've entrusted them to the library for authentication."

"Th—thank you," Eliza stammered, overwhelmed by this sudden turnabout in the other woman's demeanor. "I really do appreciate this very much, Dr. Klein."

"It's Thelma," Klein replied.

She held up the old letters like a sheaf of worthless junk bonds. "And don't thank me yet," she smiled. "If you went to Vegas the smart money would tell you these letters of yours are probably as phony as Madonna's eyelashes."

Chapter 7

"I think you should forget about this whole Jane Austen thing and stay focused on your work. You've been doing okay with the online gallery, but your property taxes are coming up pretty soon and I'd like to see you sock another few thousand into your IRA before the end of the year."

Exactly as in her dream of the night before, Eliza was sitting at a scratched Formica table in a neighborhood deli and Jerry was occupying the seat on the other side of the table. Instead of a salad he was consuming a pallid chicken breast, but just as in the dream he was dispensing dry financial advice, completely unable to grasp the romance of the letters.

Following her trip to the library that morning Eliza had excitedly called Jerry and asked him to meet her for dinner this evening. She had been anxious to share with him the news of Thelma Klein's unexpected decision to examine the letters.

Jerry's response to her announcement, however, had been less than enthusiastic and for the past twenty minutes he had been taking every opportunity to pour cold water on her carefully nurtured hopes and dreams for what he was now derisively calling her "Jane Austen thing."

"Jerry, researching the letters isn't going to do anything to my business one way or the other," Eliza interrupted defensively. "In fact, now that Thelma's taken over, there's not much else for me to do but wait, so I don't see the problem."

Jerry frowned his most serious accountant's frown and squinted at her through the panes of his gleaming round lenses. "The *problem* as I see it," he said, "isn't the research time, but all the emotional energy you're putting into this thing that you consider romantic. It's all what-if stuff, not real."

Eliza nodded sullenly. "Well *what if* the letters turn out to be genuine?" she replied, trying hard to keep the emotion out of her voice and failing miserably. "Oh, I know Dr. Klein *said* the letters are probably phony. But if you'd seen the look in her eyes, Jerry . . . I think she *believes* they are real. And if they are," she concluded on a practical note, "I imagine that they could turn out to be quite valuable."

Jerry started polishing his glasses with a paper napkin, a sure sign that he was about to deliver another lecture. "You don't fool me, Eliza," he said. "If those letters *should* prove to be real—although from what you've told me that seems highly unlikely—I'll admit that they might actually be worth something." He paused to fix her with his version of a piercing gaze. "But that's not what you're really interested in at all, is it?"

"Well, of course, I'm interested—" she began.

"What you're really interested in," he interrupted, waving away her denial, "is whether or not old whatshisname, the guy from that book—"

"Are you referring to Darcy?" Eliza intoned coldly.

Jerry nodded, stripping a piece of chicken from the under-cooked breast and popping it into his mouth. "Darcy," he re-peated, swallowing. "All you're really interested in is whether or not this Darcy character was sleeping with Jane Austen."

"Who said anything about her sleeping with him?" Eliza angrily retorted. "I only said they may have *written* to one another."

"Whatever!" Jerry shrugged to show that in his mind it really made no difference whether Darcy and Jane Austen were platonic lovers or depraved sex fiends. "The point is," he said with forced patience, "it all happened two hundred years ago, if it happened at all. So who cares?"

"I care," Eliza said. "Yes, you're absolutely right, Jerry. I care."

"See," he said, pointing his fork at her in triumph. "I can read you like a book, Eliza," he added with maddening smugness. "And all I'm saying is that you need to be careful about how much time and emotional energy you invest in this sentimental stuff." Jerry paused to stab another piece of chicken. "You need to manage your time wisely, give priority to the really important things that you need to be doing."

Eliza abruptly placed her napkin on the table and got to her feet. "You know, Jerry, I think you're absolutely right," she agreed. "Now, I'd better be going."

"Going? Where?" Jerry demanded. "You haven't even finished your smoked-salmon platter yet."

She smiled and picked up her bag. "You just reminded me of something important that I have to do," she replied. "And, as you've just pointed out, the important things should get first priority."

He squinted up at her in confusion. "But I, uh, thought we'd probably go back to your place after dinner and . . . You know, have a little 'romantic evening,'" he whimpered like a whipped puppy.

Eliza actually heard the quotes around the romantic evening part and knew that romance was not what he had in mind. "Romance? No, no, no . . . That would be a terrible waste of time, don't you think?"

His mouth fell open, revealing an unattractive view of half-chewed chicken.

"'Bye now," Eliza said, leaning to deliver a quick kiss to his forehead. "Don't forget to floss."

Then, before he could reply, she was out the door and hurrying away down the sidewalk, her heels clicking sharply against the pavement.

Fuming, she had wanted to slap the silly grin off his face when he'd said he knew her like a book. Yeah, well it was evident that he'd never gotten around to reading this part of the book and he'd certainly skipped over the chapter on romantic evenings or he would have known that a deli sandwich and lecture on her overactive imagination were not the proper prelude to romance.

Why hadn't she told him that? Because the perfect rebuke seemed to come to mind only later when she was alone and it didn't matter anymore. Sighing, she supposed it was just another stake in the fence creating the boundary that was Jerry.

Chapter 8

At home alone an hour later, Eliza stood in the middle of her living room, attending to the important task she had assigned herself for the evening. The floor had been carpeted in a layer of newspapers and she was industriously applying a thick, messy "guaranteed" French furniture restorative to the top of the vanity table.

Wickham, who had been banished from the immediate area of the easily tracked brown gunk with threats of "no tuna, ever again," sat sullenly in a chair watching her with resentful yellow eyes.

Eliza's muscles grew tired and her hands began to tingle as she lovingly rubbed the cleansing polish deep into the wood. Before long her efforts were rewarded with the warm gleam of natural rosewood slowly emerging from beneath a two hundred year accumulation of grime.

"Oh, isn't it lovely!" she exclaimed with satisfaction.

Looking up, she caught a glimpse of her comical smudged features in the hazed mirror. And she wondered again, as she had a dozen times since bringing the vanity home the night before, how many other faces before her had looked into those same misty depths.

"Just think, Wickham," she whispered, pleased with the untouchable mystery of the idea, "this table might have belonged to Jane Austen. Perhaps she even wrote part of *Pride and Prejudice* right on this very spot that I'm cleaning now."

If Wickham had any response in mind it was derailed by the sudden bright musical tones of "Mr. Postman" playing from across the room. Annoyed, Eliza wiped her hands on an old T-shirt and glared at the offending computer.

"I thought I'd turned that thing off," she grumbled, angry with herself for her inability to resist walking over and peeking at the newly arrived message.

"I *should* have taken Dr. Klein's advice and smashed this thing," she complained as she opened her e-mail folder and looked at the new message, which popped onto the screen and sat there seeming to taunt her.

"Wonderful!" she told Wickham, who had interpreted her move to the computer desk as license to leave his chair and jump up on the drawing board. "It's another e-mail from that weirdo who thinks he's Mr. Darcy."

Eliza sat pondering the twisted logic of the e-mail, trying to think of a suitably sarcastic response.

> Dear SMARTIST,
>   Even if it were true, my being a crackpot would have
>   no bearing on whether Jane Austen's Mr. Darcy was
>   a real person.
>   FDARCY@PemberleyFarms.com

"Darcy, you are becoming a royal pain in the butt!" Eliza breathed. She took a deep breath, and then began to tap out a swift and angry reply that she hoped would rid her of this pest once and for all.

Much later, despite her bone weariness, her mood vastly improved by a hot shower and the removal of most of the French furniture restorative from her hair and fingernails, Eliza sat before the little vanity table. Smelling faintly of lemon oil it was now gleaming, basking in the moonlight beside her bedroom window.

Dinner with Jerry fleetingly crossed her mind; she shouldn't really be angry with *him*, he was who he was and she knew it. The question, of course, was why she continued with anything but the business aspect of their relationship. Especially when there were men out there like . . . whoever he was at the library: a man who appreciated Jane Austen and the romance of her era. She wondered what such a man would be like to know and felt a touch of regret that she hadn't even gotten his name.

For a long, silent moment she gazed deeply into the mirror. Then tentatively she touched the cool surface of the glass with her fingertips.

"Hello, Jane!" she whispered, smiling into the haze. "Are you still in there?"

Long after Eliza had retired to her bed to dream of Jane and her mysterious lover the glow of a computer screen once again lit the luxuriously appointed study of the great country house.

Sitting at the desk, the shadowy figure leaned back in the butter-soft leather chair and closed his eyes. Several times since his trip into the city he had found himself thinking of the raven-haired beauty he'd met there. He hadn't actually met her, since he didn't even know her name, but he smiled at the memory of the light dancing in her hair. The pleasant thoughts were rudely interrupted by the coarse electronic voice of his computer telling him he had mail.

And once more he found himself gazing at an angry and provocative message from his unknown e-mail correspondent.

Dear DARCY,
    I am *not* interested in you or your silly games.
    Please stop bothering me.
                                        SMARTIST

For the briefest of moments the man's normally placid features were filled with a rage born more of the frustration he was feeling than of any true hostility toward the sender of the e-mail. His fingers poised over the keyboard, prepared to type out an antagonistic reply. Then he realized what he was doing and leaned back with a sigh. For it seemed perfectly obvious that he had just hit another dead end in his quest to verify his own experience. And the unknown person with whom he had been corresponding—a woman, he suspected— had no idea what had prompted his interest.

If she had, he reflected, then surely she would have responded differently to his first message identifying himself as a Darcy. For he believed that she would have been too intrigued by the connection his family name suggested not to have queried him further.

Regretfully—for the schedule to which he was committed during the next week would preclude any further searching for at least that long—he reached forward and switched off his computer.

Chapter 9

Late the next afternoon, Eliza again presented herself at the library's main information desk. The same gum-chewing guard was slouched behind the counter, lost in another violent, insectoid comic adventure, peopled, predictably, with more seminaked female victims.

"Excuse me," Eliza said, "my name is Eliza Knight and I have an appointment with Dr. Klein in Rare Documents."

Gum-chewer scowled at her and consulted a clipboard that lay on the counter. "I'll be damned," he exclaimed, looking up with sudden respect and pushing a laminated visitor's badge across the marble. "Mind if I ask how you figured a way to get to the old bat?"

"A little trick I picked up from a dirty comic book," Eliza grinned, pinning the badge to her purse and heading for the stairs.

The chastened guard glanced down at his book and flushed brightly. "This isn't a dirty comic book," he yelled after her. "It's an *illustrated novel.*"

Up on the third floor, with far less confidence than she had exhibited to the security guard, a very anxious Eliza slipped quietly into the document research lab.

She found Thelma Klein sitting at a lab bench, peering into a microscope and scribbling notes on a yellow legal pad. After a few seconds the big woman looked up and saw that she had a visitor. She rubbed the bridge of her nose and stood, stretching her arms wearily.

"Ah, you're back," she said to Eliza. "Good timing. I was just wrapping up the last few tests." Thelma lowered her arms and swiveled her head around, scanning the lab for something or somebody. "Rudy," she shouted over the hum of the electronic equipment, "where are my damn spectrograph results?"

Rudy, a nervous, bespectacled young man in a coffee-stained lab coat, waved back at her from across the room. "Almost done, Dr. Klein," he called.

"Bring the printouts to my office," Thelma ordered. Then she turned and jerked her triple chin in Eliza's direction. "Come on," she said.

Winding her way through a maze of lab benches, Eliza followed the older woman into a tiny office overflowing with books, piles of computer printouts and other papers. Squeezing past a bulging file cabinet, Thelma settled herself behind a desk. She pointed Eliza to a straight-backed wooden chair, indicating she should sit.

Eliza did as she was instructed, and when she was seated, Thelma held up her letters and waved them at her. "Where in the *hell* did you get these?" she demanded without preamble.

Eliza opened her mouth to explain about the antique warehouse and the vanity table. But before she could begin a knock sounded at the door. Thelma raised her hand for silence and bellowed at the intruder. "Come in, Rudy!"

The nervous young lab tech scurried into the office and leaned across Eliza to hand the researcher a thick manila folder. Frowning, Thelma opened the folder and scanned the top page of the test results and then grunted for Rudy to leave. The tech gave Eliza a strange look, then left the office quickly, closing the door behind him.

Eliza waited in silence while Thelma thumbed through the remainder of the printouts. When the older woman had finished reading, she dropped the lab report onto the desk.

She again picked up Eliza's letters and stared at them. "Okay, talk," she ordered.

"I found the letters behind a mirror in a piece of furniture I bought two days ago at an antique warehouse," Eliza said. "It's a rosewood vanity table."

Thelma Klein slowly shook her close-cropped gray head and a grin creased her sullen features. "God help us!" she mused. "Old furniture."

She thought about that for a minute or so, then again focused her attention on Eliza. "So, not only do you have letters from Jane Austen and her mysterious lover," she said, "you've got her personal dressing table, too?"

Eliza, who had spent most of the day preparing herself for the letdown of discovering that her letters were forgeries, stared at the gruff document expert. "You're saying the letters are *genuine*?" she uttered.

Thelma Klein's grin widened. "Honey, trust me. We wouldn't be sitting here having this conversation if they *weren't* genuine," she assured the shocked Eliza.

"We ran a full battery of analytical tests on the sealed letter to Darcy," she explained, the excitement in her voice growing, "and *everything* checks out." Thelma patted the lab report she had just examined. "The paper is right, the ink is correct, the style and, of course, Jane Austen's handwriting, have been compared to three different examples of original Austen letters from the library's permanent collection."

The enthusiasm in Klein's voice moderated only slightly as she held up the second of Eliza's letters. "I think we can safely assume that this letter *from* Darcy is also authentic, based on its connection to the first, as well as the age and likely origins of the paper and ink, even though we have no actual handwriting samples to compare it with."

In a daze Eliza listened to the exhaustive technical details of the researcher's report. And though she had dreamed of what it might mean if the letters could be proved genuine, she had been working hard since last night to adopt Jerry's cynical world view that miracles didn't happen and that such a thing was therefore virtually impossible.

Now a highly respected document expert and Jane Austen authority was telling her that her letters were real.

Eliza smiled, and then abruptly her bubble burst. For she had just remembered something that had been bothering her about the letters from the beginning.

"Excuse me, Dr. Klein," she interrupted as Thelma was launching into an explanation of how the oxidization of iron particles in nineteenth-century ink turned it reddish with time. "I seem to have missed something here. You say these letters are real, but I thought Fitzwilliam Darcy was a *fictitious* character."

Thelma Klein sighed like a third-grade teacher stuck with a particularly dull student, and leaned back in her chair. "Honey," she asked kindly, "how much do you *know* about Jane Austen? Beyond the TV miniseries, I mean?"

Offended by the condescending tone of the question, Eliza dug into her bag and produced the thick reference book that she had checked out of the library the previous day and spent half of last night reading.

"Well, according to *your* book on Austen," she replied defensively, "she's the greatest Romantic novelist in English literature. And she never married or even had an actual lover. At least not that anyone knows about."

Eliza's dark eyes were flashing angrily as she continued. "And, for your information," she declared, "I have read *Pride and Prejudice* at least half a dozen times, and all of her other novels as well. So I am not completely ignorant on the topic of Jane Austen."

Thelma had listened to the pretty, dark-haired artist's angry tirade without changing her expression. Now her lined features softened and she surprised Eliza by reaching across the desk to gently touch her hand.

"I'm sorry, kid," Thelma apologized. "I know I sometimes come off like the old battle ax that I am . . ." Her voice trailed away and she swiveled around in her chair and gazed out through the window at the busy street three stories below.

"If you only knew the number of creeps who come in here trying to get me to authenticate papers that prove George Washington was an alien . . ." she muttered.

Thelma suddenly turned back to face Eliza and her voice was once again strong and businesslike. "Okay," she said, "I'll admit I was talking down to you. Feel free to kick me if you catch me doing it again."

Eliza grinned. "I promise," she said.

"What I'm about to tell you *won't* be found in the standard biographies," Thelma began. "Of course, Darcy's identity is one of the great unknowns of Austen's work. But every schoolgirl who's ever gotten hooked on P&P secretly suspects that the character must have been drawn from the author's personal experience." Thelma shrugged theatrically and held out upturned palms in a no-brainer gesture. "I mean, how else could Austen have so perfectly described that unforgettable and passionate relationship between Darcy and Elizabeth Bennet, right?"

Eliza found herself nodding. "Right!" she agreed.

"The problem is," Thelma continued, her voice rising with the vehemence of a scholarly argument that Eliza suddenly realized the older woman must have been following since her graduate-school days, "that no man even vaguely fitting Darcy's description exists as a historical figure in Jane Austen's life. Not in her letters, not in the journals of her contemporaries, not in any of the several biographies written by her family members."

Eliza frowned, trying to recall some of what she had read about the author's life. "Jane did have a male admirer or two, didn't she? Wasn't there a young law student? I think his name was LeFroy or something like that."

Thelma waved off the suggestion with a swatting gesture. "Oh, there was a brief and well-documented flirtation with a penniless student—a family friend, actually—when Jane was a girl. And, later, even a couple of marriages of convenience were proposed." The older woman leaned forward, her eyes sparkling with excitement.

"But I'm talking Fitzwilliam Darcy here, a young, handsome and fantastically wealthy man with a vast estate. Now if such a person had been a force in Jane Austen's life, don't you think there'd be at least one reference to him somewhere in all her papers or in the volumes that have been written about her?" Thelma shook her head and leaned back in her chair. "But there's nothing at all in the official Jane Austen record. Not a single word."

Eliza frowned, for she was by now thoroughly confused. "Then I guess I really *don't* understand," she admitted.

"Aha!" Thelma Klein's eyes took on a mischievous sparkle and she lowered her deep voice to a confidential level. "Note that I said there's nothing in the *official* record. However, for some time now a few Austen scholars, myself included, have been developing an entirely new theory about Darcy, which may explain his absence from the official record.

"Did you know, for instance, that after Jane's death her sister, Cassandra, and several other Austen family members methodically destroyed virtually all of the letters she had written, valuable letters that they had been preserving for decades?"

Eliza shook her head in wonderment.

"It's a recorded fact," Thelma said. "Jane was already becoming recognized as a major literary figure by the time of her death. People were beginning to know her and to know of her, so why do you suppose her family started destroying their most precious reminders of her?"

"To hide something?" Eliza speculated.

Thelma slapped the desk with the flat of her hand. "Bingo! Maybe to hide something potentially scandalous!" she declared. "Like a love affair with a man who was totally unacceptable, married perhaps or even potentially dangerous to the family in a political sense."

Eliza felt her pulse quickening as she formed her next question, anxious now to delve even deeper into Thelma's intriguing theory. "Is there any proof of that?" she inquired eagerly. "I mean, besides the fact that the family destroyed her letters."

The researcher shook her head regretfully. "Oh, there have been some tantalizing hints over the years," she conceded, "a scrap of strangely altered manuscript, stories about another letter from Jane to Darcy—"

Eliza sat up straight in her chair. "She wrote *another* letter to him?"

Thelma smiled knowingly. "I have an absolutely reliable source in London—a rare-book dealer—who swears that a letter to Darcy was discovered in the library collection of an English estate two years ago." The smile faded and the researcher threw up her hands in frustration. "Unfortunately," she grumbled, "the damned letter was snatched up by a private collector before anyone in my field even got a look at it. According to my friend, the letter was sold for a price in the high six figures."

"That's incredible!" Eliza said.

"If you think that's incredible, consider this," Thelma continued, "the collector was an American named Darcy."

Eliza stared at her in disbelief. "Darcy at Pemberley Farms," she murmured aloud, thinking suddenly of her annoying Internet pen pal.

Thelma shot up out of her chair like she'd been stuck with a hat pin. "Right!" she exclaimed. "Pemberley Farms! The bastard breeds horses somewhere in Virginia's Shenandoah Valley . . ." She frowned at Eliza. "How in the hell did *you* hear about him?"

"He . . . uh, sent me some e-mail," Eliza replied guiltily. She felt her ears reddening as she remembered what Darcy had said in his e-mails. And she grimaced as she thought of the despicable way she had responded to him.

"Fantastic!" exclaimed Thelma, completely oblivious to

Eliza's pained expression as well as the evasive quality of the younger woman's answer. "I've been trying to get to this guy for two years, but he refuses to respond to my calls and returns all of my letters unopened."

Thelma's expression was positively gleeful as she leaned forward expectantly. "Eliza, what did he say when he e-mailed you?"

Eliza smiled weakly. "He said he believes Jane Austen's Darcy was a real person," she replied.

Thelma's excitement reached a crescendo as she leaped to her feet again and paced the tiny space behind her desk. "And I'm willing to bet that *person* will be found lurking somewhere in this Darcy's family tree," she declared emphatically. "Which explains why no English researcher ever discovered him."

Thelma stopped pacing and leaned over the desk. "And it could also explain why her family wanted to cover up Jane's involvement with him, and why they were perhaps forced to correspond in secret."

Eliza gave her a blank look.

"History!" the researcher said impatiently. "Jane Austen's lifetime coincides almost precisely with the one period in history when England and America were perpetually at one another's throats, beginning with the American Revolution, which began the year after she was born, and continuing right up to the War of 1812, when the British burned Washington, among other unfriendly gestures."

Thelma reached for Darcy's letter and waved it in front of Eliza's face. "Look at the date on this: 1810! Then read what it says: 'The Captain has found me out.'"

"You know who the captain was?" Eliza asked in astonishment.

"Well, two of Jane's brothers were high-ranking British naval officers whose duty in 1810 was trying to stop American ships from running guns and munitions to the French," Thelma replied. "I imagine that either of them would have been naturally suspicious of any American, much less one they suspected of dallying with their sister. And if news spread that Jane was carrying on a relationship with a man who would have been considered a potential enemy of Britain," she theorized, "their careers would surely have been ruined."

Thelma was positively dancing in place by this time. "Oh, this is positively delicious," she laughed, holding up the sealed letter. "Just think what it will mean if one of Darcy's descendants is present to confirm that his ancestor was Jane Austen's lover, when this two hundred-year-old letter is finally opened."

Eliza held up a hand to stop her, for she had completely lost Thelma's trail of logic again. "When it's *finally* opened?" she exclaimed. "Why can't we just open it now?"

Thelma gave her a look she usually reserved for her UFO-conspiracy theorists. "Sweetie, as long as this letter remains unopened," she patiently explained, "it's a mystery to die for."

The older woman closed her eyes, searching for words to adequately convey the true worth of the document in her hand. "Serious Austen collectors will pay a fortune at auction for the unique privilege of being the first to know what's inside," she said.

Eliza felt her stomach turning over as she absorbed the impact of the researcher's words. "A fortune?" she whispered.

Thelma Klein nodded, encouraging her to think big. "A fortune!" she repeated. "But they'll pay even more if we can positively link one of Darcy's living descendants to *Pride and Prejudice.*"

She paused then and looked expectantly at Eliza. "When will you be contacting Darcy again?" she asked.

Eliza sat before her computer, grimacing at the single line she had thus far managed to compose in her intended message to Darcy. She had been at it for nearly half an hour and nothing she tried to say seemed to be coming out right.

Dear DARCY,
   I'd like to apologize for . . .

"I'd like to apologize," she read aloud. "For what? For calling you a crackpot and telling you to get lost?"

She shook her head in disgust and then erased the line. From his perch on the drawing board Wickham appeared to be grinning at her.

"Why start out by *reminding* him of what I said?" Eliza challenged the cat. "I'm sure he remembers it all too well. And I'm sure it hasn't escaped your notice that he didn't even bother replying to my last e-mail."

Wickham yawned and stared out the window.

Eliza returned to the computer screen. Since leaving the library that afternoon she had been trying to think of some graceful way to reestablish communication with the enigmatic Darcy. But so far she had come up with nothing but a blank, on top of which she was embarrassed for having behaved so badly toward him in the first place.

After all, she reflected with chagrin, she had posted a question on the Internet and invited an e-mail response. But when somebody had responded—perhaps one of the few somebodys in all the world who might actually have the answer she was seeking—she had dismissed him out of hand, and in the most insulting manner possible.

Finally admitting to the cat, "Appears I blew it, Wickham." Preoccupied as he was with the shadow of a pigeon that was stalking the ledge outside the window, Wickham did not deign to reply.

But the worst part of the entire e-mail affair, Eliza decided, was that only *after* she had discovered who this latter-day Darcy was had it become important to her to apologize to him. Which made her feel precisely like one of the slimier characters Austen had taken such merciless delight in skewering in her novels. Say, the despicable cad Willoughby from *Sense and Sensibility*.

"Oh, why didn't I just tell Thelma what really happened?" she moaned. "That Darcy contacted me and I blew him off and now he probably wouldn't speak to me if I was the last person on earth."

Unable to face the empty electronic page any longer, Eliza got up and made herself a cup of tea, which she carried into her bedroom.

Sitting on the Victorian piano stool, which was temporarily taking the place of a chair at the vanity table, she regarded her unhappy reflection in the mirror.

"You're not really a bad person," she assured herself, "but you've got to face up to the fact that you have done an unkind thing. And, to make things worse, you lied to Thelma about it. Now you've got to think of some way to make it all right again."

Eliza's image regarded her doubtfully for a long time, then at last a rueful smile lifted the corners of her mouth. "Well, it's plain to see that there's nothing you can do but eat a little humble pie," she murmured.

Another hour passed before Eliza was able to compose an e-mail message that summed up both her apology and, she hoped, an acceptable explanation for her earlier behavior.

Dear Mr. DARCY,
   My rudeness was unforgivable. I hope you will accept
   my apology and try to understand that I was reacting
   mainly to the shock of receiving e-mail from you at
   Pemberley.
                                         SMARTIST

Staring at the MAIL SENT message for a few moments, she wanted to believe, but had no confidence, that it would do the trick. All she could do was hope that he was a tolerant and gracious man.

Chapter 10

The next several days flew by in a blur of activity as Thelma Klein completed her formal analysis of Eliza's letters and began making discreet contacts within the small but elite community of rare-document collectors, dealers and Austen scholars. Though she disclosed the true nature of the astounding discovery of what she had now dubbed the "Darcy Letters" to only a few trusted associates, the researcher made it clear that she was subtly preparing academia and the world at large for an announcement so momentous that it would literally rewrite the book on Jane Austen.

Far from being shunted aside in the blur of activity that began swirling about the letters, Eliza suddenly found herself being consulted by Thelma at all hours of the day and night, regarding the timing of various announcements and the ultimate disposition of the documents. For they were, after all, still her exclusive property. And when she wasn't on the phone with Thelma, she was meeting with the dynamic researcher and the representatives of various interested institutions that were expected to play important roles in the unveiling of the letters.

Timing, Thelma stressed at every available opportunity, was key. Timing and the acknowledgment of one *Mr. Darcy* of Virginia. Eliza had lost count of the number of times the researcher had quizzed her on whether contact had been reestablished with the elusive Darcy.

Unable to confess that she feared she had permanently blown the Darcy connection before even getting it started, the artist haunted her e-mail folder on an hourly basis, while putting Thelma off with a series of groundless speculations, the latest being that the reclusive horseman was probably just away from home for a few days.

Regarding Thelma's interests in the matter, and the reason she had so readily assumed the complex and demanding task of managing the release of the Darcy Letters, it soon became clear to Eliza that Thelma Klein did not expect to go unrewarded. As an Austen expert with an intriguing, albeit unproved, hypothesis about the author, the abrasive Klein had for years been an unsettling force in the snug, predictable world of Jane Austen scholars.

Now, with hard proof in hand that seemed to support her theory about the origins of Darcy, who was arguably the greatest romantic character in English literature, the cantankerous researcher was relishing the prospect of blowing her stuffy colleagues right through the roof. Toward that end, Thelma had proposed, and Eliza had agreed, that she, Klein, would be given the exclusive rights to display Jane Austen's vanity table and the Darcy Letters at the New York Public Library, until such time as the treasures were sold at auction. And, further feathering Thelma's nest, Eliza had granted the researcher exclusive rights to coauthor a book about the discovery and meaning of the letters, a book that would be ready for press before anyone else even got a peek at the documents.

Of course, all of these arrangements took a great deal of time and required numerous discussions with attorneys, library staffers and others. As a result, Eliza's online gallery business was beginning to be affected, as Jerry had so recently predicted would happen. Fortunately, Eliza had a fairly large stock of backup paintings that were easily uploaded to replace her diminishing stocks. And while she was unable to create any new paintings amid the frenzy of planning and contract signing, Eliza was able to keep up with her orders by working late at night.

The latter circumstance took its toll primarily on whatever was left of the relationship between Eliza and Jerry. Where once he had felt free to drop in for an evening, or call late for a last-minute dinner date, the investment counselor was now compelled to leave voice-mails or hurry through their occasional phone conversations. Conversations she purposely avoided the first couple of days after their disastrous dinner and then kept strictly to business when she did talk with him.

So it was that more than a week after he had openly chastised her for her foolishness in devoting so much time and emotional energy to the mysterious letters that Jerry finally got Eliza to agree to meet him for dinner.

Unlike the previous occasion when they had met for dinner at a booth in his favorite neighborhood deli, Jerry's choice of a restaurant on this particular evening was elegant, candle-lit and very French. As Eliza entered the expensive bistro wearing a positively smashing black cocktail dress, he rose from the small corner table he had reserved and ogled her though his shiny glasses.

"Eliza!" There was a nervous edge to his voice as he took her hand and actually planted a slightly damp kiss on her knuckles. "You look absolutely great tonight," he said a little too loudly. Jerry gestured grandly as he pulled out a chair for her.

Retrieving her hand, Eliza allowed herself to be seated and flashed him a dazzling smile. "Why, Jerry, thank you," she said, genuinely surprised by this sudden display of gallantry, a quality she had never even suspected he possessed.

"I've been missing you," he said regretfully. "It seems like we've hardly had a chance to speak lately."

Eliza looked at him carefully, wondering if their brief separation had at last uncovered some hidden reservoir of affection in the usually ultrareserved accountant. "I'm sorry I've been so out of touch," she apologized. "But the week has been completely crazy."

Thrilled to have someone besides Wickham in whom she could confide, Eliza leaned forward and lowered her voice to a near-whisper. "It's all very hush-hush at the moment," she told him, "but the library plans to make my letters and the vanity the centerpiece of their Jane Austen exhibit, and Sotheby's will be announcing a special auction in the fall."

Jerry beamed with enthusiasm at the news. "That *is* exciting," he agreed. "What about that reclusive collector you told me about—Darcy? Have you heard from him again?"

Eliza's smile faded and she slowly shook her head, her guilty feelings from several days earlier returning in a rush. "No," she replied, "I'm afraid I offended him too badly . . ." She thought about that for a moment and a wonderful new idea suddenly popped into her head.

"I've been thinking about going down to Virginia," she said, her words giving further form to the idea.

"Maybe if I met this Darcy and had a chance to personally explain about the letters—without his knowing I was the one who insulted him on the Internet . . ." Her voice trailed off as the thought continued to develop. Actually, she decided, it was the best idea she had had yet.

Still considering the new plan, Eliza was surprised to feel Jerry taking her hand in his. She looked up to see him scrutinizing her closely, a slightly worried expression on his narrow features.

"Eliza," he began huskily, "before you go running off in search of this romantic character . . ."

Jerry swallowed hard and his eyes darted nervously around the room. "Well," he continued after taking a sip of water, "we've known each other for a very long time. And I want to ask you something important."

She had no idea what his question might be and found his nervousness curious. "What is it, Jerry?"

He flushed and cleared his throat. He looked around the romantic little café again, then peered directly into her eyes.

"Eliza, would you . . . *Will* you . . . consider investing part of the money you get from the sale of the letters in an Internet start-up?"

She sat in stunned amazement. It took only seconds for her shock to turn to anger. The nerve! How many days had it been since his declaration that her interest in the letters was a silly waste of time? She couldn't believe it, now he wanted to cash in on them. His nervousness was obviously because he recognized his own hypocrisy, but that hadn't stopped him. She quivered with outrage; casting his hand aside as hard as she could, she rose.

Surprised, Jerry asked, "What are you doing?"

Trying desperately to stay in control and remain calm she spat out, "I'm leaving. Good night."

"But what about dinner?"

Eliza took a deep breath, picked up her water glass and threw the liquid in his face. "Go to hell, Jerry." She stormed out.

Outside the restaurant, she stopped and leaned against the wall. Still quivering with outrage, Eliza took several deep breaths. She wasn't sure why it had upset her so, it was, after all, typical Jerry behavior, completely bottom-line motivated.

Watching a couple cuddling in the back of a hansom cab, she had to admit to herself that much of the anger was directed at herself. Constructing the boundaries that relegated her passions to a relationship with someone like Jerry had in fact brought her personal life to a screeching halt.

Her mother had often told her that you can't stand still, you either move forward or you move backward. And she'd wasted the last two years in a relationship she had known wouldn't go anywhere; so by her mother's rule she had slipped back rather than moving on after her father's death. Well, that ended right now. Pushing herself away from the building she headed home with a whole new direction for her life.

Volume Two

Chapter 11

Two days after her aborted final dinner with Jerry, and nearly four hundred miles to the south, Eliza was driving a small red Toyota along a narrow state road in Virginia. The car-rental agent in nearby Roanoke, where she had arrived on the morning commuter flight, had marked a map and assured her that this was the way to Pemberley Farms, but Eliza was beginning to have her doubts.

Though it was nearly ten in the morning, the lush, green countryside through which she had been driving for the past half hour was still shrouded in morning mist, giving an eerie look to a landscape that appeared largely untouched by human habitation.

Certain that she had either taken the wrong road or somehow missed the distinctive landmark that was supposed to identify her destination, Eliza glanced at the map on the seat beside her. "Go to a pair of big stone gates," she snorted, mimicking the earnest rental agent's thickly accented directions, "Ya cain't missem, ma'am!"

Eliza squinted into the mist. "Well if ah *cain't* missem," she groused with a New Yorker's inborn sense of frustration, "then where the hell are they?"

She was on the point of turning the car around and returning for fresh directions to the last small town she'd passed through when, suddenly, a pair of tall stone pillars emerged from the fog ahead, flanking an unpaved side road.

Eliza grinned at her own impatience. "Sorry, Clem," she apologized in absentia to the friendly Hertz guy. "They're big stone gates, just like you said."

She guided the Toyota onto the side road and proceeded another quarter mile through a tunnel of overhanging trees. Emerging from the forest, she encountered a second set of gates: the real ones. They were heavy wrought iron gates intricately scrolled with an intertwining PF on each, probably created by a slave artisan right here on the plantation. Standing maybe ten feet tall and attached to brick pillars, they were secured by a large padlock. The pillar on the left held what Eliza assumed was the Darcy family crest or coat of arms or whatever they were called. The plaque on the right pillar appeared to be of patinized bronze. She slowly read the words spelled out in old English lettering, Pemberley Farms, Established 1789, then whistled softly to herself, "Oh my God!" she breathed, "I'm beginning to think that Thelma may actually have stumbled onto something here."

Leaning out of the car to examine the formidable barrier in her path, she jumped slightly, startled by the cultured tones of a deep baritone voice in this seeming wilderness. She swiveled around in her seat to find an elderly black man looking politely in at her through the passenger window of the car.

"Good morning, miss, I'm Lucas. May I help you?"

"Yes, I, uh . . ." she stammered, caught completely off guard. "That is," she began again, "can I drive in to the, uh, farm?"

The old gentleman, whom she noticed was dressed in a neatly pressed black suit, a snowy white shirt that matched his hair, and a black tie, looked regretful. "Oh, I am sorry, miss," he answered, "but there's no cars allowed up at the farm on the weekend of the Rose Ball."

Eliza tried to go with the flow. "Oh, sure, of course, Lucas!" she said, all but slapping her forehead in an overdone attempt to convince him that she knew what he was talking about. "How idiotic of me. I completely forgot about the Rose Ball."

If Lucas detected the patent phoniness of her response, he was too polite to betray any sign of it. "If you'll just drive your car around behind the gatehouse there," he said, gesturing to a fairly large stone cottage among the trees that she had somehow overlooked, "I will call up to the Great House for a guest carriage."

"A guest carriage?" Eliza had a quick vision of her impromptu meeting with Darcy going straight down the tubes as her brain filled with images of a phone call to the "Great House," whatever that was, followed by queries as to who she was and what business she had there. "Well, that's awfully sweet of you, Lucas," she quickly answered, "but I think I'd just like to walk on up to the house and, uh, admire the scenery along the way."

Lucas seemed unruffled by the request. "Certainly, miss," he replied. "Whatever you like."

Smiling graciously, the relieved Eliza drove around the gatehouse and was surprised to find several luxury cars and two pickups parked in a large, grassy meadow. Parking the red Toyota as inconspicuously as possible between a BMW and a classic Jag, she shouldered her handbag, grabbed a small portfolio from the backseat and walked to the gates. Lucas already had them open for her.

He raised his eyebrows and smiled as she stepped through. "You have a nice walk now, miss," he said as she moved past him and started up a drive that vanished into another thick stand of trees.

"How far is this house anyway?"

Despite the lingering coolness of the morning air and the movie-set fog swirling about her ankles Eliza was perspiring as she trudged wearily along the endless drive. Around her the landscape had gradually changed from dark woods to rolling meadows, then to woods again. But her destination was still nowhere in sight and her feet were beginning to seriously hurt.

"The problem with this place," she grunted as she followed the drive down a small hill, across a picturesque wooden bridge, and then started up another steep incline, "is that there's never a taxi around when you need one."

Almost before she had finished uttering those words, a deep, thundering sound rumbled at her back. Whirling around to look back at the fog-shrouded bridge, she listened for a heart-stopping moment as the thunder reached deafening proportions. Then, like magic, a rider on a magnificent black horse burst out of the mist at a full gallop, bearing directly down on her.

Screaming in terror, Eliza hurled herself into the muddy ditch at the side of the drive, to avoid being trampled. She landed facedown in three inches of soft brown muck and felt a paralyzing jolt of pain as her left elbow connected solidly with a moss-covered rock protruding from the mud.

She rolled over and sat up in time to see the rider leaping from his mount and pounding back down the drive toward her. "My God! I'm terribly sorry," he apologized. "Are you all right?"

Stunned by the force of her fall, Eliza blinked and stared groggily into his face . . . a face that seemed somehow familiar. "I . . . think so," she answered, still more aware of the gooey muck clotted in her hair and smeared across her face than of the injured elbow, which had gone mercifully numb.

"Let me help you up," said the horseman, stepping gallantly into the mud with his high, shiny boots and helping her to her feet, then gently pulling her back up onto dry ground. He stood there helplessly, regarding her filthy clothing and hair. Then he saw her badly skinned and bleeding elbow. "You're bleeding," he exclaimed. "That arm could be broken."

"I guess it was my own fault," she grumbled. "I thought

they ran the Derby in Kentucky," she added, trying for a bit of humor.

She did not resist as he pulled a spotless white silk scarf from around his neck and fashioned it into a makeshift sling for the injured arm. That done, he bent and peered into her eyes, obviously searching for additional signs of trauma.

Then he surprised her by asking, "Have we met somewhere?"

Eliza looked back into his unforgettable sea green eyes and felt the breath catch in her throat. "Darcy!" a voice was screaming from some distant corner of her brain. "This guy is Darcy, you nitwit!"

Suddenly it all made a weird kind of sense to Eliza: the e-mails, the oh-so-knowledgeable man at the library, his rumored purchase of another Jane Austen letter. Eliza blinked and looked at him again, dimly aware that he was speaking to her.

"Your elbow looks awful," he said, looking worried. "I'd better ride up to the house for help."

"No, please . . ." Eliza's feeble protest was intended to prevent him from going to any more trouble. But from the expression on his face she saw that he completely misunderstood her motive.

"Of course, you're right," he said in a how-could-I-be-so-stupid tone. "I can't leave you alone here. You might go into shock." He looked around the deserted landscape and his eyes settled on the large black horse, which was placidly munching grass a few yards away by the side of the drive. "Do you think you can ride?"

Eliza stared at the huge animal. "On a horse?" she asked with a nervous little laugh. "I don't think so. I mean, I've never been on one before," she added, by way of explaining. "So maybe I'd better walk."

He shook his head. "It's almost a mile to the house," he informed her.

"Oh!" Eliza could think of nothing more to say. So she

watched in silence as he brought the horse over to her, then knelt at her side and made a stirrup with his hands.

"There's nothing to it," he assured her in his soft, slightly accented voice. "Just grab the saddle with your good hand and put your leg over when I push."

Eliza stared wide-eyed at the horse. Up close it was even more enormous than she had previously thought. "I don't think I can do this," she protested.

"Come on," he urged, "just give it a try."

Feeling more than slightly ridiculous, she placed her left foot in his clasped hands and grabbed the saddle with her right hand. And suddenly she was looking down at him from a great height. "Who do you like in the fourth race?" she quipped in an attempt to cover her abject terror.

Laughing, Darcy retrieved her purse and portfolio from the mud, wiped them on his riding breeches and handed them up to her. She smiled appreciatively, "Thank you." Smiling back he swung easily up into the saddle behind her. Reaching around for the reins, he urged the horse into a slow walk up the drive.

Acutely aware of his body moving maddeningly against her back and buttocks as her legs tightly gripped the powerfully muscled back of the horse, Eliza managed a breathless grin. "You could get arrested for doing this in the subway," she said.

He laughed more heartily. "Well, we've established that you're from New York," he said. "What's your name?"

"Eliza Knight," she answered, feeling slightly lightheaded. "What's yours?" she added, remembering that she wasn't supposed to know.

"Fitzwilliam Darcy, at your service," he replied.

She had known he was Darcy but the Fitzwilliam caught her by surprise—the *F* in the e-mails, she should have guessed. "Fitzwilliam. Was your mother a Jane Austen fan?"

"It's a family name."

"Oh. Well, it's nice to meet you, Mr. Darcy."

"My friends call me Fitz." Darcy guided the horse at a slow pace for Eliza's comfort and the small talk slipped into silence.

Feeling slightly dizzy she unconsciously leaned back against him. His breath caught in his chest. After a few moments she realized what she'd done and sat bolt upright. "I'm sorry."

"Don't be, lean back, relax." Unequal to the upright position she did relax against him. Strange, it made her feel safe and she sighed in contentment.

Fitz looked down and had to stop himself from kissing the top of her head. Odd reaction to a complete stranger and this was the second time in less than a week that a woman had stirred feelings he had not experienced in over three years. It felt good. Warmth radiated through his body as she instinctively nestled against him. It felt right, as though she belonged there. In spite of feeling slightly silly for what seemed like a schoolboy's reaction, a small smile of contentment lit his face.

Chapter 12

The sun had already burned off the worst of the morning fog from the higher ground surrounding the magnificent Federalist-style mansion at the center of the estate.

Out on the broad front lawn, which sloped gently down to a small lake, tables and chairs of white wicker had been set up near a buffet table laden with cold meats and salads. Four of Darcy's closest friends were standing around one of the tables making small talk about the fine weather and helping themselves to drinks and coffee, before sitting down to lunch.

The most striking member of the luncheon group was an elegant blonde. Her name was Faith Harrington and her golden hair was pulled straight back into a severe bun of the type that only the extremely wealthy seem to get away with. The classic hairstyle accentuated rather than detracted from her patrician good looks and minimal makeup. In fact, Faith looked absolutely wonderful in her form-hugging, fawn-colored English riding costume, the cost of which roughly approximated three months of the nearest servant's salary.

Clutching a frosty Bloody Mary in one perfectly manicured hand, Faith raised her free hand to shade her sky blue eyes and peered anxiously out over the estate.

"Has anyone seen Fitz yet?" she asked nobody in particular. "He promised to ride with me."

Harv Harrington—a slightly disheveled young man whose

tousled hair and movie-star looks eclipsed his downscale outfit of rumpled golf shirt, old khaki trousers and topsiders
without socks—grinned and sauntered over to a table where
he slouched into a comfortable wicker chair.

"You'll have to start rising earlier if you want to catch Fitz
that way, Sis," Harv said, pausing to sip his own drink,
which was primarily comprised of Stoly with a slight hint of
orange juice for the sake of appearances. "Our gracious host
lit out of here on his horse this morning before your first
layer of natural-look makeup was dry."

Faith was not amused by his taunt. "Baby brother, remind
me to slip something toxic into your next martini," she retorted, sitting primly in a chair opposite her brother and
sticking out her lower lip in the tiny pout that had gotten her
almost everything she'd ever wanted since the age of two.

"Don't you two start," warned Jenny Brown. She was a
statuesque, awesomely beautiful black woman, and her rich,
melodious voice carried a serious undertone of warning that
instantly quelled the brewing argument between the Harringtons. Jenny's husband, Artemis, a handsome, muscular man
dressed comfortably in a threadbare Harvard T-shirt and
baggy sailing shorts, arrived from the beverage table at that
moment and diplomatically seated himself between Harv and
Faith. He and Jenny exchanged a quick, cautious glance, then
he raised his coffee mug to Harv.

"Cheers," Artemis said without preamble. "Let's eat."

Faith's lower lip extended another quarter inch, expressing
her added displeasure at his suggestion. "Artie, we will not
begin without Fitz!" she said emphatically.

"Faith, I'm hungry now!" Artemis countered. "And Fitz
may not be back for hours."

"Or at all," Harv interjected, giving his sister a meaningful
wink. "Remember that time when he—"

Faith's cheeks instantly reddened through her imported
Swiss makeup base. "Shut up, Harv!" she spat.

"Good Lord," Jenny interrupted, pointing down the curving drive, "will you look at what's coming!"

Distracted from the brewing argument, the others all turned and stared in the direction indicated by Jenny's finger, in time to see Darcy riding slowly up the drive with the bedraggled Eliza tucked securely into the saddle ahead of him. As they watched, Darcy angled the black horse onto the grass and guided it straight toward their table.

"By God, it's Fitz," Harv laughed, getting to his feet, "and he appears to have rescued a damsel. She's a real beauty, too, from the look of her."

Faith glanced at the approaching pair and sniffed disdainfully. "How on earth can you tell?" she asked. "The poor thing looks as if she's been freshly dipped in mud."

By the time the horse reached them everyone but Faith was on their feet. "Harv, Artemis, lend a hand, will you?" Darcy called out. "Miss Knight has been injured."

Harv and Artemis rushed forward to help Eliza down. When she was safely on the ground, Darcy dismounted and handed the horse over to a groom who had run up from the stables.

"We need to get your arm taken care of right away," he told Eliza, who stood forlornly dripping mud in the circle of staring strangers.

"I think it may be broken," he said worriedly to Artemis.

"I'm fine, really," Eliza insisted. She looked down and cautiously fingered her bad arm, getting a good look at the blood for the first time since her fall. She winced at the sight because her arm really did look like hell. "It's nothing, I'm sure," she said without much conviction. "Just a skinned elbow."

"Nevertheless," Darcy said firmly, "I'd like you to go up to the house and let Artemis have a look at it." He lowered his voice to a confidential tone and gave Eliza a conspiratorial wink.

"You see, Eliza, Artemis here is the leading orthopedic surgeon in our neighborhood and he will be crushed if you don't allow him to demonstrate his healing skills for us."

Darcy grinned at his friend. "Isn't that true, Artemis?"

Artemis nodded, poker-faced. "I only ever come to Fitz's weekends in hopes that someone will break something," he told Eliza. "But nobody ever does," he said glumly.

"Okay," Jenny interrupted, scowling at the men. "That's enough, you two. Let's get this poor girl into the house."

She took Eliza's uninjured arm and led her toward the front steps of the mansion, with Artemis trailing behind. "Don't pay any attention to them, honey," Jenny told the newcomer. "They're all crazy but harmless."

Darcy stood watching until the trio had disappeared into the mansion. Then he walked over to the beverage table and drew himself a cup of coffee from a silver urn. He stood silently sipping the steaming brew and gazing out at the lake as Harv sidled up beside him.

"Nice catch, Fitz," the younger man remarked. "Where did you find her?"

"She was walking along the drive, near the bridge," Darcy replied distantly. "I nearly killed her."

"Walking?" Faith exclaimed. She had joined the men at the table and was refreshing her Bloody Mary. "My God, what for?" she asked in genuine puzzlement.

Eliza sat on a small stool at an exquisite antique dressing table that blended beautifully with the other furniture in the large bedroom suite decorated in pale shades of blue. Artemis was down on one knee before her, gently examining her arm, while Jenny rummaged in a tall wardrobe behind him.

"It'll be sore," Artemis pronounced, getting to his feet, "doesn't appear that you broke anything. If it continues to give you problems we can run into my office in town later and take some X-rays . . ."

Eliza gave him a grateful smile. "Thank you," she said. "I'm sure it will be fine."

Artemis nodded and closed the small emergency bag he'd dug out of a drawer. He reached over to give Jenny a quick kiss, then started to leave the room. Pausing at the door, he turned back long enough to order Eliza to let him know if she needed anything for pain, then he left.

"That's some great husband you have, Mrs. Brown," Eliza told Jenny, who was holding up a flowered sundress for her inspection.

Jenny grinned. "Isn't my Artie something?" she marveled. "Now who would have ever thought a plain old country schoolteacher like me would have the luck to land a Harvard man, and him a damn fine doctor at that."

"From my first quick impression of you two I would say that Artemis considers himself the lucky one to have landed you," Eliza said with a smile.

Jenny's lovely ebony face glowed at the compliment. "He does act that way, doesn't he?" she smiled. "So I guess that makes us both lucky."

She offered the flowered sundress to Eliza. "This may be a little big on you but I think it'll do until we can get your luggage up here from the gatehouse."

It took a moment for Eliza to comprehend that the other woman believed she was another of Darcy's weekend guests. "Oh, I'm not going to be staying," she exclaimed, shaking her head.

"You're not?" Jenny Brown's voice was filled with sincere disappointment. "But you'll miss the Rose Ball tomorrow night."

"I came down here hoping to see Fitz . . . Mr. Darcy for an hour or two," Eliza explained. "I had no idea he had house-guests, or I would never have dropped in like this."

Jenny gave her a strange look. "Well, you might have just dropped in but you surely landed with a big splash," Jenny chuckled.

She put the sundress down on the bed. "You wear the dress anyway," she insisted. "Fitz certainly isn't going to let you get away without lunch." Jenny scrutinized Eliza's ruined clothing and matted hair. "The shower is right through there," she told her, pointing to a door. "You'll find everything you need in the bathroom, including Band-Aids. Just take your time and come on out to lunch whenever you're ready."

Eliza nodded gratefully. "Thank you, Jenny," she said. "You've been very kind."

Jenny smiled and gave her a wink. "And watch out for the icy blonde when you come downstairs," she advised. "If our dear little Faith thinks you're after Fitz, she'll plant a dagger in your heart."

"My mission is strictly one hundred percent business," Eliza assured her with a grin, "so there'll be no need for further bloodshed."

As soon as Jenny left, Eliza entered the bathroom and looked into the mirror. For a moment she was shocked by the sight of her dirt-streaked face. And then she suddenly realized that the dirt and mud must have been the reason Darcy hadn't recognized her from the library.

Removing her contacts, she stepped into the shower. Hot water pelted down on her, scouring the mud from her body and hair, stinging her elbow. She watched as the dirt swirled down the drain, reminding her that he would recognize her when she was cleaned up. She stood in the pulsating water wondering why she had denied having met him. Shaking off the guilt, she attributed the denial to her inbred New York paranoia. But that wasn't going to make it any easier when he finally realized she'd lied.

Well, she supposed that it didn't really matter right now; she would just have to cross that bridge when she came to it. Breathing deeply she accepted the fact that she couldn't stall too much longer, she was already starting to prune.

Chapter 13

The others were lingering still over their delayed lunch on the lawn by the time Eliza put in an appearance. Harv was the first to spot her coming out of the house with her purse and portfolio in hand. He grinned lopsidedly and raised his glass in her direction. "Here she comes," he announced loudly.

Faith looked up and grimaced to show her disinterest in the interloper. "Be still my foolish heart," she muttered into her third or fourth Bloody Mary.

Ignoring Faith, Darcy rose immediately to his feet and strode across the lawn to meet the new arrival. "Miss Knight, are you feeling better?" he inquired with concern.

Eliza looked up at him through the glasses she used when she didn't want to wear her contacts. Her thick black hair, still damp from the shower, was now pulled back into a flaring ponytail, and in Jenny's oversized sundress she felt fairly confident that her own mother wouldn't have been able to pull her out of a police lineup. So, for the moment at least, she was safe.

"Yes, thank you," she replied to Darcy. "It's nothing at all," she assured him. "Dr. Brown says my elbow will be fine," lightly touching her arm, "so there's no harm done."

Looking over at the table where the others sat, Eliza saw

that they had stopped eating and were obviously waiting for Darcy's return. "Please go back to your guests," she told him. "As I explained to Jenny, I wouldn't have come today if I'd had any idea I was intruding—"

Darcy gave her a warm smile and waved off her protest. "It's no intrusion at all," he assured her, nodding toward the others. "They're all old friends of mine who came out early to help me coordinate our annual Rose Ball. You can tell me over lunch why you're here."

He arched his eyebrows like a film noir detective. "I presume you did come all the way down here to see me about *something*."

"Yes, I did," Eliza confirmed. "But I can easily come back on Monday when you're free. I saw several motels in the last little town I passed . . ." She hesitated, glancing over at the table where his friends sat waiting. "My reason for wanting to see you is somewhat confidential in nature at this stage."

Darcy nodded his understanding. "You all please go ahead without me," he called to the others. "Miss Knight and I have some private business to discuss."

He guided Eliza up the steps of the mansion to an empty table, signaling for a servant to bring place settings and drinks. "We can still talk over lunch," he said, smiling. "Everyone here knows that I frequently entertain buyers who want to talk about nothing but horses, and almost always in confidence, so they'll understand completely."

Eliza allowed herself to be seated at a table on the veranda, some distance away from the others. She took a look around her while a white-jacketed waiter set places for her and Darcy. "Your house and grounds are truly beautiful," she remarked as they waited for the man to leave.

"Thank you," said Darcy. "But you haven't seen the best part yet. And since you came all this way you're more than welcome to stay on for the weekend. We're expecting something over two hundred guests tomorrow night, all in authentic period costumes from the eighteenth and nineteenth centuries. It's always a spectacular event."

Eliza reluctantly shook her head. "It's very nice of you to ask me," she said. "And it really does sound fascinating. But I wouldn't dream of imposing on you any further. Actually, I only need a few minutes of your time and then I'll be on my way."

"Very well," Darcy replied. "What can I do for you?"

At the other luncheon table Darcy's friends were speculating about Eliza and the purpose of her unexpected visit to Pemberley Farms on the eve of the Rose Ball. Never one to stand on ceremony, Harv stared over at the pair, who seemed to be engaged in a serious discussion. As he watched, Eliza made a series of broad gestures with her hands and Darcy emphatically nodded several times.

"Okay, Jenny," demanded the younger Harrington, turning back to his own table, "who is she and what's she doing here?" Harv cast a mischievous glance at Faith, who was gazing glumly into her empty glass. "My sister won't lower herself to ask you," Harv said, injecting a comic maniacal tone into his voice, "but I can see that her eyes are already beginning to take on that familiar evil red glow."

"Harv," Faith snapped, "will you shut the hell up!"

Harv grinned and raised a glass to his sister as everyone turned to await Jenny's reply. The tall black woman shrugged and, enjoying their suspense, speared a bite of her salad.

"I don't know why you're all making such a to-do," Jenny said at length. "Her name's Eliza Knight, she flew down from New York to see Fitz on some kind of business. And she's definitely not staying the weekend."

Jenny raised her right hand like the key witness in a murder trial. "That's all I know."

"Not staying, huh?" Harv looked crestfallen. "That's too

bad," he complained. "We could definitely use some new blood around here."

"Yes, but preferably not on the ballroom floor," quipped Artemis around a mouthful of ham.

Jenny giggled and jabbed him in the ribs. "That was funny, Artie darling," she laughed. "I wish you'd employ that dry Harvard wit of yours more often."

Artemis shrugged. "I would but it's a big strain," he replied with a deadpan expression.

While his friends at the other table were busy conjecturing about Eliza, lunch was being served. Eliza watched in silence as a lovely salad with blackberry vinaigrette was placed before her, followed by a beautifully grilled trout, caught right here on the estate, as her host proudly explained. The servant finished his task, leaving a delicately woven silver basket filled with warm bread and a crystal dish of butter. Once he was out of sight and, she assumed, earshot, Eliza began her story. She started with the purchase of the dressing table (excluding any mention or thought of Jerry) and ended with Thelma's confirmation of the authenticity of the letter and by extension the vanity as well.

Darcy had been listening with growing fascination to the pretty New Yorker's remarkable tale. Every word she said about her discovery had the ring of truth to it and he was certain this was the break he had been anticipating for so long. By the time she had reached the end of her narrative he was leaning expectantly across the table, his green eyes fixed raptly on hers.

"The two letters you found," he began when she had finished, "do you have them with you?"

Eliza nodded and lowered her eyes to the portfolio on the table near her. "As a matter of fact I do," she said. "Although I'm afraid that poor Thelma Klein nearly had a nervous breakdown over my taking them out of her temperature-controlled vault. I was forced to remind her that they are still my property," she added, thinking of the heated debate she had had with the stolid researcher.

She paused thoughtfully, examining Darcy's eyes in an attempt to read the surging emotions she saw there. "I felt that it was important to bring the actual documents with me so you could examine them for yourself," she told him.

Darcy nodded eagerly. "May I see them, then?" he asked, reaching for the portfolio.

Eliza's hand beat his to the leather case, pinning it firmly to the table. "On one condition," she said.

Disappointment was evident in his eyes as he leaned back in his chair and stared at her.

"You are reputed to have bought another Jane Austen letter from a British document dealer two years ago," Eliza continued flatly. "I would like to see that one."

"Who told you there was another letter?" Darcy demanded. "Oh, of course," he snorted angrily, "it was that damned Klein woman."

Darcy then realized that his tone had been too sharp. "I'm sorry," he told her, "but the letter you mentioned has been a source of immense irritation to me for some time. I paid a great deal of money for it, with the express understanding that I would remain completely anonymous," he explained. "So perhaps you can imagine how I felt when Thelma Klein, whom I had never met, suddenly began pressuring me to send it to her within twenty-four hours of the purchase."

Eliza smiled. "Sounds exactly like Thelma." Conceding in a pseudoconspiratorial tone, "She can be more than a little pushy."

"At any rate," Darcy said, calming down, "of course there's no reason you can't see the letter. I have it in my study." His handsome features lit up with a charming smile, "If you're finished with lunch we can go in now."

Almost knocking his chair over in his rush to stand, his

cheeks flushed pink and he looked away. Regaining his composure he gestured to the door. "Whenever you're ready."

Eliza was amused by the exuberance with which Darcy expressed his impatient desire to go into the house and see the letters. Trying not to reveal her own excitement, she smiled at him as she rose, "No time like the present."

Chapter 14

The enormous cherrywood paneled room that Darcy referred to as his study reminded Eliza more of a university research library than a personal workplace. Besides the massive hardwood desk holding his computer, phones and what appeared to be several stacks of business papers, and a grouping of antique furniture arranged around a large fireplace, the richly decorated study contained a long, banquet-sized table that was strewn with reference texts, piles of letters and leather bound journals and diaries, all of which appeared to be of great age.

After showing Eliza to a comfortable armchair beside his desk, Darcy walked over to a file cabinet, removed a plain manila folder from an upper drawer and laid it on the desk in front of her. She looked at him questioningly and he nodded. "Go ahead, open it."

With trembling hands Eliza opened the folder and found herself looking at a tattered fold of writing paper nearly identical in size and texture to the sealed letter that she had found behind the vanity mirror. Her voice was an awed whisper as she excitedly read the address written by the familiar hand in faded, rust-colored ink. "'Jane Austen, Chawton Cottage ~ Fitzwilliam Darcy, Chawton Great House.'"

Her dark eyes sparkling with anticipation, Eliza looked up

at him. "Yes, it looks the same as mine," she told him. "May I read it?"

Darcy nodded, then he walked to one of the study's tall windows and stared out at the lawns as she carefully unfolded the letter. Eliza read aloud:

12 May, 1810

Sir,

I have after some study located the passage that you and I were discussing last evening. If you will call on me at home at 2:00 P.M. today, I shall be glad to point it out for you.

"It's signed 'Jane A,'" she concluded.

Eliza looked up at Fitzwilliam Darcy, who had turned back to face her. "This is positively amazing," she said, examining the old letter more closely. "This letter is dated the same day as *my* letter from Darcy to Jane. In that one he told her that someone he called 'the Captain' was suspicious of him and that he had to go into hiding."

Darcy acknowledged that information with a slight nod. When he offered no further comment Eliza opened her portfolio and took out her two letters. She picked up the opened one and held it out for his examination. "Would you like to read it?" she offered.

To her utter amazement, he made no move to take the proffered letter but merely shook his head. "May I see the letter from Jane now?" he asked in a curiously subdued tone.

Eliza frowned at what struck her as his exceedingly odd behavior, but she handed him the sealed letter anyway. Darcy said nothing, but stared at it for several long seconds, slowly turning it over and over in his hand.

"Your letter from Jane says that she found the passage they were discussing," Eliza interrupted, hoping to start a discussion with him about the mysterious message she had just read. "Do you have any idea what that means?"

Ignoring her question, Darcy returned to his desk and seated himself in the leather chair. Reaching down, he unlocked a lower drawer and removed from it a large folio checkbook, which he opened on the desk before him.

"Miss Knight, let me come directly to the point," he said without looking up at her. He lifted a silver-chased fountain pen from an ornamental holder on the desk and held it poised above a blank check. "I would like very much to purchase these letters from you, as well as the vanity table in which you discovered them."

Darcy slowly raised his eyes to meet Eliza's. "What is your price?"

Taken completely off guard, both by the man's seeming disinterest in the mysterious contents of the two opened letters, and by his abrupt offer to buy her letters without further discussion, Eliza could think of no instant reply. Instead, she sat there scrutinizing him from behind her glasses, trying to imagine what was going on in his mind.

Darcy remained motionless, waiting for her to speak. Sunlight from the tall study windows glinted brightly on the silver barrel of the fountain pen hovering over the check.

"Mr. Darcy," Eliza finally commenced, clearing her throat and taking pains to keep her voice deliberately neutral, despite her growing anger. "I came here today hoping you might confirm for me that these letters were exchanged between Jane Austen and one of your ancestors. I certainly hope you don't think that I intended to *sell* mine to you."

Darcy smiled back at her with the barely concealed impatience of a headwaiter who has been insufficiently tipped. "I'm sure you had no such intention," he said in a condescending tone that Eliza interpreted to mean that that was exactly what he thought. "Nevertheless, I would like to buy the letters from you all the same." He raised the silver pen meaningfully. "You need only tell me how much you want, so that I can fill out the check."

The arrogance of this man, who was obviously used to getting whatever he wanted simply by paying for it, irritated her and she snapped back, "My letters are not for sale and you haven't answered my question: was your ancestor Jane Austen's lover?"

The determination he saw on her face and in her eyes made it clear that she had no intention of selling him the letters or relinquishing this line of inquiry. Their eyes locked and she watched as the arrogance drained away, replaced by a palpable disappointment. Not sorry that she may have caused the change, she persevered, "Well?"

Darcy slipped the pen back into its holder and closed the checkbook, and with downcast eyes and in a voice barely above a whisper said, "No."

More than a little surprised and unable to keep the skepticism out of her voice, she asked, "Are you telling me it's just a coincidence that you share the same name?"

Getting irritated himself at what he perceived as an invasion of his privacy, he shot back, "I'm not telling you anything; I simply said that he wasn't my ancestor."

"I don't understand."

"No, I don't suppose you do." He offered nothing else as an uneasy silence descended on the room.

"That's it, I don't get any kind of explanation?" Her abrasive challenge reflected her growing annoyance with his evasions.

She was surprised to see his handsome features now filled with his own frustration and barely suppressed anger. "Although I can't see that it's any of your business, I can guarantee that you would not understand the only explanation I have and you certainly wouldn't accept it."

Shocked at what she considered an insult, she said, "So you think I'm too stupid to understand."

Her statement brought back the memory of another woman saying almost those exact words.

His attention was obviously elsewhere, so Eliza accepted that the interview was over, gathered her things and stood up. Sarcastically she spat, "Well, thank you very much, I'm sorry I took up so much of your time." She walked to the door, opened it and turned to him. "If you would arrange for someone to take me back to my car, I'll leave you to the rest of your weekend."

"Miss Knight . . . Eliza, please wait." Halted by what seemed to be remorse in his voice, she closed the door and turned back to him.

Darcy stood behind his desk and gazed down at the single letter he owned. "It is very important to me *personally* to obtain your letters," he said quietly. He hesitated, and for an instant Eliza was almost certain that he was going to weep. "Especially the unopened one," he added in a humble tone.

Taking a few steps back toward the desk, "Then Jane's Darcy *was* your ancestor!" Eliza said, realizing that she was actually beginning to feel some sympathy for him. "Well, I'm very sorry, but . . ."

"Dammit! That letter from Jane was *meant for me*!" he shouted in a voice filled with frustration.

Eliza's mouth fell open and she simply gaped at him. "You *are* crazy!" Eliza accused. "I knew it the first time you e-mailed me."

Anger flared like summer lightning in the depths of Darcy's eyes. "You!" he shouted accusingly. "I should have known!"

Before Eliza could retreat he strode across the lush, rose-colored oriental carpet and pulled off her glasses. "*You* were the one at the library exhibit last week!" he said, glaring into her frightened eyes as she took a cautious step backward. "I *thought* there was something familiar about you!"

Darcy moved closer, his handsome features contorted with rage. "Did Thelma Klein put you up to this?"

He towered over her, so close she could feel the heat of his breath on her cheek. Eliza felt her knees weaken. Resolutely, although her hand was trembling, she snatched her glasses out of his hand. "I am getting out of here. Do *not* try to stop me."

Clutching her portfolio to her side, she turned, threw the door open and fled down a long white corridor decorated with classical Greek statuary.

Darcy slammed the study door after her and struck it with his clenched fist, then leaned his head against the highly polished carved mahogany. How could he have been so stupid? Alienating the one person who, more than likely, held the key to his three-year search for affirmation.

Heaving a sigh at the lost opportunity, Darcy pulled himself together and went out to join his guests on the lawn of Pemberley House.

Chapter 15

The Browns and Harringtons were still lounging at their table on the lawn. Their heads swiveled in unison as the front door of the Great House flew open and they watched Eliza run down the steps. She paused on the drive for a moment, then saw them all looking at her as she turned and hurried away in the direction of the distant gatehouse.

"Well," Faith observed with undisguised glee, "it appears that the *business* meeting has adjourned."

"Lucky break for you, Sis." Harv gave her a mock congratulatory wink. "You didn't even have to arrange for her to fall from the tower."

Far too pleased to be seriously annoyed by her brother's taunt, Faith smiled angelically and traced the rim of her glass with a blood-red fingernail. "That's right, Harv," she replied sweetly, "now I can devote myself full time to arranging *your* little accident. Tell me, dear, have you checked the brakes on that old Jag of yours lately?"

Ignoring the semiserious rhetoric of the perpetually warring Harringtons, Jenny shielded her eyes from the sun and squinted after Eliza's quickly diminishing figure. "That poor girl's never going to make it all the way back to the gates on foot," she said sympathetically. "Artie darling, see that she gets a ride, will you? And find out how I'm to get my dress back," she reminded him.

Artemis obediently started to rise but Harv jumped up from the table and placed a restraining hand on his shoulder. "Stay right where you are, Artie, old pal," he ordered. "I will personally handle this. Distraught young ladies happen to be a specialty of mine."

Artemis shrugged and resumed his seat. Jenny looked slightly alarmed.

Faith's angelic smile broadened. "Now don't you fret, Jenny darling," she exclaimed, patting Jenny's arm. "Never let it be said that I do not give credit where credit is due. My baby brother does indeed happen to be expert in these matters. There is no doubt in my mind that he will have that old Yankee girl out of your dress in no time."

Jenny rolled her eyes in exasperation. "Faith, honey," she said, "Artie and I have an ironclad rule never to take a drink before sundown. But we're going to break it just this once, for you."

She looked over at Artemis who was already getting up and heading for the beverage cart. "Make mine a martini, darling," she ordered. "A double!"

Eliza trudged wearily along the endless drive, attempting to reconstruct the details of her strange visit to Pemberley Farms. But she could make no sense of any of it. Why, she wondered, did Darcy want her letters when he seemed to have little interest in the one he already had? And what was it he had said about the unopened one? That it was *meant for him*. Sheer madness!

Of course, she glumly reflected, she should have known from the outset that Darcy was too good to be true. Dashing men as rich, handsome and charming as she had at first thought the tall Virginian to be existed only in the pages of romance novels, not in reality.

Calming down, mostly from the exhaustion of the walk, Eliza took a deep breath. She chuckled to herself; he actually was rich, handsome and charming. But there was something else, more, a gentleness, a melancholy; she couldn't quite put her finger on it but it made him extremely compelling, the insanity aside.

She stopped and leaned against a tree, sighing and smiling to herself, reflecting on the way his eyes seemed to caress her at every glance. Returning to the reality of the afternoon, she pushed herself away from the silent strength of the tree and continued the trek to her car. Saying out loud as she continued down the dirt drive, "I haven't gotten this much exercise since . . . forever."

Still muttering to herself, Eliza heard the brisk clip-clop of hooves on the road behind her. Stepping quickly to the edge of the drive, lest she be trampled twice in the same day, she turned to see Darcy's handsome friend grinning down at her from an open carriage.

The carriage drew smoothly to a stop beside her and the man stood and bowed gallantly. "Pardon me, ma'am," said its occupant, "may I offer you a lift down to the gatehouse?"

"I don't know," she said warily. "Are you insane, too?"

"Sadly, yes," Harv Harrington replied with a twinkle in his blue eyes, "but fortunately the homicidal streak in my family skips every third generation, so I believe you're relatively safe."

For the first time in hours, and despite her aching feet, Eliza found herself laughing. "In that case, I'll take a chance," she said, accepting his outstretched hand and climbing wearily into the carriage. She sank back gratefully into the soft leather cushions, wriggled out of her shoes and sighed. "This is heavenly."

"Fitz never did properly introduce us," he said as the carriage began to roll again. "I am Harv Harrington of Staunton, Virginia. And you are . . . ?"

"Eliza Knight of New York, New York," she replied.

"Well, Eliza Knight of New York, I must confess that I was longing for you to stay for the ball," he said. "The local belles that Fitz invites are always so . . . provincial."

"I'm sorry to have to disappoint you, Harv," she replied with a grin, "but I forgot to bring my dancing slippers." Eliza wrinkled her brow. "Besides," she added, "your friend Fitz is a bit . . . eccentric for my tastes."

Harv nodded his reluctant agreement. "Yeah, well, I'll admit that poor old Fitz has been just a tad strange ever since that odd business over in England a few years ago."

Eliza looked at him quizzically. "Odd business?"

Harv nodded. "Surely you remember. It was in *all* the papers at the time." Harv paused to consider his last statement. "At least for a few days. It seems that Fitz went out riding one morning on a two-million-dollar hunter named Lord Nelson and disappeared for nearly a week. Naturally, everyone thought he'd been kidnapped, including Scotland Yard."

"And had he?" Eliza asked, suddenly very interested in Harv's story. "Been kidnapped, I mean?"

Harv slowly shook his head. "Evidently not," he said. "In fact, nobody's exactly sure what happened. But Fitz finally showed up days later, wearing some kind of old-fashioned costume."

The jaunty young man looked around furtively and lowered his voice. "Of course," he continued, "that part never got into the media. In fact, the entire affair got hushed up very quickly, as such things are apt to among very rich folk."

"What did Fitz *say* had happened?" Eliza queried, her interest in this strange, new revelation about the mysterious Mr. Darcy slowly turning to fascination.

"Now that's the strangest part of the whole story," Harv replied, sounding genuinely puzzled. "You see, Fitz never would talk about it. Not even to his closest friends. Course," he added, exaggerating his soft Virginia accent, "all us Southern gentlemen are trained from birth not to question the peculiarities of our wealthier friends."

He paused and shook his blond head thoughtfully. "It was soon afterward that Fitz started haunting antique book and document auctions, buying up whole collections of old letters and journals from the early nineteenth century . . . almost as if there was something he needed desperately to find."

Shortly after Eliza's abrupt departure from the house Darcy went outside intending to send a carriage to find and take his visitor back to her car. Having been gleefully informed by Faith that Harv was already attending to Eliza, he instead poured himself a cup of coffee and sat down with the others, ostensibly to discuss arrangements for the next day.

"What a shame that your little damsel couldn't stay for the ball, Fitz." Unable to leave well enough alone, Faith pressed her Cupid's lips together and made a small, sympathetic sound. "She made such a *decorative* accent to your riding outfit this morning."

Darcy stared past her to a distant point where the drive disappeared beneath a canopy of trees, lost in private reflection. Far from having the intended effect, Faith's comment served only to heighten the painful realization that he had handled his encounter with Eliza Knight exceedingly badly.

"Well," Faith continued in her gay chatter, completely unaware of the smile that lit his face, "I guess that will leave you and me together again, just like old times—"

"Excuse me a moment, Faith."

Never glancing at her, Darcy suddenly got to his feet and walked away. Confused, Faith looked over her shoulder to see him striding toward the front of the house to meet the returning carriage.

"What is *she* doing back here!" the blonde hissed, jumping to her feet.

"Oh, oh!" Jenny exclaimed in a stage whisper intended only for Artemis.

Her laconic husband followed Jenny's startled gaze to the carriage, which was just rolling to a stop. Artemis moaned theatrically and sank lower into his chair. "Oh hell!" he said. "Somebody better call 9-1-1."

"We're out in the country, dear," Jenny reminded him.

"I'm afraid there is no one we can call," she said, taking a large gulp of her drink.

Eliza and Harv were laughing at something he had just said as the carriage came to a stop before the steps of the mansion. Harv spotted Darcy walking toward them and waved. "I brought her back, bag and baggage, Fitz. She's agreed to stay the weekend," he proudly reported.

Mildly astonished by Harv's announcement, Darcy smiled up at them and shook his head. "Harv," he said, "it is obvious that I have grossly underestimated the raw power of your Southern charm."

He stepped up to the carriage and extended his hand to Eliza. "I am very glad you changed your mind," he said.

Eliza took his hand and stepped out of the carriage with a nervous smile. "I warned him I've got nothing more formal to wear than jeans and T-shirts," she said, nodding toward Harv, who was busy gathering up the two small bags they'd retrieved from her rented Toyota.

"There is vintage clothing in the wardrobe room," Darcy assured her, "so I'm sure you can find something appropriate to wear."

His smile faded and his expression turned suddenly serious. "I was afraid I'd frightened you away for good. I hope you'll forgive my earlier outburst. It was very wrong of me to assume that you came here to sell your letters." He fixed her in his haunting green-eyed gaze. "I must confess that I'm very surprised to see you back," he continued. "My behavior was unforgivable."

"I guess that makes us even, then," Eliza said. "I'd already been feeling pretty awful about how I treated you on the Internet, so I probably overreacted myself."

She looked around to see if Harv was listening and saw that he was engaged in turning over her luggage to a portly, middle-aged woman who had come down from the house.

"I really came back to hear why you said that Jane's letter

was *meant for you*," she frankly admitted to Darcy. "That is, if you're willing to tell me."

Darcy's smile returned and he nodded. "Mrs. Temple," he called to the woman with Harv, "would you see that the Rose Bedroom is prepared for Miss Knight? I'm going to take her down to see the horses now." With that he took Eliza's arm and led her away.

Harv watched them walk across the lawn toward the end of the house, then he turned to Mrs. Temple, whose mouth had fallen open. "You heard the gentleman," he said. "The lady will be staying in the Rose Bedroom."

The astonished housekeeper followed his gaze to Eliza and Darcy. "He's putting her in the Rose Bedroom!" she exclaimed breathily. "Who on earth *is* she?"

Harv shrugged and gave Mrs. Temple a boyish grin. "Evidently an honored guest of your employer," he replied.

Knowing better than to expect any further help or information from Harv, the housekeeper clucked her tongue three times to register her disapproval of the unanticipated situation. Then she wiped her red hands on her apron in resignation, hefted Eliza's bags and disappeared into the house with them.

"I cannot believe that *woman* is going to be staying in the Rose Bedroom!" she said.

"Oh, hello, Faith!" Harv turned to look at his sister, who had crept up to eavesdrop while he was speaking with the housekeeper, and then he glanced at his watch and frowned. "It took you close to sixty seconds to get up here from the lawn," he informed Faith. "That's nowhere near your best time."

"What does that witch want with Fitz?" Faith demanded, craning her long, smooth neck to peer in the direction the couple had gone.

"Best I could make out is that she has some old letters that he wants to buy," he replied. Seeing Faith's always-suspicious eyes narrow in a way that promised big trouble was not far off, he added, "You know how Fitz is about that kind of thing these days . . ."

To Harv's great relief his last remark seemed to have had the desired effect on his combative sister—because her suspicious frown lessened noticeably and her pushed-out lower lip receded by several millimeters. "Old letters! And she's holding out on the price," Faith knowingly proclaimed.

"Well now *that* I can understand. I thought it was something serious."

Chapter 16

As Eliza walked with Darcy past the house she saw that the broad gravel drive in front of the property branched into a narrower lane. They followed the pleasant road down a slight hill toward a complex of low brick buildings trimmed in green and ringed with white rail fences. Several of the fenced enclosures adjoining the lane contained horses, which came trotting expectantly to the rails to watch the couple passing by.

Looking at the converging scenery of lush countryside and distant mountains, Eliza was reminded of Jane Austen's description of Pemberley in *Pride and Prejudice*. What was it? Something about how man had not interfered with what nature had done. That's how Fitz's farm seemed to her and she remarked, "I'd love to paint here sometime," and meant it.

"You're an artist," Darcy replied, sounding pleased that she approved of his property. "But then, I suppose I should have figured that out from your online screen name. Smartist, isn't it?"

"Yes," she laughed, wondering just how smart she was being in having agreed to spend the weekend as the guest of the strangely obsessed horseman. "I paint idealized country landscapes."

Darcy raised his eyebrows. "In Manhattan?"

"I guess that does sound a little odd," Eliza said, though

she had never thought of her way of working as particularly odd until he had implied it. "Though they're based on actual places I've visited, most of the landscapes I paint are imaginary," she explained. "I often compose them entirely in my mind beforehand, so I suppose you could say they're really fantasies."

Darcy thought about that for a long moment. "That could turn out to be an advantage," he said, "when I try to explain to you about the letter."

She cast a questioning glance his way but he kept walking, so she said nothing and waited for him to go on.

"What I meant was that it may be helpful that you work with your imagination," he continued. "Because I'm absolutely positive that what I'm about to tell you would be automatically rejected by anyone without a receptive mind."

"About why you said Jane's letter was meant for you?" she asked.

Darcy nodded. "I've never discussed the reasons for my interest in Jane Austen with anyone."

Eliza wasn't quite sure if another response was expected from her. So when Darcy did not say anything further for several more seconds she nudged him. "Well, I'm all ears," she said.

"Perhaps, but it's difficult to know where to begin, considering the fact that you obviously already think I'm deranged," he responded, looking grave.

"I'm so sorry about what I said to you before!" she apologized, determined not to provoke him again, at least not until she had heard him out. "I have *such* a big mouth," she added. "I'm afraid tact has never been one of my virtues."

Darcy raised a hand to preclude any further admissions of guilt on her part. "Please don't apologize," he said. "In fact, there was a long period of time when I wondered myself whether I was merely delusional, or if . . ."

He left the thought hanging as the enormous black stallion he had been riding earlier extended its head over the fence and whinnied for his attention. Stepping off the road, Darcy walked over to the enclosure, patted the animal's nose and fished in his pocket for a handful of something. Eliza came over and leaned on the rails beside him and watched the horse gratefully nuzzling the treat from his open palm.

"Before I begin my story," Darcy said, turning to look at her, "you should probably know that my family has been breeding champion hunters and jumpers on this same land for generations."

Deprived of Darcy's full attention, the black horse fixed a jealous eye on Eliza, then tossed its noble head impatiently in an obvious plea for more of whatever the treat had been.

"I saw the plaque on your gates," Eliza said, keeping a wary eye on the magnificent animal, which still frightened her, mostly because of its size. "The idea that it's been in your family since—is it 1789?—is amazing."

Darcy nodded. "We've always been proud of our heritage. And we've been buying and selling horses across the Atlantic since the late 1800s," he told her. "So my visit to England three years ago began as an ordinary business trip." He hesitated for a moment. "It wasn't really ordinary, I suppose. You see I had gone to England specifically to attend a breeder's auction at which a particular horse was to be sold. A champion among champions." He rubbed the velvety nose of the big black stallion again. "Lord Nelson, meet Eliza Knight."

Darcy looked over at her and smiled. She couldn't help but return the smile.

Turning back to the horse, he hesitated, wondering just how much to tell her. The memory of the auction excited his senses but the exhilarating images dimmed as Darcy also remembered the cloying closeness of Faith Harrington that long-ago afternoon. She had been hanging on his arm all day, the sweet smell of too much champagne on her breath as she screamed encouragement into his ear every time the blue lighted numbers on the electronic auction board went up and up . . .

Over Darcy's objections, Harv had insisted his sister accompany them to England. Darcy, however, had been concerned that a trip abroad with him would simply fuel the tabloid reports of their impending engagement; reports, which seemed to be more and more frequent. He often wondered, in spite of her declaration of innocence, if Faith wasn't the source of the reports. She often allowed her fantasies to get the better of her and he didn't want to add to them. But, as was often the case with Harv, he had acquiesed and so she had joined them.

Shaking off the unpleasant thoughts he said, "I wanted that horse very badly." Darcy resumed his narrative, suddenly remembering that Eliza was still there, "primarily to improve the bloodlines of my stable." He shook his head ruefully. "The only question was whether or not I could really afford him."

There had been an Arab princeling in a box opposite Darcy's, the third or fourth son of the royal house of some oil-rich Gulf dynasty. With no appreciable chance of ever attaining his country's throne, and with unlimited money to spend, the handsome young prince had become a notorious international playboy and womanizer, and a renowned horseman as well. That particular afternoon, surrounded by a bevy of pale English film actresses and his huge retinue of bulky bodyguards and simpering retainers in well-cut suits, the flamboyant prince had been Darcy's only serious competitor for the black horse.

The bid had escalated well past the million-pound mark—Darcy's absolute upper limit—when, thankfully, the youthful potentate had suddenly lost interest in the proceedings and dropped out.

"In the end," Darcy told Eliza without elaborating, "I won the bid and the horse was mine, but for far more than I had planned on spending. I immediately had Lord Nelson transported down to a friend's country place in Hampshire, about fifty miles out of London, to be stabled there until I could arrange to have him flown back to the States.

"That night," Darcy continued, "my friends rather unwisely decided that a victory celebration was in order. I'm afraid there was a great deal of drinking and general carousing . . ."

His voice trailed off again as he prudently edited his story, leaving out the details of the drunken evening that had ensued in the echoing drawing room of the vast Edwardian manor house his friends the Cliftons had rented for the summer. Also leaving out the fact that the evening had ended very late as he tottered up the stairs, with Faith still hanging on his arm.

Throughout his halting preamble Eliza had been closely watching Darcy, certain from his long pauses and hesitant delivery that he was modifying the story for her benefit as he went, but uncertain what any of it had to do with Jane Austen, or her letters.

Now he caught her quizzical expression and flushed with embarrassment.

"Well, I suppose you're wondering what all of this rambling about a horse auction and a country house has to do with the Jane Austen letters?" he asked, as though he'd been reading her mind.

Eliza grinned and pointed her chin westward. "The sun *will* be going down in a few hours," she noted.

The small joke seemed to relax Darcy slightly. "I'm sorry," he said, "I warned you that I'd never discussed this with anyone before. I had no idea it was going to be so difficult."

"I get the impression that you're trying to be selective in what you're telling me," Eliza replied, trying to put him more at ease. "Maybe if you just told me everything that happened and left out all the long, reflective pauses."

Darcy nodded. "You're right," he said. "It's just that some of what took place is a bit personal in nature."

Eliza solemnly raised her right hand. "I promise not to tell another soul," she said.

"Okay," he agreed. "The only point of the story so far is that three years ago I went to England to buy a very expensive horse and ended up with him at a friend's country place in Hampshire."

Eliza nodded. "Fair enough."

"One more thing I should explain before I go ahead," he said. "Some of what I'm about to tell you—things I didn't know as they were happening—was related to me afterwards . . ." Darcy hesitated, choosing his words carefully, ". . . by someone else who was there."

Eliza nodded her understanding.

Darcy gazed off into the distance again. "Though it had been a very late night, I awoke before dawn the morning following the auction," he began.

He closed his eyes, remembering how he had slowly come awake in the big, ornately carved and canopied bed in one of the many guest rooms of the friend's country house and found Faith sprawled unattractively in a tangle of sheets beside him.

Shakily getting out of the bed, Darcy had gone to a window and looked out over the gray, fog-shrouded Hampshire countryside.

"I had a splitting headache," he told Eliza. "I wanted to be outside in the cold morning air . . ."

He looked back at the bed; he had been afraid Faith's traveling with him would send her the wrong message and now too much drink and his own arrogance had created what would surely become an untenable situation. In another time he would have been considered a cad, taking advantage of a woman who had had too much to drink, using her. He was heartily ashamed of himself and feared that he would pay the consequences of his impetuous and stupid actions many times over. His eyes returned to the window and the mist-covered meadow beyond the grounds of the house; at that moment he wanted nothing more than to be away from her.

Darcy paused, deciding that there was no reason to tell this stranger how seeing Faith in his bed made him cringe, adding only, "I wanted to get out and ride Lord Nelson, to feel him underneath me, to see what he could do." Darcy smiled. "I also think I needed to convince myself that I hadn't made a very expensive mistake. After all, I'd never before spent two million dollars on a single animal.

"So," he continued, "I got dressed in some proper English riding clothes, went down to the stables, woke up one of the grooms and had him saddle Lord Nelson."

"Wow!" Eliza breathed. "Two million dollars' worth of horse! And you just got up with a hangover and decided to take him out for a little prebreakfast gallop."

"It was an incredibly stupid thing to do," Darcy admitted. "The sun wasn't even up yet and I was completely unfamiliar with the surrounding countryside."

Darcy began to speak freely then, describing to Eliza the momentary feel of the horse's warm breath on the back of his hand as he took the reins from the sleepy groom, the emptiness of the silent, gray English landscape as he had vaulted up into the saddle and started across a stubbled field in the direction of the gradually lightening sky.

Then suddenly, as he spoke, he was back in that meadow on that gray English morning, urging the willing horse forward, feeling the cold, damp wind in his face.

And, just as the great animal's muscles had seemed to loosen and stretch with the sheer joy and freedom of the run on that long-ago day, so the story that Fitzwilliam Darcy had kept to himself for three long years began to spill from his lips in an unstoppable torrent of words.

Enthralled and mystified by the intensity of his narrative, Eliza listened in silence, not daring to interrupt, lest she break the spell.

Chapter 17

Riding farther and farther from the house, lost completely in the speed of the run and the nearly mystical agility of Lord Nelson, Darcy was unsure how much time had passed as he rode. But at some point he noticed that the sky was rapidly brightening ahead of them and the heavy veils of mist were slowly beginning to part.

Then, directly in their path at the far end of a long meadow, he spied a wall of stacked field stones overhung with the intertwined branches of two tall trees.

As man and horse drew nearer, the rising sun began to climb into the steeply arched frame formed by wall and trees. The illusion of a natural doorway of stone and living wood was so perfect that Darcy suddenly took it into his head to jump the wall, which was low and did not appear to be particularly wide.

Certainly, he thought as they hurtled onward, the low stone barrier presented no serious obstacle for a champion jumper as accomplished as Lord Nelson.

Leaning forward for the hurdle, Darcy pushed the eager horse to its limit, smiling in anticipation of the instant when Lord Nelson's fleet hooves would leave the ground and they would be momentarily flying.

Then, a heartbeat before they reached the wall, the great red orb of the dawning sun rose higher, all at once clearing the tree-filled horizon and flooding the natural archway with a blaze of dazzling light.

In that same split second Darcy realized his mistake, for he could see nothing of the terrain that lay ahead of them in the next meadow. He considered trying to stop Lord Nelson but it was far too late. For the horse was already lunging up and over the wall, into the blinding window of sunlight.

Then, with a sudden, bone-jarring jolt Darcy was flying alone, flying headfirst over the horse toward a hard, uncontrollable impact with a patch of muddy ground on the far side of the stone wall.

Vaguely he heard the frightened horse's scream, followed by the receding sound of its hoofbeats.

Then, nothing.

"I think he's dead."

"No. See, he's breathing. Quick, run for help!"

The voices were high and musical, like angel voices, he thought. Whether minutes or hours had passed Darcy could not be sure. His eyelids slowly fluttered open and he blinked into strong sunlight.

He seemed to be lying on his stomach, his head turned awkwardly to one side, half-resting on his shoulder. Automatically he started to rise, but his limbs would not obey.

Strange, he thought.

Directly in his field of vision lay an outstretched arm—his own, he realized with a start. He could clearly see the hands of his watch glinting in the dazzle of sunlight, slowly ticking off the passing seconds.

A shadow blotted out the sun and Darcy found himself looking up into a small, worried face. Again he thought of angels, for the apple-bright cheeks and wide blue eyes of the tiny blonde girl regarding him might have belonged to a cherub.

The beautiful child cocked her little head and spoke. "Oh you *are* alive, sir!" A heartbreaking smile of relief curved the perfect bow of her pink lips and she knelt beside him on the dew-damp ground, reaching out to dab at his bloodied forehead with the hem of her long, ragged dress.

Darcy opened his mouth to speak but only a soft moan escaped his lips. The worried child leaned closer to whisper in his ear as he felt himself plunging downward into unconsciousness, her sweet, plaintive cry echoing as through a vast, dark tunnel. "Please, sir, don't die!"

More time passed before he struggled up into the light again. Now his head was throbbing with gouts of liquid fire and he felt the pull of rough, work-hardened hands flipping him over onto his back like a beached sea creature.

"Well, he's a gentleman, that's for certain," said a stranger's deep voice. "Look at his hands." The speaker had an unfamiliar country accent and he was methodically feeling and prodding his way through Darcy's pockets.

"Queer, though, them boots," said a second man. "And what's that on his arm?"

As the words were spoken Darcy felt his right arm being lifted. He opened his eyes to see two men in shapeless woolen caps, muddy boots and filthy leather breeches examining the gold watch on his wrist.

"It's a cunning little pocket watch, that," observed the first speaker, his voice filled with sudden awe. "Smallest one I ever seen. Oh, he's a gent for sure, this one."

Darcy briefly lifted his head, and then he fell back into the dark tunnel again.

He awoke once more, certain this time that he must be dreaming. For there were green tree branches passing over his head, interspersed with patches of bright blue sky speckled with cottony puffs of cloud, and the sound of creaking wagon wheels somewhere beneath him.

Looking down past his own chest, Darcy caught a glimpse of Lord Nelson, his reins looped to a wooden post on the lurching farm wagon, following placidly along behind his prone master.

"I say we take him up to Chawton Great House," said the

deep voice of the man who had been examining Darcy's watch. "We're like to get a bigger reward up there, from the master."

"Don't be daft," argued the second man. "The cottage is closer. And there'll be no reward for the likes of us if the poor gent expires in the back of this here cart."

Once more Darcy tried to lift his head, for the two men he could hear so calmly discussing his possible demise in the back of their wagon were somewhere beyond the range of his vision. And, once more, raising his head proved to be a serious mistake. Darcy was swept by a dizzying wave of nausea and he felt himself sliding inexorably back into the dreaded echoing tunnel of darkness.

When consciousness next arrived he was being carried on a board into a large stone house. The voice he heard this time was that of a cultured Englishwoman. Without attempting to raise his aching head Darcy opened his eyes and saw her standing off to one side, issuing stern orders to the two men.

"Take him upstairs to the first room. Careful! Mind the steps."

She was slender and, he thought, somewhat pretty, though her fine features seemed drawn with worry. But he noticed that the two rough men, who seemed to be taking great pains to follow her instructions, were also handling him far more gently than they had earlier.

Before he could get a better look at the woman she disappeared from his field of view. Then the board was tilted at a sharp angle and Darcy was being carried up a flight of broad stairs. But he could still hear her on the floor below, giving orders to another woman.

"Maggie, send to the village for Mr. Hudson," she said with just a touch of panic in her voice. "Say that he is most urgently required here."

"Yes, Miss Jane!" The woman called Maggie must have responded quickly, because a hurried shuffling of feet and the slamming of a door almost immediately followed her reply.

Darcy was carried into a pleasant upstairs room and laid on a feather-soft bed that smelled faintly of roses. It was the dark-haired woman's own bed, he guessed, remembering that her name was Jane. He idly wondered if her skin smelled of roses as well. A moment later her face moved into his field of view and he looked up into her luminous brown eyes.

From this vantage point he discovered that she was much prettier than he had previously thought, with a firm but sensuous mouth, regular features framed by beautiful dark brown hair that gleamed with highlights of sunshine from the open window.

But her best feature, he thought, was her large brown eyes, which sparkled in the light and seemed to contain infinite depths of intelligence and understanding.

Darcy smiled weakly at her and was rewarded with a lovely smile in return.

"I feel a bit foolish about all of this," he said, finding his voice at last. Momentarily forgetting his earlier experiences with gravity, he attempted to boost himself up onto one elbow. The effect was immediate and severe, as a jagged spear of pain impacted like a Scud missile just above his right eyebrow.

"Please remain still," she pleaded, placing a strong but gentle hand on his shoulder and pushing him onto the pillows. "I have sent for a doctor."

Groaning, Darcy allowed his head to loll back, then turned it slightly to the side to gaze past her into the room. To his surprise, he saw the two shaggy men who had rescued him still standing beside the open doorway, woolen hats clutched nervously in their dirty hands.

"What happened?" he asked self-consciously. "I feel like I've just been slammed by an express train."

The men at the door exchanged confused glances but said nothing. The dark-eyed woman, however, noticed the movement and turned to them. "Thank you," she said, addressing them as if they were particularly good children. "You have both done *very* well. Now please go up to the manor house as fast as you can and summon my brother."

Jane paused for a moment, then added with a smile, "And you may tell him I said you are to have a reward."

Rather than being insulted at what seemed to Darcy to be her condescending tone, the two rough-and-dirty men both beamed and touched their foreheads respectfully. "Yes, Miss Jane. Thankee, miss," they chorused, backing awkwardly out of the bedroom.

Darcy heard their clumping footsteps on the stair as Jane returned her attention to him.

"You were thrown from your horse," she said in response to his earlier question. "Do you not remember that?"

All in a rush it came back to him. "Lord Nelson!" Darcy exclaimed. "Oh damn, how could I have been so stupid."

"I beg your pardon! Did you say Lord Nelson?" Jane was regarding him very strangely now and he saw her drawing back from the bed in shock.

"My horse?" Darcy anxiously inquired. "Where is he?"

"The horse is uninjured," she said uneasily, her bright brown eyes darting to the empty doorway. "Those men brought him here with you."

"Thank God!" Darcy's sense of relief was palpable as he considered all of the horrible things that could have happened to the extremely valuable animal as the result of his ill-advised sortie.

"Please try to rest now," his attractive guardian urged, cautiously coming a little closer to the bed again. "The doctor will be here soon."

Darcy's eyes were darting nervously about the room, taking in for the first time the candlestick on the night stand by the bed, the antique furnishings everywhere and the woman's high-waisted, floor-length gown that exaggerated the enticing swell of her breasts. "What is this place anyway?" he asked. "Some kind of historical theme park?"

The intelligent dark eyes followed his as he continued to

scan the quaint furnishings of the bedroom, and again her expression was strange. "You are at Chawton Cottage," Jane replied at length. "Is there anything I can do for you?"

"Could you possibly phone the people I'm staying with?" he asked. "They may be getting worried about me."

"Fone?" She repeated the word with a puzzled look.

"Yes, the Cliftons," Darcy said. "They're leasing that gigantic old Edwardian brick pile a mile or so to the west of where I fell."

Darcy smiled ruefully, thinking of the ribbing he was going to get when Faith and the others turned up in the Land Rover and discovered the mess he'd gotten himself into.

"My name is Fitzwilliam Darcy," he told Jane, who continued to stand there staring at him. "Just ask the Cliftons to get over here with a horse trailer, and tell them I'm okay," he requested.

"Okay?" She was still staring at him with that strange, slightly disbelieving look in her eyes. "I am very sorry," she said slowly. "But I do not believe that I comprehend your precise meaning, Mr. Darcy."

Convinced that for some reason of her own she didn't want to make the telephone call for him, Darcy sat up and swung his legs over the side of the bed.

"Oh please, do not try to move," Jane pleaded, rushing forward with obvious alarm.

"I think I'm okay now," Darcy said, trying to get his feet under him. "If you'll just show me where your phone is, I'll call the Cliftons myself . . ."

He got unsteadily to his feet, stood tottering beside the bed for a moment, then suddenly toppled to the floor like a bag of dropped cement.

Jane fell to her knees beside him. "Mr. Darcy!"

Like the tiny cherub before her, Darcy heard her cry of alarm echoing from a long way off. "Maggie," she called, "come here! I need you."

Maggie, the red-faced housekeeper, hurried into the bedroom and stared in confusion at the unconscious man lying on the floor.

"Don't just stand there," said Jane, bending over him. "The gentleman has fainted. Help me get him back into bed."

Together the two women managed to haul Darcy back onto the bed. When it was done, they both stood panting from the effort. Maggie fanned herself with her apron for a few moments. Then she went around to the foot of the bed and started removing Darcy's boots.

Jane watched her, then reached over and unbuttoned his waistcoat and shirt, revealing a chain holding a gold medallion emblazoned with the Darcy family crest. She curiously lifted the pendant in her hand, looking at the detail in the design, then returned to the business of unfastening his shirt.

"Now you leave all that to me, Miss Jane," fussed Maggie, placing Darcy's boots in a corner and returning to the bed. "I'll look after the gentleman properlike."

"Nonsense, Maggie," Jane replied. "I grew up with six brothers. So I believe I am perfectly capable of managing one unconscious gentleman. Now do go down to the kitchen and put on the kettle for Mr. Hudson. He'll want hot water, basins and clean muslin for this wound when he arrives."

Frowning and muttering at the impropriety of her mistress dirtying her hands on the muddy stranger, Maggie nevertheless scurried off, as she had been ordered to do.

When the fretful housekeeper was gone Jane lifted Darcy's gold medallion from his chest and examined it more closely. Then she covered him with a blanket.

She stepped back from the bed, and noticed a glint of light from something on the floor where Darcy had fallen in his attempt to stand. Her curiosity aroused, Jane picked up a small, rectangular object no larger than a gentleman's calling card. She frowned and looked closely at it, scarcely believing her eyes. With the strange card held high in her hand, she walked straight to the window and extended it into the bright shaft of midmorning light pouring into the room.

"Such a thing as this cannot be!" Jane gasped as a perfect, three-dimensional hologram of a prancing horse danced and wheeled in the sunlight before her disbelieving eyes. Squinting to better see the magical picture, she saw behind the tiny horse the same golden crest that she had observed just moments before on Darcy's medallion.

Jane read aloud the words "'Fitzwilliam Darcy, Pemberley Farms,'" impressed in graceful black type below the hologram on the clear plastic business card—a box of which had been a gift to Darcy from Faith Harrington the previous Christmas.

Jane scanned the senseless jumble of e-mail, fax and telephone numbers beneath Darcy's name, unable to decipher their meaning. Then she ran her fingertips over the flat surface of the hologram once more, confirming for herself the reality of the thing.

Turning, she stared at Darcy, who lay unmoving on the bed. "Who are you, sir, to possess such a wondrous, nay, *impossible* object?" she whispered to the helpless stranger. "And what will others think of you when they see such an astonishing thing?"

She was startled out of her rumination by the sound of carriage wheels on the drive below. Looking out the window she saw Mr. Hudson's modest black surrey pulling to a stop before her gate. To Jane's surprise, her sister, Cassandra, whom he must have met along the way, was riding beside the white-haired doctor. She heard the urgent sound of their voices as they hurried into the house and started up the stairs.

Wracked with indecision, Jane looked from the impossible card in her hand to the unconscious man on the bed. Footsteps were sounding outside the bedroom door as she stole another look at the clear plastic card, then tucked it into her gown.

Chapter 18

It was midafternoon before Darcy again awoke. This time there was an intense, steady throb in his head and a strange tingling sensation in his right arm. He opened his eyes and blinked up at a high ceiling finished in swirls of dazzling white plaster. Grimacing at the pain, he tried to recall the strange dream he had just had. He vaguely remembered falling from his horse and being brought to some sort of theme park where the employees all wore old-fashioned costumes.

Turning his head, Darcy looked at his right arm, curious to discover the cause of the itchy, tingling sensation. He was horrified to see three glistening black leeches, each the size of his thumb, greedily sucking at the soft flesh on the inside of his forearm, which was suspended over a porcelain basin containing several more of the engorged nightmare creatures.

Darcy's scream of terror immediately brought a white-haired gentleman wearing a bloody apron to his bedside. "There, there, sir!" said the startled old gentleman. "Steady now. As your physician I must caution you against any abrupt—"

"What the hell are those *things* doing on me?" Darcy shouted, struggling to rise.

"Sir, you were badly in need of bleeding to reduce the dangerous humours occasioned by your injury," the doctor patiently explained.

Finding that he was too weak to sit up, Darcy again interrupted the man by screaming, "Get them off of me! Now!" His eyes darted wildly about the room, seeking someone to help him, but he saw that he was alone with the demented old man. "Get them off!" he again ordered.

Obviously distressed by the vehemence of his patient's outburst the doctor quickly removed the leeches from Darcy's arm and retreated, muttering, with his horrible basin to the far corner of the room.

At that moment the bedroom door flew open and a handsome, middle-aged man entered. He was wearing a splendid tailcoat of wine-colored velvet over spotless doeskin breeches tucked into a pair of gleaming knee-high boots. Peering through the doorway behind the new arrival Darcy glimpsed Jane, the pretty brunette, and a taller, slightly older blonde woman.

"Everything all right, Hudson?" The man in the velvet coat had a pleasant, cheerful voice and the tenor of his question suggested he might have been asking if the tea was satisfactory.

"No! Everything *is not* all right!" Darcy shouted. He pointed his finger accusingly at the elderly man in the bloody apron, who was protectively cradling his basin of wriggling leeches. "I woke up to find this . . . witch doctor sticking those *things* on me—"

Darcy broke off his complaint to take a closer look at the odd assemblage in their long dresses and funny suits. They were all staring at him as if he was mad. "Who are you people anyway?" he demanded.

"Sir, I beg you to remain calm," said the handsome gentleman in the tailcoat. He stepped forward and bowed slightly at the waist. "My name is Edward Austen," he continued, "and upon my word as a gentleman, Mr. Hudson is an eminent member of the Royal Academy of Medicine."

Stepping over to the white-haired man, Edward Austen placed an approving hand on his shoulder. "Mr. Hudson has for years been entrusted with the care of my own dear family and is of the highest repute," he assured Darcy.

"Your confusion of the moment is understandable for you have suffered a severe blow to the brain, which has temporarily addled you, sir. But for your own welfare you must remain calm."

Darcy struggled to sit up in the soft featherbed but Mr. Hudson rushed over and placed a restraining hand on his shoulder. "Please, sir!" he cautioned. "The bleeding will have made you quite lightheaded. Now, if you will just lie back quietly while I stitch up your wound with cat's gut—"

His eyes widening, Darcy feebly pushed the old man away. "Cat's gut!" he moaned. "Are you insane? Let me up!" He rose a few inches from the pillows, and then fell back, unconscious.

The other occupants of the room gaped as Mr. Hudson walked quickly to a small table and returned with a large, curved sailor's needle and a length of twisted suture material and began expertly sewing up the large gash in Darcy's forehead.

"My word!" Edward exclaimed, peering over the doctor's shoulder. "He is indeed completely out of his head, is he not, Hudson?"

"Not unusual following an injury of this sort, sir," the elderly gentleman replied as he continued to stitch with swift, practiced movements. "Complete rest and quiet is what he wants now."

Hudson paused to fish a new piece of cat's gut from the silk waistcoat beneath his apron. He wet the end with his tongue and threaded it into the needle.

"He's a lucky fellow," Hudson chuckled as he resumed his needlework on Darcy's head. "Fainted *before* I came to the stitching, you see."

Averting her eyes from the doctor's gruesome task, Cassandra raised her voice to ask a timid question. "Do you think he will recover, then, Mr. Hudson?"

"Oh, I should think so," Hudson replied. He bent to bite off the end of the last suture, then crossed the room to dip his bloody hands in a basin of water. "He's a strong, healthy fellow," the doctor continued.

He winked at Cassandra. "Someone will have to keep an eye on him, though, lest he decide to go walking. Great care should be taken to keep him abed until the bleeding has stopped."

"You may rely on it, Hudson," Edward volunteered, stepping forward. "We have not yet located the friends he mentioned, but the moment Jane told me his name and the place he comes from I knew who this man Darcy was."

Hudson folded his bloody apron away and raised his bushy white eyebrows in surprise. "Indeed, sir?"

While this conversation was taking place, Darcy, who had been drifting in and out of consciousness, and who was by now more than half-convinced he was trapped in a bizarre nightmare from which he would soon awake, opened his eyes. He touched the freshly sutured gash on his forehead and winced in pain. At the sound of his name he turned to look at the others who were gathered by the door, unaware that he was listening in on them.

"Fitzwilliam Darcy is a wealthy American with a great estate in Virginia," Edward was telling the doctor. "I know this because my younger brother's bank, in which I have a considerable personal investment, has, I recall, transacted letters of credit for a client who each year purchases several fine horses from this Darcy's farm, for use on his own plantation."

"An American? How extraordinary!" exclaimed the doctor. The old gentleman turned to glance back over at the bed where Darcy lay listening with his eyes tightly shut, so the others would believe him to still be unconscious.

"The man's being an American would explain his rather odd clothing and that peculiar timepiece he wears on his arm," Mr. Hudson observed with a chuckle. "I daresay we haven't been treated to many Yankee fashions since the in-grates rebelled back in 1776."

Bewildered by this talk of the year 1776, which Hudson's tone seemed to indicate had been fairly recent, Darcy peered through slitted eyes at his gold wristwatch, which seemed to fascinate these people. Then he covertly scanned the bedroom again, searching for electrical outlets or fixtures, or some other sign of modern times, but could find none. He quickly resumed his unconscious act as footsteps approached the bed.

Edward Austen stopped at the footboard and leaned over for a better look at his helpless guest. "American or not," he told Hudson, "this fellow Fitzwilliam Darcy is a wealthy and powerful man. And he shall receive nothing but the most considerate treatment at my hands."

"Commendable, sir," the doctor harrumphed. "Quite good of you."

"I should like to move the man to larger, more comfortable accommodations at my manor house as soon as possible," Edward suggested.

Mr. Hudson frowned at that. "Considering the gentleman's present state of unconsciousness, I would prefer to wait and see how he fares through the night," he said.

The physician cast a glance at Jane and Cassandra, who were still hovering near the door. "That is, of course," he told Edward, "if your sisters do not object to his remaining here until he may be safely moved."

Without waiting for Edward's reply, Jane stepped forward. "Certainly we could entertain no thought of turning out a rich and powerful gentleman," she said, smiling at her brother, "especially one who might possibly become a favored client of our dear brother's new bank."

Jane turned to Cassandra for affirmation of her statement. "Could we, Cass?"

Cassandra smiled and shook her head. "Certainly not," she replied. "Poor Mr. Darcy shall be welcome in our home for as long as need be."

"Then it is settled," Jane told the two men. "Cassandra and I will watch over our American guest with the greatest of care."

"Splendid!" said Mr. Hudson. "I shall come and see him morning and evening until he is better. And of course you must send for me at any hour if his condition changes for the worse."

Digging into his worn leather satchel, Hudson pressed a small vial into Jane's hand. "Give him this draught in a little wine if he grows agitated, but just a little, mind, for it is very powerful."

"We shall take care," said Jane, closing her palm on the vial of alcohol laced with opium.

"I am exceedingly obliged to you, Mr. Hudson." Edward escorted the elderly doctor to the bedroom door and slipped a gold sovereign into his hand.

"Your servant, sir." With a broad smile at the unexpectedly large fee, Hudson bowed deeply from the waist and took his leave.

When the doctor had gone Edward kissed Jane on the cheek. "Dear Jane, you are, as always, all kindness and understanding," he effused.

Turning, he gave Cassandra a kiss as well. "And having a handsome and wealthy invalid to attend may not be without its compensations, eh Cassandra?" he teased.

Cassandra, whose temperament Edward believed tended exclusively toward somberness and melancholy, reacted predictably to his affectionate jibe. "Brother, the way you speak!" she exclaimed, blushing deeply. "Until he is strong enough to be moved we shall look after poor Mr. Darcy with no motives beyond our duty as good Christians."

Moving to the window, Cassandra pointed down to the front garden where Lord Nelson was tied to the gate, calmly munching on a bunch of daisies. "Pray do however take the gentleman's horse away to your stables," she entreated, "before the beast consumes everything in our garden."

Edward looked out the window at the black horse. "Yes, yes, of course I shall," he laughed. "My word! What a splendid creature it is."

Late that night, long after Darcy had fallen into an exhausted sleep, Jane sat at her mirrored vanity table by the fireplace. Removing a sheet of paper from the center drawer, she dipped her pen in the inkpot and began to write, as was her usual occupation each evening.

Hardly had she begun, however, when she was disturbed by the sound of a low murmuring from the bed behind her.

Picking up the single candle by which she worked, Jane got softly to her feet and walked over to look down at Darcy. She saw his lips moving, as if he was speaking, and as she leaned closer she heard him giving orders to some unseen employee.

"We'll move the horse back to Virginia on the seventeenth," Darcy was saying, "if you can arrange a flight. We can have him home in five hours by private jet . . ."

Imagining his nonsensical ramblings to be the result of one of the mysterious fevers that invariably accompanied any open wound, Jane placed a hand on Darcy's cheek and found it hot.

"I am going to insist on heavy security," he continued in his sleep, "because I *do not* want any television . . ."

Darcy's speech died away, leaving Jane staring at him in complete puzzlement. For though she was able to derive little meaning from his actual words, neither did they sound to her like the rantings of one who is deranged. It was altogether quite mysterious.

While Jane was pondering the mystery of Darcy's peculiar mutterings, the bedroom door quietly opened and Cassandra stepped into the room. Dressed in her nightgown and carrying a candle of her own, she came over to the bed and stood beside her sister.

"Is he any better?" Cassandra whispered.

"He is very feverish, I fear," Jane told her.

"Poor man," Cassandra sighed. "Has he spoken again?"

Jane hesitated before replying. Then, without knowing exactly why, she shook her head. "No," she lied, "he has said nothing more."

Cassandra looked around the dimly lit bedroom. "It must be most inconvenient having this stranger occupying your bedroom," she sympathized. "Shall I stay and sit a while with you?"

Jane kissed her sister's cheek. "No, thank you, dear Cass. I shall work on *First Impressions* a while longer," she said.

Cass's eyes lit up at the mention of the novel, an older work that Jane had lately begun to rewrite. "Oh, I'm so glad you've decided to get back to that one," Cass whispered, "it's always been my favorite of all your works. Tell me, have you yet decided the fate of all the Misses Bennet?"

Jane smiled, for her sister was the one person in the world with whom she felt completely at ease in discussing her writing. "I have decided that I want both of the elder Bennet sisters in my book to be happily married in the same ceremony," she confided to Cass. "Do you think that will seem too contrived?"

Cassandra laughed delightedly. For, despite Edward's brotherly view of her as a somber old maid without a trace of passion in her soul, Cass never tired of discussing Jane's wildly romantic stories. "A double wedding will make a *perfect* ending," she said. "And I never care if an event in a novel is slightly contrived, as long as the contrivance leads to a blissfully happy ending."

Cass paused for a moment, then continued. "But I still do not like the title *First Impressions*," she informed Jane. "I think you should call it *Improper Pride*. For that is what the story is really about."

"It is about pride, yes," Jane grudgingly conceded. "But more than that, my novel is about the prejudices that often unfairly attach to persons merely because of circumstance beyond their control.

"However," she promised Cass, "I shall think about a new

title if it will make you happy. Now go to bed," Jane ordered. "I will come to your room and sleep later. After you have rested."

Cassandra nodded her agreement but she remained standing beside Jane's bed, looking down at the tall man. "Mr. Darcy is very handsome, is he not?" she asked quietly.

"Yes," Jane agreed. "Very." By the candle's glow she saw a tear glistening in the corner of Cassandra's eye, and from it she knew that her sister was thinking of her late fiancé, a dashing young naval officer who had died of fever in the Indies, just months before he and Cass were to have been wed. Though nearly two decades had passed since the young man's tragic death, theirs had been a deeply passionate and loving relationship, and one from which the beautiful Cassandra had never recovered.

At least, Jane reasoned as she read the grief on Cass's face, there had been one great love, however brief, in her dear sister's life. And, though she would never have dared mention it to Cass, Jane sometimes envied her that.

Long after Cassandra had gone to bed, Jane stood silently regarding Darcy's face. Presently, she retrieved from the bodice of her gown the transparent card that looked like glass but was not. She marveled again at the cunning portrait of the tiny prancing horse frozen in the depths of the soft glass by some unimaginable magical process.

"I cannot believe, Mr. Darcy," she said aloud to the still figure on her bed, "that you are what my brother thinks you are. But whatever else you may be, you are by far the most fascinating personage *this* house has ever entertained. And my honor as well as my own curiosity about you demands that I keep your secrets until you are able to explain them for yourself."

Jane smiled down at Darcy, reaching out to lay a soft hand against his cheek. "Cass is right on one count, though," she told him. "You are a very handsome rogue."

She left him then, walking across the room to a tall wardrobe and removing her nightgown from it. Casting a self-conscious glance at the masculine form on her bed and feeling slightly foolish, she stepped behind a thin screen of sheer muslin and began to disrobe.

Darcy, had in fact been wide awake for all but a few moments of the evening, when he had dreamed he was giving orders to his trainer about Lord Nelson. Now he opened his eyes and silently studied the slender feminine form, which was clearly silhouetted by the firelight, enchanted by the image.

Chapter 19

"So I lay there in the darkness of that strange room," Darcy said, "unable to move and afraid to speak to her . . ." He was still leaning on the fence, talking.

Eliza, who had listened silently to his story until now, could not resist interrupting. "Afraid . . . of her?"

Slowly Darcy turned at the sound of Eliza's voice, as if he was emerging from a dream. "Yes," he replied without evident embarrassment. "You see, I was wholly convinced that my head injury had triggered some sort of delusional state and that I would snap out of it at any moment and find myself in an ordinary hospital room, babbling to some poor bewildered nurse."

"But you were *really* somewhere back in the nineteenth century . . . with Jane Austen." Eliza could not keep the cynicism out of her voice.

"May of 1810, I soon discovered," Darcy responded matter-of-factly. "But there were far too many other things concerning me at that moment to have immediately connected her with *the* Jane Austen. In fact, Jane's first novel had not yet been published in the year 1810."

Eliza was still dubiously shaking her head. "You'll forgive me if I find all of this extremely hard to believe," she said.

"Miss Knight, you insisted on knowing why I said that

Jane's letter was meant for me," Darcy brusquely reminded her. "I had very little expectation that you *would* believe my explanation. Which is also why I've never told anyone else what happened."

"Then why tell me?" Eliza countered argumentatively.

"Because," Darcy responded with rising frustration, "you have something that I desperately want. And I am not ashamed to confess that I will do anything I can if there is even the slightest chance of convincing you to let me have that letter."

"Ah, yes! I forgot," she shot back. "A letter from a lover you abandoned two hundred years ago. Well, it *is* a wildly romantic concept."

Darcy's cheeks were flushed with anger. "You don't understand at all!" he said vehemently.

"What doesn't she understand, Fitz?"

They both turned to see Faith Harrington walking down the lane toward them. Darcy cast a warning glance at Eliza, then smiled at the new arrival. "Eliza doesn't understand the many difficulties of breeding champion jumpers, Faith."

Playing along with his deception, Eliza looked down at the ground and kicked at a clump of grass. "I guess I'm just a dumb old city girl," she admitted. Then, raising her eyes to Darcy's, she put on what she hoped was her dumbest expression. "Now it's the mares that have the foals, right?"

"I'm terribly sorry to interrupt poor Eliza's equestrian education, Fitz," Faith abruptly cut in, "but the caterer from Richmond is in the ballroom, screaming about your ban on electricity for tomorrow. The poor man insists it's not possible to serve hot guinea fowl to two hundred guests without his precious microwaves."

Darcy sighed and pushed away from the fence. "I'll take care of it," he told the blonde.

"Perhaps," he suggested, turning back to Eliza, "you'd like to go up and see your room now. I'll ask Jenny to show you the way." He paused and then added, "We can continue our discussion later, if you still want to continue . . ."

Eliza's eyes sparkled mischievously and she gave him an enthusiastic nod. "Oh, I wouldn't miss it for the *world*."

They all started walking back toward the house. But before they had proceeded ten paces Faith linked her arm possessively in Darcy's and led him out ahead of Eliza, pointedly excluding the visitor from all further conversation.

"The florist is here looking for pots or something," Faith rattled on to Darcy. "She says you promised they'd be ready."

"I *told* that woman yesterday that Lucas would have the planters at the gatehouse." Darcy sounded genuinely annoyed. "Will you point the florist down there while I see to the caterer?"

"Poor darling," Faith crooned. "Of course I will. Anything I can do to help."

After a few seconds of eavesdropping, Eliza tuned out the mundane discussion and followed silently behind them. As she walked she attempted to accord some level of credence to any part of Darcy's bizarre tale. But aside from the seeming sincerity of his delivery and his own professions of bafflement over what had actually happened to him, she could think of nothing solid on which to ground a belief that he could have simply blundered into another century.

"Hope you like roses."

At the end of a richly carpeted upstairs corridor hung with dark ancestral portraits Jenny Brown flung open a door and stepped aside. Looking into the large, antique-filled room beyond, Eliza saw that the decor was entirely themed around roses. From the rose-patterned wallpaper and carpet to the curtains at the windows and the intricately carved roses on the wooden bedposts, everything was roses.

Stepping into the Rose Bedroom Eliza saw that her bags had been placed on a blanket chest at the foot of the bed with its embroidered rose-colored satin coverlet. "Incredible!" she gasped, overwhelmed by the scene, which vaguely reminded her of the bedroom set from *Gone With the Wind*.

"Yeah, kind of takes your breath away, doesn't it?" Jenny was grinning as she walked to a pair of tall French doors. She opened them to reveal a broad balcony overlooking the lawns and fields of Pemberley Farms. "You can see most of the estate from up here," she reported.

"They say Fitz's great-great-great-grandmother, Rose, used to sit here and watch for her man to come riding across those hills." Turning back to the amazing bedroom Jenny switched on a small bronze lamp, illuminating a deep alcove that Eliza had not yet noticed.

Hanging on the wall of the alcove, above an ornate copper bathtub, was a lifelike painting of a slender, dark-haired woman, her full, sensuous lips seemingly on the verge of smiling.

Eliza thought that the subject of the portrait was the most exquisitely beautiful female she had ever seen, especially dressed as she was in a marvelously revealing gown of rose-colored silk. "Is that her?" she asked in awe.

"The grand lady herself," Jenny confirmed. "They say when the master's horse was sighted Rose would step into a bath filled with rose petals." The handsome black woman smiled and pointed. "She'd be sitting naked right there in that tub, waiting for him when he reached her door."

"Hmmm, sounds kinda kinky!" Eliza laughed.

Jenny joined in with her laughter. "I think that all depends on your point of view," she said. "You see, *my* great-great-great-grandmother was the one who had to *pick* all those damn rose petals. But the times do change, don't they?" Jenny continued. "Now Artie and I are *guests* here at Pemberley, and we stay in whatever room we choose."

"Do you ever choose *this* room?" Eliza asked, smiling.

Jenny shuddered theatrically. "Honey, I get the *hives* when I walk into this room. You're welcome to it." She threw herself backwards onto the satin bed coverlet and crossed her ankles. "You'll have to pick your own damn rose petals, though."

"Point me to them gardens," Eliza laughed, falling onto the bed beside her. "This is so bizarre," she giggled, looking around at the roses that surrounded her on every side. "I came down here to talk about some old letters and I feel like I've fallen through the looking glass."

"This room will do that to you, sure enough," Jenny chuckled. "They say you should stop to smell the roses, but this bedroom is a definite case of overkill."

"What do you recommend we do now?" Eliza asked between spasms of laughter.

"Well, Alice," Jenny giggled, "if you're up to it, this might be a good time for us to go find something for you to wear to the ball tomorrow night."

"The ball," Eliza gasped, choking on her own laughter. "Do you know I've never even been to a single ball in my life?"

"Girl, you have been *deprived*!" squealed Jenny.

Twenty minutes later, their giggling finally under control, Jenny and Eliza stood together in a huge, air-conditioned and cedar-paneled attic room, looking through long racks of neatly labeled antique clothing of all types.

"This is incredible," Eliza said, indicating the contents of the vast wardrobe room with a sweeping gesture of her arms. "Did the Darcys save every piece of clothing they ever owned?"

"No, these things didn't belong to the Darcys, the vast majority didn't anyway," Jenny replied. "Sometime back around 1960 Fitz's grandmother discovered a trunk filled with antique gowns. She decided to see if she could restore them to their original condition so they wouldn't be lost to history. When she succeeded, the word got around. Folks started bringing her other old things, men's clothing included. And before she knew what was happening she had a collection."

Jenny rolled out a rack of exquisite ball gowns from the early nineteenth century, all looking as fresh as if they had been newly made. "After his grandmother died Fitz's mother kept the restorations going," she explained. "When she passed away, the collection went into moth balls. A few years ago Fitz set up and funded a foundation for the ongoing preservation of the collection. He had this room built, hired a full-time curator and two seamstresses just to keep all this up, as an homage to his mother and grandmother. Mostly the clothes are lent out to museums and schools now," Jenny added, holding up a shimmering blue silk gown and passing it to Eliza for inspection.

Eliza examined the dress appreciatively, once more slightly revising her early opinion of the enigmatic Fitzwilliam Darcy. She realized with a start how he had happened to know so much about Regency-era clothing that first day when they had met at the library.

"Mr. . . . I mean Fitz, seems to be quite an extraordinary person," Eliza said, hoping to draw an unguarded opinion from Jenny. "Is it really possible for one man to be rich, handsome and as genuinely nice as he appears to be?"

Jenny put down the gown she was holding and her voice turned suddenly serious. "I have known Fitz my entire life," she said without a moment's hesitation. "And he's probably the best man I've ever known."

Eliza raised her eyebrows at this seeming exaggeration of a good friend's character, but Jenny wasn't finished yet.

"The times might have changed," observed the beautiful black woman, "but you still don't find that many Southern aristocrats hobnobbing with the descendants of the family slaves. And besides his other work and contributions to a number of causes, Fitz puts on this charity Rose Ball at his own expense every year, just so the poor kids around here—many of them from former slave families like mine—can go to college."

Jenny was obviously speaking on a favorite theme and she reached her conclusion with near religious fervor, "The man is a saint in my book."

"Yet he seems to be somewhat . . . obsessed, too," Eliza timidly observed.

"Oh, you mean the Jane Austen thing?" said Jenny. "Isn't that why *you're* here after all?"

"Well, yes," Eliza admitted.

"I can't honestly claim to be a big fan of that Austen lady," Jenny said, "considering the fact that she was bemoaning the problems of the not-quite-rich-enough back in England while my people were chopping cotton and being sold by the pound. Though to be fair," Jenny went on, "Miss Austen did from time to time write a few things disapproving of slavery." Jenny lowered her voice to a conspiratorial whisper. "I have my own private theory as to why Fitz is so hung up on Miss Jane Austen."

Eliza leaned forward eagerly.

"First," Jenny explained, "you have to understand that this place almost came apart two hundred years ago, when Rose Darcy read that woman's book naming *her man* and a place he owned called Pemberley. I suspect that if Rose hadn't known that no Darcy had set foot in England for forty years or more, the rose-petal baths would have come to a screeching halt."

Eliza stared at the other woman. "Are you saying that Fitz's ancestor *wasn't* in England around the time that Jane Austen was writing?"

"Lord, no!" Jenny snorted. "The Darcy family were American patriots back in 1776, and not a one of them ever went back to England again until well after the end of the Civil War."

Jenny suddenly hesitated, almost as though she feared revealing embarrassing family secrets that had come to light yesterday, rather than two centuries earlier. "But after *Pride and Prejudice* was published here in the U.S.," she said in a low voice, "there was scandalous gossip that the first Fitzwilliam Darcy, the man who built Pemberley Farms, must have been Jane Austen's lover, else why would she have used his name in her book?"

"Good question," said Eliza, remembering the haunted

look in Darcy's verdant eyes as he had related his extraordinary tale to her. "Why do you think Jane Austen used those names?" she asked Jenny. "I mean, the mere fact that she linked two rather odd names like Fitzwilliam Darcy and Pemberley together would seem to rule out coincidence."

Jenny laughed. "Well, if the same thing happened today," she said, "my first guess would have been that she must have picked them out of the phone book . . . or off the Internet. But where or how she might have run across them two hundred years ago is anybody's guess.

"All I know," Jenny said, "is that because of *Pride and Prejudice* there were no Austen lovers in the Darcy family. And though Fitz doesn't talk about it, I think his obsession with Austen's letters and papers may have something to do with proving once and for all that there was *never* any connection. You know, family honor and all of that."

Jenny paused and her eyes lit up as she pulled another gown from the rack. "Oh, my! Look what I just found for you!" she breathed, holding up an emerald green velvet Regency-era ball gown that was strikingly similar to the one that Eliza had seen and discussed with Darcy at the library exhibit.

Eliza took the gown from her, turned to a full-length mirror on the wall and tried to imagine how she would look in the shocking garment. "Well, it might fit me," she reluctantly admitted, "but I have it on good authority that Jane Austen would *never* have worn anything this revealing."

"Maybe not," Jenny grinned, "but then she didn't have access to the Wonder Bra either. You have just *got* to try it on," she insisted, standing back and scrutinizing Eliza. "And we need to do something with your hair."

Having minutes before calmed the frantic caterer, Darcy was now standing out on the front lawn, facing the Great House. As was his custom each year before the ball, he was going over last-minute details with the two dozen employees and volunteers who had assembled on the drive. It would be their responsibility to transport arriving guests by carriage from the gatehouse parking area to the house.

The men, most of whom were local grooms and trainers, would be transformed for one evening into liveried carriage drivers, footmen and attendants, and many of them were nervous or uncertain about their roles in the grand costumed drama of the Rose Ball.

Eliza stepped out onto the balcony wearing the green Regency dress, her hair swept up, with soft tendrils framing her face. She stood there for a moment and watched Fitz on the lawn with his employees, joking and having a good time. She smiled at his seeming ability to fit into any situation with ease.

"Now, as the guests arrive tomorrow night," Darcy said, pointing to two younger men near the front of the group, "Jimmy and Larry here will help them from their carriages as quickly as possible. Speed is very important," Darcy stressed, "because we only have a limited number of carriages and they must be turned around and sent immediately back down to the gatehouse to . . ."

Attracted by a flash of movement, Darcy let his eyes wander up to the second story of the house. He stopped talking at the site of Eliza at the balcony railing. She looked like a snapshot out of time. Their eyes met, they stared at each other, bewitched. Eliza recovered first and quickly vanished into the bedroom.

Darcy remained frozen to the spot, gazing up at the balcony as if he'd seen a ghost. Several of the men turned to see what had distracted him, but there was nothing to be seen. Jimmy, one of the two young stable hands whom Darcy had been addressing a moment before, cleared his throat for his employer's attention.

"Uh, Fitz, are we footmen supposed to escort the guests up to the steps, or what?" Jimmy asked.

Darcy slowly lowered his eyes to the group of men patiently waiting for him to resume speaking. "What?"

"After we get them out of the carriages," Jimmy began again, "do we walk them over to the steps?"

"Sorry, Jimmy. No," Darcy replied, trying to remember exactly what he had been saying before Eliza's ghostly appearance. "One of the hostesses will be waiting to escort each group into the house," he resumed. "It's your job to get those carriages turned around as fast as you can."

"Fitz, what about these here *costumes?*" whined another young hand. "Do I really gotta wear them tight fancy pants they give us?"

Darcy smiled at the predictable question that was always prompted by the men's first sight of the red satin breeches that went with their bright green coats of Pemberley livery. "Ben, this is your first year in costume," he replied. "But the other guys here can all tell you that once your girlfriend sees you in those tight red pants she'll never let you go back to wearing overalls again."

Ben nodded miserably. "That's exactly what I'm afraid of," he groaned, prompting a good-natured outburst of laughter from the other men standing on the drive.

Inside Rose Darcy's bedroom Eliza leaned against the beveled glass of the French doors trying to catch her breath. God, the way he looked at her, the butterflies were going crazy in her stomach.

Walking to the bed she sat down and looked around the room, taking note of the lush rolling hills outside the window. Sitting here in this exquisite old house, wearing a ridiculous but beautiful vintage gown she really did feel like Alice in Wonderland. Were there mushrooms in the salad? Laughing at herself she decided that this would be a good time to see more of the estate. With Jenny gone off on some Rose Ball business she was alone and free to walk the beautiful grounds of Pemberley.

Chapter 20

The sun was sinking behind the stables as Faith and Darcy watched a team of gardeners placing ornamental pots filled with crimson roses along the drive. Though Darcy had intended to return immediately to Eliza after taking care of a few pressing matters related to the ball, several hours had passed during which Faith had professed that no detail could possibly proceed without his personal approval.

Eliza had changed into jeans and a T-shirt after finally collecting herself. She had to keep her wits about her; fresh air and a change of scene would help. She had told Darcy that she wanted to paint some of the vistas he'd shown her and this might be the perfect time to take advantage of the opportunity to commit some of Pemberley's magnificent views to paper; she took her sketch pad from the leather portfolio and headed downstairs and out into the warm afternoon air.

Wandering the magnificent estate Eliza tried in vain to reconcile Jenny's logical theory of Darcy's obsession with his own bizarre tale of time travel. Jenny's idea was far more rational but Fitz's story seemed to have the ring of truth to it, although maybe she was just being swept away by the romance of the whole thing. Trying to keep her wits about her, she walked down to the lake at the bottom of the broad lawn.

Smiling to herself at the absurdity of the situation, she lay down in the soft grass on the shore of the small lake and watched puffy clouds float above her in the hot summer sky. She realized that she welcomed the temporary respite from the intensity of Darcy's narrative, the incredible details of which continued to swirl through her mind, embellished by her own vivid imagination.

Though she found it quite impossible to take seriously her soft-spoken host's account of his accidental trip into the past and his subsequent encounter with Jane Austen, Eliza was nevertheless intrigued by the handsome millionaire.

She felt a sudden flush of heat rising to her cheeks as she recalled the intensity with which Darcy had gazed up at her when she had stepped onto the balcony of the Rose Bedroom.

She smiled inwardly; Jerry wouldn't have been capable of such a smoldering look. And yet, with Darcy, that look of barely restrained passion had seemed almost natural. It must be the way, she imagined, that he looked at all women and was perhaps the reason poor Faith found him so irresistible. For certainly nothing had passed between him and Eliza to indicate that it was a look reserved exclusively for her.

She reflected that, his strange obsession aside, Fitzwilliam Darcy was possibly the most fascinating and attractive man she had ever met. "Careful now," Eliza cautioned herself as she found a comfortable place to sit by the lake, "you're already beginning to sound like Jenny. Fitz Darcy may be a hunk and an extremely nice one at that, but the bottom line seems to be that the poor guy is just slightly out of his tree. Besides, this is real life, not a romance novel."

Romance wasn't likely to happen here anyway. There was an aloofness, a standoffishness in him that Eliza suspected was often taken for arrogance. Jenny had theorized that the loss of the three people he was closest to—his grandmother, father and mother—before he was eighteen had made him wary of intimate relationships. The pain of loving and losing again was simply not worth the risk. That was something with which Eliza could easily understand and sympathize.

She had determined after the death of her father that she would never again love anyone that much and realized now it was the reason that the only relationships she'd allowed herself had been like the one with Jerry. Completely unsatisfying. But now, as Darcy's face drifted through the clouds, she questioned that decision. Maybe happiness with someone you love, who loves you in return, was worth the risk of pain.

Shaking off the daydreams Eliza plunged her feet into the still water of the lake and started drawing.

While Eliza was thus engaged, Jenny, who had taken an immediate liking to the high-spirited New York artist, had already decided it would be good for Darcy to develop a relationship with her. She suspected that Eliza might just be the right woman to bring him out of the shell he'd inexplicably slipped into three years ago. Having made up her mind, Jenny, who despite her Southern Baptist upbringing had the soul of a Jewish yenta, set out to promote the relationship in any way she could.

Faith's painfully obvious maneuvers to keep the couple separated throughout the afternoon had resulted in the artist going off by herself while Faith had ensnared Darcy in a series of increasingly mundane tasks. Now, as the gardeners finished aligning the planters along the drive, Jenny stood nearby, determined to block Faith's next move.

The blonde socialite was ticking off items on a clipboard for Darcy as Jenny edged closer to listen in.

"The driveway roses are done," Faith was saying. She blew a stray wisp of hair from her carefully made-up face and adopted a martyred look. "Of course," she added wearily, "I've got a thousand things left to do."

"You're doing just great," Darcy said, consulting her clipboard and pointing out two more items for her to check off. "We've now got all the carriages rolling and ready for tomorrow, and Lucas and his men are setting up a trough and feed supplies for the horses at the gatehouse."

He paused and looked around, suddenly aware of the lengthening shadows falling across the lawns. "Have you seen Miss Knight?" he asked.

Fearful of resorting to outright lying, especially when it was likely that she would be immediately found out, Faith reluctantly pointed toward the small lake at the bottom of the lawn. "I believe I saw your little guest walking down to the lake a while ago," she peevishly allowed.

Darcy scanned the lakeshore and spotted Eliza sitting by herself on a cluster of rocks at the water's edge.

"She looks like such a solitary soul," Faith observed in a mock pitying tone. "To tell you the truth, Fitz, I don't think that girl cares for company at all."

Ignoring the remark, Darcy turned and started walking toward the lake. "I'll just go down and see if she needs anything," he said.

Faith hurriedly fell into step beside him. "I'll go with you, then," she offered as sweetly as she knew how. "After all, we wouldn't want *poor* little Eliza to feel neglected."

Darcy started to protest but he was interrupted by Jenny, who suddenly came running down from the house. "Oh, Faith, there you are!" she called with evident relief in her voice. "I have been looking *everywhere*."

Faith screwed up her pink, doll-like features into an approximation of a disbelieving scowl. "For me?" she asked suspiciously.

Jenny nodded urgently. "There's a crisis with the seating chart for tomorrow night's dinner and I don't trust anyone's opinion but yours," she lied. "It's a matter of etiquette," Jenny explained, setting the hook firmly.

Faith, who had long before set herself up as the final authority on all matters mannerly, especially as they related to the Rose Ball, was trapped. "Can't it *wait* a little while?" she pleaded.

"We're doing the place cards *now!*" Jenny insisted, taking her firmly by the elbow and guiding her toward the house.

Looking like a pup that's just been plucked from its litter, Faith reluctantly allowed herself to be led away.

Darcy grinned as Jenny glanced back over her shoulder and winked at him.

He found Eliza sitting on a large flat rock with her jeans rolled up and her bare feet in the placid green water. She was holding a pad in her lap and intently drawing with pastels. He stood unnoticed, watching her work. The image of her on the balcony only a short time before flooded his memory. She was breathtaking; he wondered at the strong emotions this woman seemed to evoke in him. Once again raven-haired beauty came to mind, as the sunlight played among the highlights in her hair, much like the candlelight had at the library exhibit. Sighing deeply, he smiled at the pleasant warmth that permeated his body.

Stepping closer, Darcy asked, as he sat down beside her on the rock, "May I see your drawing?"

Eliza grimaced, then handed over the pad. He looked at it and raised his eyebrows in surprise.

"Do you like it?" she asked.

Without immediately answering he closely examined her brilliantly colored rendering of himself astride the black horse. To Darcy's utter amazement this complete stranger had perfectly captured the precise moment when he and Lord Nelson had leaped over the stone wall into the blinding dazzle of sunlight.

"Very much," he said after a long pause, "but not at all what I was expecting." Darcy's mind was working furiously in an attempt to derive some meaning from the fact that his visitor had composed this startling picture based on nothing more than his verbal description of an event that had taken place three years before.

Eliza took back her pad with a smile. "I told you," she said before he could form the question he longed to ask, "my specialty is *fantasy*."

Her reply sounded enough like a taunt to make Darcy's face suddenly redden. "Meaning?" he asked defensively.

"Meaning," she answered with no hint of mockery in her tone, "that I'd like to hear the rest of your story now."

Sighing, Darcy gazed down at her reflection in the shimmering surface of the lake. On the one hand he felt like jumping to his feet and screaming at her to go back to New York and leave him in his misery. But there was something else that stopped him, some powerful message in the expectant way she scrunched her shoulders forward, waiting for him to begin, that told him Eliza Knight was willing to be convinced.

"I remained in Jane's bedroom at Chawton Cottage for the next three days," he said, "eavesdropping on her conversations and pretending to be asleep or unconscious."

Darcy closed his eyes, remembering the smell and feel of the soft, rose-scented featherbed, the same intoxicating scent that he had come to associate with Jane herself.

"Very gradually I reached the impossible but inescapable conclusion that I was neither dreaming *nor* insane," he continued, forming a new picture in his mind of Jane's gentle countenance and lively, sparkling eyes. "By then, of course, I had also realized *who* she was."

Darcy smiled. "God knows I had heard enough while I was growing up about Jane Austen, the great English novelist who had nearly ruined the distinguished Darcy family name. But where had she gotten the name in the first place? The family always naturally assumed that she had somehow heard of my ancestor and liked the sounds of his name and estate. But there I was, lying in her bed. The implications of that were maddening, especially since it seemed evident that she had never heard the name Darcy until my arrival at Chawton.

"Anyway," he said, "for three days Jane and her sister, Cassandra, took turns sitting with me. And whenever they left me alone for a few minutes I would get up and take a few halting steps around the room, praying I would become strong enough to escape before the kindly Mr. Hudson subjected me to fresh medical horrors."

Chapter 21

As he had done morning and evening for the past three days, the bombastic Mr. Hudson stood over Darcy's bed, thoughtfully examining the forehead of his apparently unconscious patient. "His wound is healing splendidly," the physician pronounced, running his none-too-clean fingers over the tender, pink tissues of the wound on Darcy's scalp.

Hudson turned to Jane who was standing apprehensively beside the fireplace, watching. "The scar will be completely hidden by his hair," the old doctor happily predicted. Then, with a worried frown for what her august brother might think if a cure was not soon effectuated, he asked, "But you say he hasn't spoken again?"

Jane shook her head. "He has said not a word since the first night," she affirmed, this time having no need to lie. For it was true that the handsome American lying in her bed had uttered not a sound since she had heard him murmuring in his fever three nights earlier.

She did not mention to Hudson that late at night, when she was alone at her writing, she sometimes experienced an eerie sensation that the stranger's eyes were upon her, watching and secretly scrutinizing her every move. Once or twice the feeling had grown so strong that she had actually whirled about to look at him.

But always she had found Darcy's eyes tightly shut, his breathing deep and regular. Odd, she thought. So very odd.

Distracted as she was by those thoughts, it took a moment before Jane realized that Mr. Hudson was again speaking to her. She returned her attention to the old doctor and found him leaning over Darcy.

"Hmmm, an extraordinary case," Hudson muttered, stroking the tuft of snowy whiskers on his chin. "Extraordinary." He finally straightened and cocked his head. "Perhaps I should treat him with an injection of mercury or stinging wasps," he ruminated aloud. "Well, we shall see how he looks this evening and then decide which treatment shall be better. For it is a sad fact that many patients cannot tolerate the effects of such strong systemic poisons, though they often have the beneficial effect of shocking the brain back to activity."

Jane wisely said nothing, but waited until the doctor closed up his bag and then escorted him out of the room.

The instant the door closed behind them Darcy's eyes popped open and he got out of bed, feeling both ridiculous and vulnerable in the long linen nightshirt he wore.

He shuffled barefoot to the window and pulled aside the lace curtains to peek outside. In the garden below he saw Cassandra standing at the gate, speaking with Hudson. Beyond them, a heavy post coach rumbled through the tiny village, scattering a cloud of squawking ducks and chickens in its wake. Then all was silent again.

"Mercury and stinging wasps!" Darcy whispered the frightening words in abject terror as his mind conjured up horrible visions of the bumbling Mr. Hudson working his medieval tortures.

Though the gash on his forehead was indeed healing nicely and hardly gave him any pain at all now, he was still unsteady on his feet. He had been hoping to become just a little stronger before seeking out his clothes and departing from Chawton Cottage under cover of darkness, hopefully to reclaim his horse and return to the spot where he had stepped into this nightmare.

But Hudson's last pronouncement had convinced the unwilling patient that he must escape before the old doctor returned and managed to do him some lasting harm. Darcy had, over the past few days, come to understand that he had been incredibly lucky so far. Because it was clear that Mr. Hudson's outrageous treatments with catgut and leeches actually represented the cutting edge of early nineteenth-century medical technology. However, Darcy had no confidence that he could even survive another round of bleeding, much less wasps and applications of mercury.

While he was having these thoughts and wondering where to begin looking for his clothes, Darcy heard the bedroom door opening behind him. He turned to see Jane Austen angrily regarding him.

"Just as I suspected!" she said, pointing at the bed. "Get back in that bed, sir!"

"Now just a minute . . ." Darcy blustered, managing to feel both guilty and foolish at the same instant.

"Immediately!" she commanded. "You may be an artful deceiver but you are still a sick man."

With her dark eyes flashing dangerously she watched as Darcy sheepishly climbed into the bed and covered his naked legs with a quilt. "Now, sir," she demanded, "tell me without delay *who* you are and how you came to be here in Hampshire."

"My name is Fitzwilliam Darcy and I am from Virginia," he began, reciting the carefully rehearsed story he had put together over the past three days of listening to his hosts discussing him. "I was visiting friends nearby when I—"

Jane cut him off with a disgusted look. "You have *no* friends in this neighborhood, sir," she coldly informed him. "Nor is there any large house such as you described closer than twenty miles to the west of this village."

Darcy felt his cover story disintegrating before he could get it all out. "I, uh, perhaps it was to the east, then . . ." he stammered, relying on his head injury to account for his seeming confusion. "Look, you've been very kind, but I think I should just get dressed and leave now. May I have my clothes?"

At first he thought Jane was going to let him go, for she immediately stomped over to the same tall cupboard in the far corner of the room where she kept her nightgown and flung open the door. "Yes," she said, "let us begin with your clothes." She turned to face him in a swirl of skirts and held up his gray knit boxer shorts. "How do you explain *this*!"

Confused, Darcy stared at her. "My underwear?"

As if she was handling a deadly reptile, Jane held the shorts out in front of her with two hands and stretched the elastic waistband, releasing it with a loud snap.

"Not the garment!" she said, stretching and snapping the elastic band again. "*This fabric* that springs and stretches like gum arabic! Never has such a thing been seen or heard of, even in London. Poor Maggie nearly fainted in the laundry."

Darcy's mind raced. "Oh, the elastic," he said smiling. "Elastic, it . . ." the smile faded as he realized that if she was holding his underwear, then he wasn't wearing them. He looked down at the nightshirt he'd had on since his first night in her house, her bed.

Darcy looked up at Jane, a deep blush coloring his face and more than likely his entire body. "Who undressed me?"

Jane, still holding the boxer shorts, dropped her hand to her side. Taken aback by the question she could only respond, "I beg your pardon?"

The blush receding Darcy asked again, "Undressed me, who did it?"

Jane looked at him, unable to say anything.

"Miss Austen?" he nudged.

Still not sure how to respond, she said, "I have six brothers."

"And none of them lives here."

She stood looking into the depths of his green eyes; she saw embarrassment and anger. He'd been brought into her house bleeding; it had seemed perfectly natural to get him out of his dirty clothes. How many times had she helped her mother do the same with one of her brothers? But now she questioned the propriety of having done so to a perfect stranger. She wasn't prepared to admit it. But he wasn't going to let her escape so easily.

"You did it, didn't you?" he challenged.

Now she felt the heat rise in her own face as her cheeks went crimson. No longer able to withstand his penetrating stare she looked away, but couldn't hide a small smile at the memory of his strong, athletic body.

For what seemed many minutes but was actually only a few seconds an embarrassed silence fell on the room. In the hope of changing the subject Jane turned to anger. "I demand that you tell me who you are and where you come from."

"I'm not sure you're in any position to be making demands," was his own angry reply.

Her tone turned serious. "You must explain yourself to me now, sir, else I must think you a spy."

Darcy stared at her. "A spy? Who would I be spying on?"

Jane's expression did not change. "It is no secret that our two countries have many quarrels and have often been at war," she said. "Even now American ships continue the illegal trade in slaves and supply our French enemies with cannon and munitions . . ."

Again Darcy felt like slapping his head at his own stupidity. This was 1810, the era of the Napoleonic Wars between Britain and France. Wars in which the new, maverick American nation had sided firmly with France.

"I am *not* a spy," he said weakly. "Okay?"

A flash of anger shone in Jane's dark eyes. "Okay!" she mimicked the strange new word. "What does that *mean*? I speak several languages and the word okay is not included in the vocabularies of any of them."

Darcy suddenly swung his feet out of the bed, realizing that he was on increasingly shaky ground with this lovely but dangerous woman. He stood and held out his hand to her. "First let me have my clothes," he demanded with as much dignity as he could muster.

Still holding his undergarment in her hand, Jane stood her ground for a moment. She wanted to know about the brass contraption that opened and closed his trousers, the buttons that looked like bone but were not, as well as the fabric he called elastic. She watched him and found that she was unwilling to revisit the uncomfortable scene regarding how she came to know about those things. Heaving a sigh she turned to the cupboard and retrieved his pants. Turning back to him, she wordlessly handed the items to him, then turned away as he slipped them on.

He sat on the bed and began pulling on his boots. "Okay is an American slang word," he told her. "You *are* familiar with slang . . . made-up words from the people in the streets?"

"Yes, I understand your meaning," she said, as he strode over to the cupboard and found his freshly laundered shirt folded neatly inside.

With his shirt in his hand he looked over at Jane who was still standing by the cupboard. She looked up into his haunting green eyes. He saw in her face a jumble of emotions. Although she was embarrassed by what had just passed between them, what he saw behind the anger was excitement, passion. He was enchanted once again by this wonderfully complex woman.

Finally finding his voice, he said, "Okay means all right, or fine," he explained, pulling on more clothes and walking over to the window to look down at the empty village road junction.

"If you *are* a spy they could hang you." It was a flat statement.

"I am *not* a spy!" he again insisted, turning back to her. "To tell you the truth, I don't really know *how* I got here. As a matter of fact I'm not even sure where *here* is, though I'm pretty certain I'm a very long way from my own . . . home."

He paused then, watching her eyes for some sign, realizing as he did how extraordinarily attractive she was, bearing not the slightest resemblance to the poorly done sketch of a frumpy sixteen-year-old that was the only known portrait of Jane Austen to have survived into his time.

"I'm very sorry that I deceived you," he apologized again. "I was hoping to leave here quietly, recover my horse, and then try to find my way back—"

"Back to Virginia in—five hours?" Despite the obvious tone of her cynical question, Jane's dark eyes were filled with evident curiosity.

"Oh God! Did I say that?"

She nodded slowly. "Along with many other strange and unexplainable things. Things you called phones and jets and some sort of telling vision."

Darcy was shocked and disturbed to learn that he had managed to reveal so much in his brief unconscious state. "My God, were you taking notes?" he asked sarcastically.

"How can you explain all of these strange words and the devices that you carry with you," she said, gesturing at his watch. "Like your watch that never needs winding. Virginia is but a few months, sailing time from England; surely such wonders could not long remain hidden from the world if they were not the tools of some secret and sinister mission . . ."

"Yes, you're right," he replied, cutting her off. Darcy paused for a minute, trying to think of some way to explain without making his position any more precarious than it was. "Very well," he said after a moment, "I'll try to explain if you'll promise not to repeat what I'm going to tell you."

Jane stiffened at the suggestion. "I shall make no such promise to protect your foul secrets," she proclaimed.

Darcy glared at her in frustration. "Fine!" he retaliated.

"Then let me tell you a few secrets about *yourself*, Miss Austen. At night, after you have removed your clothing and put on your nightgown, you sit at that dressing table by the fire to write. Often before you actually begin writing you carry on imaginary conversations between your characters, or wonder aloud how they might react to a lover's intimate touch. You are presently working on a novel about five sisters who are all hoping to marry well. Two of them do in fact, but another one is seduced and deceived by an infamous scoundrel you've named Wickham."

For a fraction of a second Darcy toyed with the idea of informing her that the hero of her romantic novel would be named Fitzwilliam Darcy. But he saw with grim satisfaction that his unexpected disclosures had hit home and he had no wish to reduce the effect. For Jane's face had turned pale as he spoke and she'd stumbled a step backward, as though he had physically struck her.

"Sir," she murmured resentfully, "you have been spying on me, and reading my most intimate private papers—"

"I have not read anything!" Darcy said coldly. "How could I when you never have more than a few sheets of your writings with you at any time and you never let them out of your sight?"

She turned away in confusion. "You . . . only think to confound me with more riddles," she accused. "You *cannot* know what is in my book, which I am not yet finished writing."

"But I do know," he insisted, regretting the need to resort to such crude, bullying tactics but unable to think of any other way to keep her under control until he could find a way to escape from his dangerous situation. "We *both* have secrets we'd rather keep, Miss Austen, and I know some of yours. That is my only point," he concluded.

He moved closer to her and spoke as gently as he could. "Now, if you will only listen calmly and with an open mind, I'll try to explain myself to you. But I must have your pledge of secrecy."

Pointedly stepping away from him, Jane walked to her vanity table and sat weakly in the chair.

"I'm sorry," he said, "but once I've explained, I think you'll understand my reasons." He tried a reassuring smile on her. "If it makes you feel any better, I also happen to know that you're an extremely gifted writer."

Defeated by his disclosures, Jane shook her head. "Please, just tell me who you are," she said wearily.

Before Darcy could reply, the bedroom door opened and Edward Austen walked in unannounced. His eyes widened in surprise at the sight of Darcy awake and fully dressed.

Jane immediately rose and went to her brother's side.

"My dear Mr. Darcy," Edward exclaimed with evident pleasure, "I came down to look in on you because Mr. Hudson reported that you were still abed. But happily I see that you are instead greatly improved. Excellent, sir! Excellent!"

"Yes, I'm feeling much better, a bit weak but definitely better," Darcy replied, keeping a wary eye on Jane, who stood like a statue coldly regarding him from the sanctuary of her brother's side. Darcy continued to Edward, "I was just thanking your sister for her great kindness in looking after me."

To Darcy's relief Jane curtseyed slightly in his direction. "You are *most* welcome, sir," she murmured.

Edward was all smiles. "Well then, Darcy, you must move up to Chawton Great House. I insist upon it." He moved to a window at the far end of the room and pointed out across the fields to a forest of chimneys and the top of a mansard roof rising above a line of distant trees. "My house is only a short journey away on the other side of the meadows that you see beyond that small wood," he said proudly. "There you may complete your recovery in greater comfort whilst we continue our efforts to locate those friends of yours."

Darcy's eyes darted to Jane, who was watching him with a grim little smile that seemed to say, *Let's see you get yourself out of this one, pal.*

"Oh, my friends!" Darcy stammered. "Yes, well, it's rather

embarrassing, but as I have just explained to Miss Austen, that knock on the head really confused me."

He looked at Jane and saw her triumphant smile fading. "In fact," he continued, "I know no one in this part of the country. I was simply riding through on my way to London when my horse bolted and ran into the fields."

"Ah, I see!" said Edward, seemingly satisfied with the American's nebulous explanation. "I suppose that explains it, then."

Chapter 22

A short time later they stood at the front gate of Chawton Cottage, where Edward's carriage waited.

"Miss Austen, I am obliged to you," Darcy said, bowing at the waist to Cassandra, as he had seen Hudson do earlier.

"Not at all, sir." Obviously pleased to have the handsome stranger in her debt, Cassandra rewarded him with a radiant smile and returned his overly formal bow with a polite curtsey.

"I hope we'll meet again before I return home," Darcy told Jane, who was standing beside her sister and making no effort whatsoever to conceal her irritation.

"I would take great pleasure in such a meeting," she said, raising her eyes to his and looking straight into them. "For I still have many unanswered questions to ask about your fascinating life in . . . Virginia."

Darcy fidgeted nervously beneath her steely gaze, certain that she was about to give him away. He breathed a sigh of relief as Edward stepped forward and addressed her.

"You two shall *indeed* have another meeting, Jane," Edward cheerfully informed her. "Have you forgotten that my brother Frank is arriving today at Chawton Great House? You and Cassandra are to dine with us this very evening. And several of your friends will be there as well."

Edward suddenly broke off his cheerful discourse and cast

an apologetic look Darcy's way. "Of course," he continued, "we had thought to delay those jolly plans because of Mr. Darcy's incapacity, but if he is now well enough . . ."

Forced to make some polite reply, Darcy tried to sound enthusiastic at the unsettling prospect of dining with all the Austen clan and their friends. "I feel quite well now," he assured Edward, quickly adding, "however, I wouldn't want to impose on your hospitality, sir."

In fact, Darcy wanted nothing more than to be taken to his horse so that he could flee from these people at the earliest opportunity. He most decidedly did not want to be forced into a social situation where his ignorance of early nineteenth-century customs would surely mark him as an impostor.

Edward, however, was having none of his feeble protests. "Nothing of the sort, sir," he assured Darcy. "We shall enjoy a fine dinner of excellent fish and fowl, and then be charmingly entertained by the ladies."

Turning to Jane and Cassandra, he said, "Shall I send my carriage at seven?"

The ladies both smiled in appreciation of their brother's thoughtfulness. "Yes, thank you, Edward," Cassandra replied for both.

With a sinking feeling in the pit of his stomach, Darcy climbed into the open carriage with Edward and it drove away. He looked back through the etched glass backlight to see Jane waving good-bye to him, a little smirk of satisfaction pasted on her lovely face. And he realized that she was actually looking forward to his undoing.

Leaning back against the padded leather seat cushions, Darcy only half-listened to Edward, who was enthusiastically describing the local hunting conditions. Between polite nods, the anxious American covertly surveyed the passing countryside in a futile search for the low stone wall with its distinctive arch of overhanging trees.

*   *   *

"Sister," Cassandra said excitedly as the carriage rolled out of sight, "I did not know that you had been so much in conversation with our guest." The elder Miss Austen frowned to express her own disappointment. "I confess he did nothing more interesting than to sleep and groan while I sat with him."

With a disinterested shrug Jane dismissed Cassandra's evident desire to begin gossiping about Darcy. "We had only a little brief discussion . . . about his home in Virginia, after I found him awake a short while ago," Jane lied, wondering now if she had perhaps only imagined the strange, combative conversation with the American in her bedroom.

"And yet you seem most eager to meet with him again," Cass said with a sly smile. "Did he tell you if he has a wife at home in Virginia?"

Jane, who usually loved to engage in such delicious but harmless prattle with her beloved sister, was in no mood for such foolishness today. So she pretended to be shocked by Cassandra's intimation. "Cass, what a thing to say!"

"Well, he is very handsome and, as Edward tells it, very rich, too."

Jane sniffed irritably. "Yes, and I expect that like most rich American landowners he also keeps slaves and is thus thoroughly wicked," she replied, silently conjecturing whether it might actually be true. "Mr. Darcy is probably the sort of man who beats his servants and loves his dogs and horses to distraction," she concluded, turning and going into the house.

"Well, hello there, big fella. How are you doing?"

Darcy grinned with genuine delight as a young groom led Lord Nelson out of Edward's commodious stable for his inspection.

"He's in tip-top condition, sir," said the groom, handing the reins over to Darcy. "Can't say I ever seen a healthier beast."

Edward Austen, whose fine team of matched chestnut geldings demonstrated that the man obviously had an excellent eye for horseflesh, was clearly impressed by Lord Nelson. "What a marvelous creature, Darcy!" the older man exclaimed. "Where on earth did you find him?"

"I bought him at auction . . . a few days ago," Darcy warily replied. "I plan to, um, take him home . . . to improve the bloodline in my own breeding stable."

To Darcy's dismay, Edward seemed shocked by this innocent revelation. "Home? You mean to say you plan to sail to America with this magnificent horse?" he bellowed. "Good Lord, man, is that not highly risky? I mean, the army regularly moves cavalry and livestock by sea, but confining a superior animal like this for months below decks in a heaving, rat-infested ship's hold . . ."

Realizing that he had stepped into another minefield, for he had forgotten that this was still the age of sail, with steamships not due to revolutionize ocean travel for another sixty years or so, Darcy quickly backtracked. "Well, I'm still only thinking about it, actually. We'll see."

Slightly mollified by his answer, Edward nodded in the direction of the large Jacobean mansion they had passed on the way to the stables. "Shall we go up to the house now?" he suggested. "I daresay you will want to rest before dinner."

"Yes, thank you," Darcy replied. "But I'd like just a little more time with the horse, if that's all right."

"Certainly," Edward agreed, seeming to readily understand a man putting the welfare of his horse before his own comforts. "I shall have your rooms prepared and some fresh clothes laid out for you."

Edward indicated the young groom who had been standing patiently by the stable door while they talked. "Young Simmons here will show you the way up when you're ready."

"Sir!" Simmons touched his peaked hat in acknowledgment of his master's order.

With a nod to his guest, Edward left the stables and Darcy began to check the horse over carefully.

"Begging your leave, sir," said the groom, coming over to stand beside Lord Nelson. "I think there's something you should see."

Darcy looked at the youngster. "There is?"

Taking hold of Lord Nelson's halter, Simmons deftly rolled back the horse's upper lip, exposing the electronic barcode symbols that had been tattooed there by the previous owner. "Look at this, sir!" the groom exclaimed. "What can it be?"

Another minefield, thought Darcy, wondering how many of these situations he was going to be able to talk his way out of before making a fatal slip.

Looking quickly around to see if anyone else was listening, Darcy placed a warning finger to his lips. "Simmons," he said in a low, confidential tone, "you seem like a good fellow. Can you be trusted to keep your mouth shut if I let you in on a secret?"

Simmons's plain country features lit up with pleasure. "Oh, yes indeed, sir," he whispered.

"This is a good-luck charm that was given to me by a very noble Indian chief when I was a boy," Darcy said, pointing to the barcode identifier, which listed the horse's international registry number, age, country of origin, lineage and owner.

"No!" Simmons's eyes were as large as saucers.

"I have that charm secretly tattooed on all of my horses, for luck."

The look of awe on Simmons's face gave Darcy an idea and he decided to embroider the ridiculous tale just a bit more. "In fact," he told the wondering groom, "I believe that Indian charm is the only reason I wasn't killed in the fall I took going over that wall the other day."

"That's amazing, sir," Simmons breathed. "For I heard tell you took a very bad tumble indeed."

Darcy was just on the point of congratulating himself

when the youngster frowned and said, "But I thought maybe it was there so you'd know the horse was yours if he was ever stole."

Shot down again for having underestimated his supposedly unsophisticated listener, Darcy couldn't help laughing out loud. "Simmons, my friend," he told the observant groom, "something tells me that you'll go very far in this life."

His clever plan to coax the location of the stone wall from the young man in tatters, Darcy went for broke. "Tell me, though, how can I get back to the spot where I was thrown?" he asked. I'd like to ride out there and take a look at the ground."

"Oh, I'm sorry, sir," said the lad, looking genuinely pained that he did not have the answer Darcy sought. "I don't believe I've heard it mentioned exactly where it was they found you. Perhaps Master Edward knows."

The sun was dropping toward the horizon as Jane sat before the mirror at her dressing table. She had been taking advantage of the waning daylight to examine the handwritten manuscript that she kept hidden under lock and key in a chest downstairs. To her great disappointment she had been able to find no evidence that either her chest or the pages stored within had been tampered with. "Oh that *horrid* man!" she spat, still convinced that Darcy had somehow gained access to her manuscript.

Looking into the mirror, she saw that Cassandra had quietly entered the bedroom and was standing behind her, looking very worried.

"Jane, what is the matter?" Cass inquired.

Jane turned and regarded her. "Why *must* we be forced to dine with that arrogant American?" she demanded to know.

Cass's worried look changed to one of confusion. "But you said you looked forward to meeting him again," she reminded Jane. "However, if you do not wish to see him I will send word that you are ill. Edward knows that you have not slept properly since—"

"No!" Jane interrupted, coming to a sudden decision. "We shall go to Edward's," she defiantly declared. "For I will not miss an opportunity to see Frank and all of our friends." She turned back to the mirror and mischief sparkled in her eyes. "And I do genuinely wish to learn more of this Darcy."

"Oh, sister," whispered Cassandra, suddenly anxious to share her own thrilling speculations about the handsome stranger, "you do not think that Darcy has deceived us, do you? Perhaps he is a brigand," she breathlessly suggested, "or an American spy, and not a gentleman at all."

"Perhaps!" Jane said, reaching up to arrange her hair. "But if he is not a gentleman, then let the society of my brother's drawing room be his undoing. For only a true gentleman will know how to dress and behave in company."

Chapter 23

Chawton Great House was ablaze with light. Several fine horses stood in the traces of the carriages waiting in the drive before the huge brick mansion. The drivers and footmen of the equipages sat or stood about on the lawn, enjoying the excellent supper of roast venison that had been sent out to them from Edward's well-stocked kitchens.

While the drivers happily ate and quaffed ale outside, up in the manor's large, oak-paneled dining room more than a dozen Austen relations and friends were being treated to a sumptuous repast of fresh trout and roasted game birds, enhanced by a dizzying selection of soups, meat, salads and fresh fruits.

The food was being served on a gorgeous, delicately patterned china service just arrived from the East Indies courtesy of Jane's seagoing elder brother, Captain Francis Austen.

Dressed uncomfortably in a foppish suit of Edward's best evening clothes, into which he had barely managed to squeeze his large frame, Darcy found himself seated near the head of the long, linen-draped table, directly across from Frank—a handsome, middle-aged officer of the line, who was dressed in the splendid blue-and-white uniform of His Majesty's Royal Navy.

To Darcy's absolute horror, Frank had been plying him

with ever-more probing questions throughout the evening. And it had been to the visitor's great relief when Edward had mercifully broken in, insisting that his brother repeat for all the company the story of how he had brought the priceless set of china through a violent storm at sea by cushioning the fragile crockery in the bags of gunpowder stored deep in the magazine of his warship.

"The gale was blowing ninety, with waves so high they were topping our mainmast," Frank was now telling his enthralled listeners. "We were being knocked about so badly that every article in the ship was smashing itself to pieces against the bulkheads, when here comes the gunner, his eyes as round as cannonballs."

Frank paused dramatically, his ice-blue eyes scanning the table to be sure he had everyone's absolute attention. "'Cap'n, Sir,' says the gunner," Frank continued his story, mimicking the high-pitched voice of the frightened man, "'everything's bashing about so terrible below I fear the powder may spark and blow us all to kingdom come.'"

Frank paused again and a sly smile creased his deeply tanned features. "'Well man,' said I, 'thank God for all that good china down there among the powder. For if it's to kingdom come we're bound, at least when we arrive there we'll be able to put on a decent British tea.'"

The guests laughed and clapped appreciatively. But no sooner had the applause died down than Frank returned his attention to Darcy. "Well, sir," he said a bit too loudly, "Edward tells me you had a close call of your own the other day. Thrown from your mount, eh?"

Darcy nodded as all eyes turned to him. "Yes," he replied, smiling. "But I was fortunate enough to be rescued and taken to the home of your lovely sisters who nursed me back to health." He inclined his head in a bow toward Jane and Cassandra, who were seated together a little ways down the table.

Frank, who had been drinking copious amounts of wine, raised his glass to his sisters. "My own dear Jane and Cass, God bless 'em. Are they not angelic creatures?" he asked, his gruff voice filled with genuine affection.

The sea captain winked and leaned closer to Darcy. "Yet I declare the poor lasses have not a husband between them," he said in a loud stage whisper, "though not for want of offers. But both of them have vowed they will marry for love alone, fortune being not a matter of consequence to either."

Jane smiled tolerantly at her brother's good-natured teasing, but Cassandra's fair complexion flushed bright pink. "Frank!" she exclaimed, scandalized. "Mr. Darcy will think you are in earnest if you insist on baiting us so."

"What you say is true, brother," Jane playfully rejoined Frank. "But you know full well that we have only vowed never to take husbands until you have brought us a shipload of pirate treasure, so that we may have fortunes large enough to marry whomever we choose."

Frank's broad shoulders shook with laughter and wine sloshed over the rim of his glass. "Then, dear Jane, I shall scour the world over in search of pirates," he declared. "For sisters as genial and accomplished as you and Cassandra deserve nothing but happiness."

Without warning the tipsy captain turned back to Darcy. "And you, sir, what think you of the married life?"

Relaxing slightly, for his adversary seemed now to be merely having fun, Darcy glanced over at Jane and pretended to ponder the question. "They say that marriage is a wonderful institution," he finally answered. "But who wants to live in an institution?"

There was a long moment of deathly silence in the room as everyone at the table pondered the threadbare joke that Darcy had last told as a freshman in college.

Jane was the first to laugh. Then the entire company broke into loud, appreciative howls.

"Quite right!" Edward chortled uncontrollably from his winged armchair at the head of the table. "An excellent jest, sir! Excellent."

Darcy smiled at their reaction, wondering if it was possible that his audience might have just heard the joke for the very first time. In the same instant, though, he realized that he had committed yet another serious blunder.

Frank, his blue eyes rimmed in red from the effects of the wine, was glaring at him. For a moment Darcy couldn't imagine what he had done, then it dawned on him that he was guilty of having gotten a bigger laugh than the Austen family's heroic favorite son.

"And what think you of the politics in France these days, Mr. Darcy?" The humor had drained from the captain's voice and he was eyeing his victim like a hungry gull making ready to swallow a sardine.

Another uneasy silence descended upon the candlelit dining room as Darcy smiled disarmingly. "I'm afraid I know more of horses than of politics, Captain," he replied.

"Hmmm!" Frank grumbled, unappeased. "Would that all your countrymen felt so. Even now my ships patrol the American coast in an attempt to halt the godless Yankee slave trade and quell your shipments of munitions to England's enemies."

Frank paused and took another long draught of wine, dribbling a few blood-red drops onto the front of his snowy shirt. "We may soon be at war with you Americans, you know," he growled menacingly.

Glancing down the table, Darcy saw that Jane's face was filled with alarm, and he wondered if she was now regretting her earlier promise to keep his secrets.

"Frank! I fear you are making our guest uneasy with this talk of slaves and war." Edward was on his feet, clearly embarrassed by his brother's rude behavior toward a potentially valuable new banking client.

To Darcy's surprise, Frank abruptly stood and bowed stiffly

to him. "My apologies, sir, if I have said anything to offend you. I fear I am not often enough in gentle society."

Seizing upon the opportunity to put to rest the dangerous subjects of slavery and war with America, Darcy leaped to his feet and returned the bow. "No offense taken, Captain," he said. Then, raising his glass to the assembled guests, he offered a toast. "May our two nations be forever joined in friendship and prosperity."

Darcy could feel the tension in the room magically dissolving as all present smiled with evident relief and raised their glasses.

"Hear! Hear! Well said, sir!" Edward cried out.

Darcy looked back over at Frank, but the abrasive captain had already turned away and was conversing with a buxom young lady at his side.

From her position farther down the table Jane sat thoughtfully scrutinizing Darcy. Cassandra leaned close to her and whispered with a little smile, "What think you of Darcy now, Jane? Is he not after all a gentleman?"

"He makes a good show of it," Jane grudgingly conceded, "but I observe that he is far too nervous in this informal atmosphere. See how his eyes dart constantly about the room. And I saw him before, rubbing at his fork with a napkin, as if he thought the thing to be unclean."

Jane paused to watch the American a moment longer, then she slowly shook her head. "No, sister," she concluded, "I think there is too much of the cornered fox in Darcy's look. And he is sorely in need of a valet to tie his cravat."

"Oh, Jane, you exaggerate as usual," Cassandra retorted.

"Do I?" asked Jane. "Watch this, then." She pointedly stared at Darcy until he glanced her way. When she had his attention, she touched her throat with her fingers and shook her head slightly. Darcy immediately looked down self-consciously and fumbled with the broad silk scarf tied in a clumsy bow at his collar.

Grinning delightedly at his flustered reaction, Jane inclined her head toward her sister and raised a hand to cover her mouth. "See," she whispered.

Cassandra looked from Darcy to Jane and back again. "But whatever can it mean?" she asked.

Following supper, the members of the dinner party retired to a large drawing room on the second floor of Edward's manse for conversation and light entertainment. Jane, who was soon coaxed and teased by the others into taking her place at the piano, played a series of increasingly difficult pieces by Mozart and Haydn, all of which she performed with admirable style.

Hoping to avoid both of the Austen brothers, but most especially the volatile Frank, Darcy sought out Cassandra, whom he discovered sitting alone at one side of the room, and took a chair beside her. "Your sister is very accomplished," he said quietly, for he was genuinely impressed with Jane's mastery of the instrument.

Cassandra accepted the compliment to her sister's musical talent with evident pride. "She does play beautifully," Cass agreed, adding, "music, I think, is Jane's only true passion. She practices every morning at the pianoforte at home, you know."

Before Darcy could say that he did not know that—for he could not recall having heard any music during his stay at Chawton Cottage—Jane finished her last piece to enthusiastic applause. He and Cassandra both rose as she walked over to join them.

"That was wonderful, Miss Austen," Darcy told her, pointedly touching his poorly tied cravat. "You are *full* of surprises."

Jane accorded him a little curtsey. "I thank you, sir," she replied with laughter sparkling in her eyes. "You are all politeness."

"Is it true that music is your *only* passion?" he asked with a mocking smile.

"Not at all," she retorted sharply. "Is it true that horses are yours?"

Cassandra, who had been listening to the conversation with growing bewilderment, took advantage of the momentary lull to step back and curtsey to Darcy. "If you will excuse me, I think I must visit with my brothers now," she said, beating a diplomatic retreat to the other side of the room.

Alone at last, Darcy and Jane both looked around to see if anyone else was within earshot. To Darcy's dismay, he saw Frank scowling at them from his post beside the mantel.

Jane read the anxiety written on Darcy's features and asked him a little too loudly, "And how is dear Lord Nelson, your horse?"

"Please, not here," Darcy begged her. "I believe your brother would gladly run me through with that saber he's carrying."

Jane accorded him an angelic smile. "Yes, I'm sure he would, given cause," she agreed. "In which case, perhaps you had better explain yourself to me now, sir, so that I may properly consider whether I would wish to stop dear Frank if he tries."

"Very well," Darcy said. He glanced nervously around the crowded room. "Is there someplace we can go?"

She stared at him, not certain of his meaning. "Go?"

"Somewhere private," he said impatiently, "where we can speak without being overheard."

Jane wrinkled her brow at the odd request and she also looked around the drawing room. Then she slowly shook her head. "Not here in my brother's house," she told him. "Certainly not with Frank about."

"Where, then?" Darcy pleaded. "It is urgent that I speak with you immediately."

Caught off guard by this unexpected turnabout—for Jane had expected to be the one who would force him to reveal his secrets to her, and in her own good time—she could think of no suitable private meeting place.

And at any rate she was not at all certain that she wished to be alone with this mercurial and possibly dangerous man.

"I do not know . . ." she replied, playing for time. "You must give me a moment to think."

Darcy waited impatiently. Across the room, Captain Francis Austen was speaking in low, serious tones with Edward and Cassandra, turning around from time to time to openly glare at Darcy.

Chapter 24

"I stood there waiting for her to think of a private place where we could speak, the whole time with her brother's suspicious eyes burning into me like lasers."

Darcy looked up at Eliza in the growing gloom of early evening. Though she had long since taken her feet out of the water and folded them beneath her, she was still leaning eagerly toward him, as if she was afraid of missing some minor detail of his story. "So where did you go?" she asked expectantly.

"Jane couldn't think of anywhere at the moment, and then we were interrupted by another of her many relatives," Darcy replied. "We didn't have another opportunity to be alone for the rest of the evening. But later, as she was leaving Edward's house, I—"

"Fitz? Y'all down there?"

Darcy left the sentence hanging and whipped his head around as the shrill cry split the quiet evening.

"Perfect!" Eliza groaned. She tore her eyes from Darcy and saw Faith Harrington stumbling toward them across the lawn.

Darcy got up, gave Eliza his hand and helped her to her feet. "I'm sorry," he said. "I'll finish this later."

"Oh *there* you are!" Faith waved and hurried down to the lakeshore. She had changed from her riding outfit into a frilly pink summer dress, which somehow made her look even harder and less feminine than she had before. "Now y'all aren't having a little secret affair, are you?" the tall blonde chirped, leering at Eliza.

Annoyed by the sudden interruption, Eliza stooped to retrieve her sketch pad and her shoes. "If we were it wouldn't be a secret for long around here, would it?" she murmured resentfully.

"My goodness, aren't we cranky? I just came to tell you that dinner is being served." Faith's manner was full of wounded innocence. "I wouldn't have dreamed of *interrupting* your little soiree otherwise," she pouted, turning and stomping back toward the house on her own. Darcy and Eliza waited a moment before following her at a safe distance.

"Do you two have a *thing* going?" Eliza asked him when the other was out of hearing range.

Darcy shook his head and smiled. "No, old family friend and Harv's sister," he told her as if to explain Faith's presence, although he wasn't sure why that was important. He looked up at the retreating pink figure flouncing through the dusk ahead of them. "I'm afraid that poor Faith just can't stand not being the center of attention."

Eliza laughed at the ridiculous explanation of the other woman's bad manners. "You don't really think that's all it is, I hope."

"What do you mean?"

"I mean," Eliza said, pointing at Faith, "that the woman looks like a disgruntled postal worker who just got a pink slip." She lowered her voice to a dramatic whisper. "You don't have any automatic weapons lying around, do you?"

"Well, not any that are loaded," Darcy replied with a grin. "Shall we go up to dinner now?"

Eliza shrugged and rolled her eyes. "Sure, why not?"

Eliza, Harv, Jenny and Artemis were clustered at one end of the huge table in the echoing dining room, eating a delicious meal of crab bisque and cold fried chicken. Faith, meanwhile, had once more appropriated Darcy for herself. She had moved him to the opposite end of the table, where she had been chattering nonstop for the past half hour about some arrangement or other.

"Admit it now, aren't you glad you stayed?" Harv Harrington was pointing a partially consumed drumstick at Eliza.

She cast a deadly glance in Faith's direction. "Let me get back to you on that one, Harv," she replied, attacking the savory pink soup with an antique silver spoon, the bowl of which was cunningly formed to resemble a miniature seashell.

Harv's handsome features contorted into an expression of mock concern at her reply. "Oh, my! I do hope my big sister hasn't been bothering you," he said.

"No more than your average case of bubonic plague," Eliza assured him. "What is *with* her anyway? I mean, it's not like she caught Fitz and me playing doctor behind the barn."

"Artie, I *told* you I liked this girl," Jenny piped up.

Artemis looked up thoughtfully from his bisque. "Playing doctor behind the barn? I must have missed that course in med school," he commented dryly.

Jenny leaned over and kissed his neck. "I'll fill you in on it later, dear," she solemnly promised. Then she turned to Harv. "Harv, why don't you be a darling and explain to Eliza about Fitz and your sister," she said.

Delighted at actually being invited to speak for once, Harv quickly finished demolishing his chicken drumstick and washed down the last bite with a large swallow of scotch. "Fitz and Faith," he said at length. "Well, that's simple enough. You see, Eliza, Faith has dreamed of becoming the mistress of Pemberley Farms since she was old enough to read a Gucci label—"

"And she *learned* to read from the Neiman Marcus catalog," Artemis interjected, reaching for the chicken platter.

Harv shot the handsome doctor a pained look, then turned and refocused his attention on Eliza. "As I was saying, Faith's most ardent wish is that Fitz will marry her. A wish Fitz isn't likely to grant. But I suppose I should start at the beginning. Although our family—mine and Faith's—is old and aristocratic, our wealth isn't what it once was. So, unless one of us should ever decide, God forbid, to go to work, our only track to genteel prosperity is for me or Faith to marry somebody rich enough to keep up with our spending habits."

"Which together roughly rival those of Argentina," interrupted Jenny.

Artemis threw Harv a pitying glance. "The man is in a *tough* position," he told Eliza. "I'm talking about using his mansion's swimming pool to raise *catfish*." Artie managed to look suitably solemn. "It's *very* sad to see a once-rich-and-powerful white family reduced to such a state," he intoned.

"Thanks, Artie, I knew *you'd* understand," Harv said gratefully. "And despite what you've heard from the AMA, catfish contains almost no fat. It's the beer and cornmeal batter that really puts on the pounds."

"Now *that's* a true fact!" Jenny declared.

Harv turned back to Eliza. "At any rate, Eliza," he continued, "I have tried my level best to secure a bride who would restore the family fortunes and, incidentally, put a new roof on the summer house, but alas the only suitable candidates all rejected me, including one who actually *looked* like a catfish . . ."

"She did, too!" Jenny giggled. "It was a match made in heaven."

Harv ignored the remark and, clearing his throat, continued in a mournful tone, "I struck out in the marriage bowl. My sister hasn't fared any better and continues to hope that Fitz will reconsider his stand and marry her. But the only way that might happen is to get him blind drunk so he forgets how obnoxious she is long enough for us to whisk him off to Juarez or someplace where they still perform fifteen-dollar weddings without a blood test."

By this time Eliza had caught the giggles from Jenny. "Wow! I'm sorry I asked," she told Harv, whose nose was back in his glass. "And Fitz doesn't have any inclination to go along with this program?"

Snorting into his drink, Harv rolled his eyes but kept drinking so Jenny attempted to interpret for him, "Absolutely not."

Finally coming up for air Harv added, "We couldn't actually get him that drunk."

Eliza queried, "Doesn't he like her?" Wondering why the woman was there at all.

Artemis joined the conversation. "Well, he liked her enough to take her to England with him."

"She was with him?" startling herself with the quick stab of jealousy she felt.

Jenny seemed to sense Eliza's alarm and was pleased that things were moving in that direction. "The tabloids had a field day with it but it was Harv's idea, to keep her out of trouble here alone."

Harv added, "Yeah, turned out she wasn't the one we had to worry about."

Eliza questioned the meaning of his cryptic statement, so Jenny explained, "That was when Fitz pulled his vanishing act. The tabloids had a field day with that, too."

"Well, the tabloids got it all wrong," intoned Harv. "I'm convinced he disappeared because he'd had just about enough of my darling sister as any sane person could take. I considered running away myself, he just beat me to it."

Being reminded now of Fitz's own explanation, she remembered the look on his face when he was talking about his first meetings with Jane Austen, and another small stab of jealousy surprised her.

Still in her own thoughts she mumbled aloud, "No, but he had fallen in love . . ." She stopped short, the three other diners turned and looked at her. Glancing at each in turn she realized that she couldn't explain why she'd said it, so she hastily got up and excused herself. Bidding a good night to everyone at the table she retreated to the Rose Bedroom.

* * *

Later, Eliza sat cross-legged on the floor of her room, reviewing the events of her peculiar first day at Pemberley Farms. Because she always did her clearest thinking while she was working, her sketch pad was in her lap. Why had she felt jealous over a man she'd known only a few hours? Jealous of a woman he didn't like and another who'd been dead almost two hundred years. She had to laugh at herself for the absurdity of it all.

Glancing up from time to time at the lovely portrait of Rose Darcy, Eliza drew the first mistress of the Great House precisely as Jenny had described her, standing on the balcony of the Rose Bedroom dressed in her silken gown, watching the distant fields for the return of her man.

Trying to sort out the strange thoughts swirling around her head, Eliza mentally recapped as she sketched. Darcy's ancestor had been ruled out as a candidate for the character in Jane Austen's romantic classic. And Jenny and the others had all marked his trip to England three years before as the beginning of Fitz's obsession with the writer.

Eliza tried to seriously consider the possibility that her host's incredible story might actually be true. Closing her eyes, she envisioned once more Darcy's trancelike expression as he had seemingly relived events for her that, in his mind at least, had taken place two centuries before. Could it all possibly have happened just as he said? Eliza struggled to come up with an alternate explanation, one that could be tested with logic and reason.

She was startled out of her musings by the sound of a light knock. Eliza got up, laid her sketch pad on the bed and went to the door. "Who is it?" she asked softly.

"It's me, Fitz."

She opened the door to find him standing in the dark hallway with a tall silver candlestick in his hand. "Nice candle," she said, smiling. Then, sticking her head out into the corridor, she looked up and down, halfway expecting to see Faith

Harrington lurking behind a potted palm. "Where's Lady Macbeth?" she asked.

"Locked safely away in the dungeon," Darcy replied with a good-natured smile. "Would you care to go for a walk?"

Eliza returned his smile, realizing that it was almost impossible not to like this man. "A walk!" she exclaimed. "Isn't this the point in one of those Gothic Romance novels where the master of the house—that's you—is supposed to force his way into the heroine's room—I'm the heroine—and rip her bodice?" she asked, feigning disappointment.

Darcy laughed. "Maybe," he replied, pretending to consider the possibility. "I just usually come by and ask if they'd like to take a walk. However, if your bodice is in need of ripping I can call Harv for you."

"That's okay," she grinned. "I actually only have the one bodice with me this trip anyway."

Darcy stepped back. "As you wish," and indicated the broad hallway with a sweeping bow. "Walk this way, then."

Eliza stepped out into the darkened passage and followed him. "Where are we going?" she whispered.

He turned and winked at her, his finely formed features disturbingly handsome in the flickering light of the candle. "To the one place where we're almost certain *not* to be disturbed," he replied.

After several minutes of walking down narrow back staircases and through the silent house they emerged onto the lawn through a side door.

By the light of a full moon Darcy led Eliza down a worn path to a barnlike wooden structure that loomed ahead in a grove of trees. Darcy grabbed a pull handle and a large wooden door slowly opened with an appropriate horror-movie creaking of iron hinges. Eliza hesitantly followed him into a pitch-black space and stood nervously at his back while he fumbled to light a lantern he removed from a peg inside the door.

"Am I going to like this place?" she asked. "Or are there bats?"

"There might be a few bats living in here," he replied, peering up into the pools of inky darkness filling the space between the dimly outlined rafters, "but they're probably all out feeding at this time of night."

"Oh, thanks," she replied with a shudder. "Now I feel *much* better."

The lantern suddenly flared, illuminating the interior of what appeared to be an ancient barn filled with large, box-like shapes. Eliza blinked in the glare and her mouth fell open as she realized what she was looking at.

For parked along the walls in two neat rows were no fewer than a dozen horse-drawn conveyances, their polished brass and painted woodwork gleaming like new in the lantern light.

"Oh, they're beautiful!" she gasped.

"Family heirlooms one and all, and all quite comfortable," Darcy said. He raised the lantern high and walked slowly down the aisle, past racy chaises, heavy traveling coaches, and light buggies with wheels as spindly as cobwebs. "Take your pick," he told Eliza.

She wandered among the elegant vehicles, pausing from time to time to peer in at soft, hand-stitched leather seats and ran her fingers over shining red and black lacquer and delicately carved sills. At the end of the aisle she stopped before a graceful burgundy traveling coach with glass windows etched in elaborate floral patterns and an interior of spotless dove-gray suede.

"I pick this one," she announced.

"My personal favorite!" said Darcy sounding pleased. "This coach belonged to the very first mistress of Pemberley Farms—"

Eliza clapped her hands. "Rose, your great-great-whatever-grandmother!"

"The very same," he said, opening the door with a flourish to admit her to the roomy interior of the coach. "Climb in and make yourself comfortable. I'll be back in a moment."

Stepping up into the high passenger compartment, Eliza sank luxuriantly into the feather-soft cushions of the forward-facing rear seat and closed her eyes. "Now I know how Cinderella felt," she uttered into the darkness. "But I'm warning you. I could get used to this."

When no response was forthcoming she peered out into the barn through the open door, looking for some sign of him. "Hello?"

Darcy suddenly appeared at the window on the opposite side of the coach. He opened the door and climbed in, taking the seat facing hers. In his hands were an open bottle of champagne and two fragile wine glasses.

"Here you are," he said, handing her a glass.

Eliza watched as he deftly filled first her glass and then his own and placed the bottle on a small wooden shelf. "Are you *sure* this isn't a decadent prelude to some wild romance novel hanky-panky?" she asked, gazing at the golden effervescent wine.

"On my honor as a gentleman," he pledged, touching his glass to hers with a musical ring. "I just thought you might enjoy a little authentic nineteenth-century atmosphere to go along with my tale."

"A dashing gentleman, champagne and candlelight!" Eliza sipped the chilled golden wine, found it delicious and sipped again. "Every woman's dream."

His raised eyebrow made her blush at the exuberance of her reaction to the romantic gesture but his warm smile made the hair on the back of her neck stand up. Needing to be in control, she sat up a little straighter in her seat, cocked her head and searched his chiseled features. "Fitz, may I ask you a personal question?"

"Eliza," he replied, "so far you don't seem to have asked any questions that *haven't* been intensely personal." There was a pause that made her fear he might say no. "But yes, you may go ahead."

"Were you falling in love with Jane?"

Darcy's eyes lit up with a sudden surge of hope that tugged at Eliza's heart. "Does that question mean you believe my story?" he asked.

"Let's just say I'm beginning to believe that *you* believe it," she answered, struggling to keep the warring emotions that she was feeling out of her voice. "But you were falling in love with her, weren't you?"

"I'm not sure I can truthfully answer that question," he replied. "It's easy to fall in love in a dream. And that's what it all seemed like to me then."

Darcy took another slow sip of his wine and closed his eyes, remembering. "As I was saying when we were interrupted earlier, Jane and I weren't able to speak alone again, so as she was leaving Edward's house that night . . ."

Volume Three

Chapter 25

The stately Edinburgh grandfather clock in the marble foyer of Chawton Great House was striking half past ten as Jane and Cassandra stood outside beneath the portico with several other guests, waiting for their carriages to arrive.

There was a chill in the night air and Jane was searching through her bag by the flickering light of the pitch torches affixed to wrought iron sconces at either side of the porch. The tension caused by Darcy's earlier demands for a private meeting had been wearing on her and she had successfully avoided him only by remaining close to members of her family for the remainder of the evening.

Now the evening was at an end and Jane wished only to flee to the cozy safety of Chawton Cottage, there to reflect on what to do about the brash American. "My gloves, my green gloves," she exclaimed, rummaging through her bag in frustration. "I am certain I put them in here . . ."

At that moment Darcy emerged from the house, a pair of ladies gloves in his hand. "Miss Austen, are these yours?" he politely inquired.

"Oh, yes," Jane said, her eyes flashing with a fury that was not reflected in her voice. "I am grateful to you, Mr. Darcy," she said for the benefit of Cassandra, "for these are my favorite pair. A gift from my brother Frank."

Jane reached for the gloves. But as she did, Darcy stepped

close and pressed them into her hand, along with something else. She looked down and saw a small square of paper lying in her upturned palm.

Before she could speak, Darcy stepped back and bowed. "I hope we will meet again *very* soon," he said with a broad smile.

Across the portico Jane saw Edward and Frank engaged in conversation with one of her many cousins. Shooting Darcy a final hostile look she closed her fist over the scrap of paper and stiffly acknowledged his formal bow with an abrupt inclination of her chin.

A moment later Edward's carriage rolled to a stop before the steps. Simmons, the groom, helped Jane and Cassandra into the closed landau and then climbed up to the driver's seat. With a cluck to the horses the coach rumbled away. Jane looked back to see Darcy slowly waving to her from the portico.

"Obnoxious man!" she hissed under her breath. "I do not think I have ever known a more arrogant and disagreeable person than Mr. Darcy."

"Do you not, Jane?"

Jane looked up to see Cassandra regarding her with a stony countenance. "Surely you cannot believe I was deceived by that pitiful charade of the gloves," Cassandra said.

"I cannot imagine what you mean," Jane replied, fidgeting with her bag.

Cassandra sighed tolerantly. "Jane, I *saw* Darcy put that note into your hand a moment ago."

When no reply was forthcoming Cassandra pointed to her sister's tightly closed fist. "Well," she demanded, "are you going to read it?"

Defeated, Jane unfolded the note and held it up to the dim light of a carriage lamp to read the few hurriedly scrawled lines. "The insufferable Mr. Darcy writes that he wishes urgently to see me. At midnight," she reported to her stunned sister. "Further, he specifies that he will be waiting in the small wood behind Chawton Cottage, and that I am to come to him alone."

"The wood? Alone at midnight!" Cassandra's utter disbelief at what she was hearing was reflected in her hoarse whisper. "Surely the man is demented."

Jane considered her sister's shocked statement for several seconds and it slowly dawned on her that Cass mistakenly believed that Darcy's intentions toward her were of a romantic nature.

"Yes, he must be mad," she replied with an enigmatic smile. "For the grass is certain to be damp at that hour of the night and I shall probably catch my death."

The already scandalized Cass nearly choked. "Jane, have you, too, taken leave of your senses?" she gasped. "You *cannot* actually be thinking of going out to meet him."

"I can and I *must*," Jane declared, and wondering idly what Darcy's lips would feel like pressed to her own, she felt her pulse beginning to race as Cass spluttered indignantly.

"But *why*, Jane? You have said yourself that you despise this man."

Jane, who was by now playing to her sister's obvious discomfort, waved her off with an angry flick of her gloves. "Oh, Cass," she said irritably, "do not ask me any more about it. I shall explain everything to you later. Tonight, though, I must meet with the cocksure Mr. Darcy."

Obviously injured by this abrupt rebuff, and certain that her younger sister was plotting a dangerous liaison with the handsome American, Cass herself turned irritable. "Well, I think you are behaving very stupidly indeed," she proclaimed, sniffing loudly. "Such romantic foolhardiness as you intend may occasionally be overlooked in very young girls who are not yet sensible of the world, but you have long since passed that age."

Jane nodded in acknowledgment of the harshly stated fact and turned her face to the shadowy landscape rolling past the window. For even in girlhood she had experienced precious few romantic adventures. "Of that you need not remind me, sister," she said regretfully.

"And what of your reputation?" Cassandra pressed on, more intent now on pointing out the sheer folly of a clandestine tryst with Darcy than she was sympathetic to Jane's emotional state.

Jane laughed bitterly. "Cass, an unmarried woman's reputation is valued only by her prospective husbands," she retorted bitterly. "And, as I *have* no such prospects, my reputation can be neither improved nor greatly damaged by meeting with Mr. Darcy."

Looking out at the clear, star-filled sky, Jane gradually became aware of the small smile that was creeping across her scowling features. For, despite the circumstances under which the despicable Mr. Darcy had intimidated her into accepting the terms of his outrageous meeting, she suddenly realized that she was quite enjoying Cass's mistaken conviction that she and the presumptuous American were about to become lovers.

"At least there's a good moon out tonight," she cheerfully observed, this last bold remark deliberately calculated to further her poor sister's scandalous impression.

As the coach rolled on through the night Jane occupied herself by conjuring up a wicked vision of Darcy's lean body lying in her bed and imagining the words he might speak if they were lovers in fact.

The moon was almost directly overhead by the time Simmons led Lord Nelson out of the stables and walked him over to Darcy. Pleading a headache, and anxious to avoid another confrontation with the irascible Captain Austen, Darcy had earlier declined Edward's offer of a nightcap and had instead retired to his room upstairs immediately after the other guests had departed.

Fully clothed he had waited in the darkness until shortly before midnight, then crept through the silent house and down to the stables to get his horse. To his great surprise he had found Simmons awake and waiting for him.

"Do mind the ground now, sir," the young groom cautioned as he placed Lord Nelson's reins in Darcy's hand. Simmons affectionately patted the black horse's nose. "Easy for him to step in a hole in the dark."

Darcy took the reins and placed them over Lord Nelson's neck. "Thanks, I'll be careful, Simmons."

He paused, trying to read the groom's expression in the dim light. "How did you know I would be going out tonight?"

Simmons grinned, exposing a row of even white teeth. "I guessed you might be off to meet a lady, sir," the youngster tactfully ventured. "It's what many gentlemen do of an evening."

He gave Darcy a knowing wink. "Even my good master sometimes went out riding of a night, when Mrs. Austen was close to her confinement," Simmons confided. "Master Edward says a gent must not impose too much on the ladies at such times, if you take my meaning, sir."

Darcy nodded without commenting, amazed at how casually and openly the matter of marital infidelity was treated in this very early part of the nineteenth century. But then, he reminded himself, the sexually repressive Victorian age still lay several decades in the future.

"Your master seems a very good man," Darcy finally offered by way of a noncommittal reply. For though he was anxious to be on his way, he did not wish to offend the talkative groom, who might easily report this midnight adventure to Edward.

Simmons's head bobbed enthusiastically. "Oh, yes, sir," he declared. "All that's in his service will tell you there's no kinder gentleman than Mr. Edward. For didn't he let his two poor sisters have Chawton Cottage for themselves and their old mother," Simmons went on, obviously reciting a well-worn tidbit of village gossip, "when most men in his position would've made the unmarried ones live up here in the Great

House where they'd have nothing of their own and never a moment of privacy."

Simmons hesitated. His canny eyes darted up to the darkened windows of the silent manor house and there was a note of warning in his next words. "Now *Captain* Austen, he's a different sort of man altogether from his brothers Edward and Henry," he continued. "The captain's very protectful of his sisters, and he's got a fearful temper, sir."

Darcy acknowledged the groom's well-intentioned counsel with a grateful smile. "You don't miss very much that goes on around here, do you Simmons?"

Simmons winked. "You just leave the horse in his paddock when you return, sir," he said. "I'll see to him for you." He watched Darcy mount Lord Nelson and ride slowly away into the moonlit night.

Keeping to the soft grass at the edge of the drive, Darcy rode silently past the lawns and gardens and out through the gates of Chawton Great House. When the tall chimneys of the mansion had disappeared behind the hedgerows he guided Lord Nelson onto the narrow dirt road and urged the black horse to a brisk canter. Though the ride to Chawton Cottage was a short one, he did not want to keep Jane waiting any longer than necessary.

Jane. Recalling the angry look she had given him when he had placed the note into her hand, Darcy grimaced. He was uneasy with himself for attempting to force her into a meeting that he knew would be distasteful and possibly even dangerous to her and wondered if she would be there. But he was growing more desperate by the hour and hoped that her intelligence and curiosity would win over her sense of propriety. Because, as his encounter this evening with Francis Austen had demonstrated, it was only a matter of time before he would be denounced as a fraud, or perhaps something worse.

"A matter of time!" Darcy spoke the words aloud and was struck by their full irony.

He had to find a way to return to his own time and Jane Austen held the key. Lovely Jane. He closed his eyes and envisioned her once again as he had watched her in the bedroom at Chawton Cottage, her dark eyes gleaming in the candlelight as she leaned over her writing. Something stirred within him as he recalled another, even more powerful image of her: naked behind the thin dressing screen, her slender, full-breasted figure limned in the dancing firelight.

Darcy felt a sharp, sudden pang of regret that he would never embrace that lovely body, nor stay to unlock the secrets hidden behind those brilliantly shining eyes.

Half a mile from Chawton Cottage Darcy guided Lord Nelson off the road and into a long, grassy meadow. Moving at a slow walk across the uneven ground, he rode cautiously toward the line of dark woods at the far end of the field. To his great surprise, as he neared the trees Jane stepped from the shadows and stood waiting for him to dismount.

"I was afraid you wouldn't come," he said when they stood face-to-face. He saw that the hood of a light cloak covered her hair; looking up at him in the cold moonlight, her unsmiling face was even lovelier than he had remembered.

Forcing from her mind the foolish romantic fantasies that she had allowed herself to entertain in Edward's carriage, she replied abruptly, "Could you not at least have waited for daylight?"

"I'm very sorry but I couldn't," he apologized.

Darcy looked around at the empty meadow. "I know this must be very awkward for you—"

Defiantly she said, "The only awkwardness that I feel is for the inconvenience of the hour and the desolation of the place that you have chosen."

He nodded, stung by her coldness. "I won't keep you long," he promised. "I just need to know how to get back to the spot where my horse threw me. Then I'll be gone."

"The place is nearby," she said. "I will happily show you

the way . . . after you have fully explained yourself and your exceedingly odd behavior."

Darcy cringed, for he had been afraid of something like this. He had insulted Jane by forcing the inappropriate meeting on her and she was not going to cooperate without first saving face, and perhaps in the process satisfying her own curiosity. "Miss Austen, I really *can't* explain," he stammered. "You wouldn't understand."

Jane stared at him for a moment and he saw the anger flashing anew in her eyes. "And because you are a man," she spat, "it is obvious that you think me too *stupid* to understand."

She turned abruptly on her heel and walked away, calling back to him over her shoulder. "As you wish, Darcy! You may find the place you seek by riding about in the dark until you come to it." There was mockery in her tone as she added, "The meadows hereabout can have no more than two score sections of stone wall overhung with trees."

"Miss Austen . . . Jane, wait!" he called in near panic.

She turned back and regarded him fiercely.

"I don't think you're stupid," he said, running to catch up with her at the edge of the wood. "On the contrary, you're by far the most intelligent woman I have ever met!"

She suspiciously scrutinized his face as he hurried to explain. "I know that you began writing your novels nearly twenty years ago, when you were still a young girl," Darcy told her. "For years you believed they would never be published, but you were very wrong, Jane. Next year *Sense and Sensibility* will become one of the most popular books of the year. And even now you are reworking and editing the book you call *First Impressions.* Your sister is right about the title, though. And that isn't the title you will ultimately give the book," he continued breathlessly.

"Jane, one day your name will be known throughout the world and people will be reading your works two hundred years from now. Scholars in great universities will devote entire careers to studying them, to studying *you*."

As he spoke those words Darcy saw her head slowly moving from side to side, her eyes darting nervously to the shadowed woods, calculating her chances of escaping from him. "You are *mad*, sir," she exhorted, edging away from him. "I cannot account for your intimate knowledge of my past, but I am certain that no one can *know* the future!"

"You're right," he said quietly. "We can only ever know the past."

Darcy hesitated, for she had left him with no alternative but to reveal the truth. "I have somehow fallen into the past, Jane. That's *my* secret."

Her momentary fear of him turned to outrage. "You insult my intelligence, sir. I will not listen to this nonsense one moment longer," she cried. "Good night, Mr. Darcy!"

"If what I've said is nonsense, then you will have no trouble explaining this." Left with little choice but to do something he had promised himself he would not do, Darcy raised his left arm to her. He saw the fear return to her eyes as she cringed, anticipating a blow.

Of course he had no intention of striking her—could never have done such a thing.

Instead, he touched the case of his gold watch and pressed a tiny button. The watch beeped. The crystal lighted, casting an eerie green glow onto the lower branches of the trees as a seductive female digital voice announced the time: "Twelve-zero-nine and six seconds, seven seconds, eight seconds . . ."

Jane stared at the electronic watch in awe. After several seconds of frozen silence, punctuated only by the sound of the tinny, synthetic voice counting off the seconds, she slowly backed away a few paces and sat down hard on a fallen log.

Darcy went to her side, tore the watch from his wrist and pressed it into her trembling hand. He showed her the tiny buttons, quietly explaining their functions.

After a few moments she experimentally pushed a button, making the watch light again and prompting more computerized beeps and voice messages.

"Sorcery!" she said.

Darcy shook his head. "No, Jane, it's something called electronics. The watch is only a machine, a distant relative of that great clock in your brother's house, but still just a machine. Nothing more, nothing less. Articles like this watch are as common in my time as horses and carriages are in yours."

She looked up at him then. The anger had fled and now her shining eyes were filled with wonder.

"Phones, jets . . . those other things you mentioned in your fever," she asked, "what are they?"

"More machines," he replied. "Ways of communicating, of moving about faster—"

"Machines that go from England to Virginia in *five* hours?" she interrupted.

He nodded. "Yes, we have machines that fly now."

"Good God!" she exclaimed, gazing into the glowing face of the watch. "And with such machines as this you are able to travel through time itself?"

"No," Darcy said, "that we can't do."

"Yet you are here with this astonishing timepiece," she said with perfect logic. "And I can think of no other explanation for your presence and the wonders you possess. How, then, is it possible?"

Darcy had been pondering that very question for days and he had come up with only one possible answer. Now he shook his head and wearily sat down beside her on the log. "I'm not a scientist," he said, "but there is a popular theory that time is not what it appears to be."

Darcy furrowed his brow, trying to remember details from an article he had recently read in *Scientific American* while waiting in his dentist's office.

"The past and the future aren't separate rooms we occupy only at this moment we call the present," he explained. "Rather, past, present and future exist together as a winding path that we are constantly moving along, never turning back or running ahead."

He paused, watching her face for some sign that he had lost her, but Jane was nodding eagerly, her shining eyes urging him to continue expounding the fascinating theory.

"According to some physicists," he continued, "we *could* turn back down that path of time, if we only knew how. And these same scientists think that sometimes two parts of the path may curve and touch, and that such points may open portals to other times. I believe I accidentally entered into your time through just such a portal," Darcy concluded, realizing how incredible his explanation must sound to someone from an era when the concept of human flight was still in the realm of fantasy.

Jane, however, did not disappoint him by discounting his theory out of hand. She considered his explanation for several seconds, and then frowned. "If you are a visitor from another time," she asked, "who is this man Darcy in Virginia, the person my brother thinks you are?"

Darcy smiled. "My ancestor," he replied, "the founder of Pemberley Farms, which is the estate I own in my time . . . two hundred years from now."

"Your own time . . . two hundred years into the future . . ." Jane's composure finally slipped and she buried her face in her hands. "I am sorry, it is too much to comprehend."

He gently lifted her chin and looked into those beautiful eyes. "Jane, please," he whispered, "I need you to tell me how to get back to the exact spot where I was thrown from my horse. Maybe the portal is still open and I can step back through to the world I know."

"And if you cannot?" she asked.

He threw up his hands helplessly, for hers was a frightening question, and one that he had dared not ask himself. "I don't know," he said grimly. "I only know I can't stay here. I beg you to help me."

"Yes," she replied without hesitation. "I shall, of course."

Relief washed over him. "Then please tell me how to return to the place where I was found."

"Tomorrow," she said haltingly. "I will tell you then."

Jane saw the sudden confusion in his eyes and felt hot blood rushing to her cheeks. "The men who brought you to me said only that you'd been found about a mile from Chawton, nothing more," she timidly explained.

"What?" He was staring at her in shock. "But you said you knew the place."

"I was angry," she told him. "I wished to force you to reveal your secret to me." She suddenly turned away, unable to bear his look of bitter disappointment.

She murmured, "Please forgive me. But you were so arrogant and deceitful—"

Darcy leaped to his feet and stared down at her. "Deceitful?" he snorted, cutting off her rationalization.

"You spied on me, eavesdropped on my most private conversations . . . And *you* lied to me first," she accused in a tremulous voice. "Tomorrow I shall send for the men who brought you to me and discover from them the location of the place where you fell," Jane promised.

"That's just great!" Darcy groaned. "Let's hope your brother doesn't decide to put my head on a spike in the meantime. Or have you English given up that lovely practice yet?" he asked sarcastically.

"Has civilization advanced so much in your time that criminals are no longer executed?" she retorted.

"No, I guess not," he reluctantly admitted. Then, unexpectedly, he found himself grinning. "But our executions *are* very much neater than yours," he added lamely.

Realizing that he had made a joke, though a very poor one, Jane began to laugh. "Lord, what a fine dialogue this will make for a new novel," she told him. "I must make a start on it right away."

Suddenly mindful of the extreme jeopardy in which he had placed her, Darcy extended a hand to help her up from her seat. "I'm afraid I've kept you here far too long," he apologized. "Please send word to me the moment you've located those men."

"On that you may depend," she assured him.

Jane reached out to take his hand, but his touch so electrified her that she remained sitting. "Will you not stay yet awhile?" she softly inquired, inviting him with a slight tug of her hand to sit again. "For there is much about your future world that I would like to know."

Chapter 26

Darcy looked over at Eliza, who was curled up comfortably with her feet beneath her on the gray suede coach seat, listening intently to his every word.

"So she asked me to stay with her and tell her all about the place I came from, and to explain what the future would be like."

He paused in his narrative to take a sip from his nearly full glass of champagne. Noticing that Eliza's glass was empty, Darcy retrieved the bottle from its shelf and refilled it for her.

"I did as she asked," he continued, replacing the bottle on the shelf, "but it wasn't easy because, if you think about it, for all of its obvious shortcomings her time was still in many ways far more innocent than ours."

Eliza frowned at that. "It sounds like an awful time," she said. "A time of wars, slavery, barbaric medical practices . . ."

He nodded slowly. "Yes, but in 1810," he continued, "the skies and oceans of the world had not yet been polluted with industrial wastes. Great expanses of unbroken primeval forest still covered much of Europe and North America. There had been no world wars or nuclear bombs. No Hitlers had yet thought of constructing factories for the sole purpose of wiping out entire races of human beings . . ." Darcy's voice trailed off.

"So was that how you described the future?" Eliza asked. "World wars and nuclear bombs?"

Darcy smiled and shook his head. "Fortunately, Jane wanted to know about other things, the kinds of things she wrote about. She asked me how society would change, customs, the role of women in the modern world . . ."

"And love?" Eliza inquired archly.

"Yes," he said quietly, "love, too."

Eliza slowly sipped her champagne and gazed thoughtfully into his eyes, wondering. "And what did you tell her, about love, Fitz?"

Darcy shifted uncomfortably in his seat. "Before I tell you that," he said, "try to remember that I was speaking to a woman from a world where most women, especially women of her elevated class, were virtual prisoners of men. Generally they entered into loveless marriages based on property and money. Or they simply didn't marry at all. In fact, something like sixty percent of women in Jane's circumstances didn't."

Eliza's eyes widened in surprise at the startling statistic, wondering where he had gotten it. But she said nothing.

"And even if an English Regency-era gentlewoman was lucky enough to find a suitable husband," he continued, "her troubles were often just beginning. In that time and place, women were routinely kept pregnant, bound to their husbands, unable to inherit if there was a potential male heir anywhere in their family line—"

"I don't think I understand where you're going with this," Eliza impatiently interrupted. "What about love? Jane Austen wrote constantly of love."

Darcy nodded excitedly, thrilled by her evident interest in what he was saying. "Yes, but always she wrote about love as an ideal, an ideal that was only very rarely realized in life. Try to put yourself in her place. How old are you, Eliza?"

"Thirty-four," she replied hesitantly.

"And how many lovers have you had in your life?"

Eliza felt her face reddening. "That is none of your damned business," she snapped.

Darcy appeared to be genuinely startled by her hostile response. "Sorry," he said, reaching for the champagne bottle again. "I was only trying to illustrate my point. By age thirty, an Englishwoman of Jane Austen's time would generally have been considered unmarriageable . . . an old maid, a spinster."

Darcy considered his next words for a moment, then went on speaking in a quieter tone. "She would never have had *any* lovers at all, Eliza. Because the risk of pregnancy was just too high, and giving birth out of wedlock may well have resulted in her being literally cast into the streets and abandoned by her family and friends. Remember Lydia, the younger sister from *Pride and Prejudice* who ran off with Wickham, who then had to be bribed into marrying her? Well, that was actually no joking matter. In real life, both the girl and her family might well have been ruined as the result of her indiscretion."

Eliza nodded. She tried briefly to imagine what living such a life might have been like, and failed. "I think I get the point," she said after a moment of further reflection. "In Jane Austen's world love was truly a luxury. And sex was playing with fire . . . But is that really so different from the way things are today?"

"Oh, yes," Darcy said emphatically. "In 1810, even sex in marriage was preposterously dangerous. More women died in childbirth than from any other single cause. And there was almost as much risk of contracting an incurable venereal disease from husbands who, more likely than not, frequently consorted with prostitutes in order to relieve their sexual urges."

Eliza grimaced at the thought. "Lovely!"

"God knows our society today is far from perfect," Darcy said, "but I was afraid that telling Jane how very different things would one day be might make her own world seem intolerable by comparison."

He hesitated for a brief moment before continuing. "It would have been far easier for me to make up some safe, fictionalized future version of her own society," he said.

"But you didn't do that, make up a safe version of the future." It was a statement, not a question.

Darcy shook his head. "In the end I told her everything, about birth control, women's rights, female CEOs . . . In short, I told her the truth."

Alarmed, Eliza suddenly reached out and gripped his hand. "Good God, why, Fitz?" she asked, her voice filled with genuine compassion for the long-dead English writer.

"Because she *wanted* to know," he softly replied. "Because I didn't want to leave her with a lie. And because . . ."

Darcy halted his narrative and looked down at Eliza's hand. He slowly covered it with his own and leaned forward until their faces were almost touching. "Like you, Eliza, she was only thirty-four years old," he whispered, "and though she didn't know it, her life was almost over."

His voice broke and he retreated, shaking his head. "I wanted her to know that the future held something better for women than what she knew."

"And how did she react to your revelations?" Eliza was intensely aware of the pressure of Darcy's hand squeezing hers. She squeezed back, encouraging him to go on.

He closed his eyes, savoring the feel of her touch. "Considering the fact that she had marked me as an arrogant, insufferable scoundrel, Jane reacted in the most unexpected way imaginable," he told her.

"Then a woman in the society of your time may choose and discard her lovers at will, all without fear of censure?" Jane had listened in wonder to everything that Darcy had had to say about love and society in the twenty-first century, interrupting him frequently to ask pointed, intelligent questions, for which he had not always been able to supply ready answers, questions like that one, that were central to the freedom of all modern women.

"It's not quite as simple as you make it sound," he said, attempting to carefully qualify his answer, as he had several others before it. "But, essentially, yes, a woman of my time has that choice. Because for the most part lovemaking is no longer regulated by church or state, or even one's relatives."

He smiled then. "The individual's right to privacy and personal choice in matters of love and sex theoretically applies to any activity that occurs between consenting adults."

Jane silently considered the alien concept of a society filled with consenting men and women who were free to make love to one another whenever and however they liked.

"But what of morality?" she suddenly asked, following a long pause.

Darcy shrugged. "Oh, I suppose that morality is still around in my time," he said thoughtfully. "God knows people still talk about it enough. But then, what we call morality is always only relative to the standards of a given society. In my world it's a word that's come to be applied more to corrupt politicians and bankers than to lovers."

He saw her frowning at that and he knew that in her rigidly structured, class-conscious society morality and sexuality were mutually exclusive terms.

"Consider the plight of one of your own fictional heroines," he said, hoping to draw for her a clearer distinction between the two words. "She is forced by mere circumstance and social custom to choose between love and fortune. Now where's the morality in that?"

"Where indeed?" asked Jane, turning at last to smile at him. She sat there quietly for a moment longer, seemingly lost in thought. Then she abruptly stood.

Darcy immediately jumped to his feet, fearful that he had told her far too much. "I hope that I haven't offended you with my frankness," he said.

Still smiling, Jane shook her head. "No," she replied, "you have been most delicate in your phrasing, sir. It is only that I find the swift and shining modern world that you've described nearly impossible to envision. It is like the telling of a dream."

She paused, again seemingly lost in deep thought, then softly whispered to the cool breeze that had begun sighing through the trees. "Astonishing! The feminine spirit freed."

"Jane . . ." Darcy was suddenly gripped with an overwhelming desire to pull her into his arms, as if he might somehow be able to protect her from the stark reality of her own rapidly approaching death in this age of primitive medicine and suffering, a reality that he alone in all that world knew awaited her.

"I should go now," she said, interrupting his grim thoughts by looking up at the lowering moon. "It is very late and I must think on all that you have told me."

Fighting his impulse to enfold her in a warm embrace, Darcy instead stepped forward and took her arm. She froze and gazed down at his hand on her. "Let me take you home," he begged.

To his utter astonishment she raised her face to his and said, sounding for just an instant like a small girl, "Will you not kiss me good night first?"

He hesitated, then kissed her lightly on the lips. Jane pulled back from him and looked into his eyes, and for the first time he saw the woman that she truly was.

"Is that the manner in which you would kiss a lady if you were on a—what was it you called it—a date?"

Suddenly he was smiling, his tensions of a moment before running away like summer rain. "Well, maybe a *first* date," he said.

Her voice was teasing, her face perfection in the moonlight. "And for a second date," she teased, "or a third?"

Then Darcy did pull her to him, and kissed her more thoroughly. She responded eagerly.

For long seconds they remained locked together in the moonlight. When their lips finally parted, Jane leaned her head against his heaving chest and softly sighed. "Please forgive me. I only wished to taste a lover's kiss in the moonlight."

She raised her sparkling eyes to his and seemed embarrassed by her sudden abandonment of all propriety. "Henceforth you may regard me as a foolish old maid who had never before been properly kissed by a man," she whispered.

"No, dear Jane," he whispered, placing trembling fingers on her lips to stop the self-deprecating litany. "For the rest of my life I'll remember only the beautiful and desirable woman that you are at this moment. And in my thoughts you will never grow old."

"And I shall dream of a man who loved me once," she vowed in return, "if only for a moment. And in my dreams, dear Darcy, you shall be ever strong and kind and most exceedingly noble."

She misread his look of wonder at those last beautiful sentiments. "Oh, do not be alarmed, sir," she said, smiling happily. "For I know that you do not really love me. How could you when I have so harshly misjudged and vilified you?"

Jane sighed again, sounding like a contented kitten, and again she raised her face to his. "I am merely building up a store of dreams," she told him. "So may I have another, if you please, dear Darcy?"

Gently he took her chin in his hand caressing her lovely face, he grew giddy from the scent of roses in her hair as they kissed in the waning light of the moon.

Chapter 27

"We stood there in the chill night air and I kissed her again . . ."

Darcy's voice slowly trailed off and he gazed down at his hands, flexing them helplessly before him. Eliza remained frozen in her seat, attempting to gain some sense of deeper understanding from the intensely private reverie that had entranced him so. But the combined effects of the champagne and his story had taken their toll on her as well, and she gradually became aware of the hot tears streaming down her cheeks.

"Dammit, Fitz, if you're making all this up, I swear to God . . ." she sobbed.

Darcy looked up at her, and in his tortured green eyes she at last saw the naked truth. Impulsively she took his face in her hands and stared into his eyes.

"It *is* true, isn't it?" she demanded.

"Yes," he replied, his voice barely audible.

Certain that she was going to be ill, Eliza fumbled with the door of the stately antique coach. It popped open and she stumbled clumsily to the ground. "I need some air," she gasped as she ran through the darkened carriage barn and out into the cool night.

Darcy caught up to her on the lane leading to the house. "Eliza . . ." he said.

"Just don't say anything for a minute," she begged him. I need to think about all of this."

They walked along together in silence for several seconds. The cold breeze on her face began to dry her tears and the queasiness in her stomach slowly subsided. At length she cast a furtive glance at the tall, handsome man keeping pace at her side. His features were lost in shadow, his emotions unreadable.

Uncertain whether it was his strong, unyielding determination to convince her of its truth or the sheer pathos of his impossible story, Eliza understood that something had changed, something within herself. That small fragile part she had so vigilantly protected all these years. And fear grabbed her heart.

Stopping, she looked up at Darcy. "Did you make love to Jane that night?" she boldly inquired.

He considered her question for a long moment. "Why do you want to know?" he finally asked.

"I'm not sure," Eliza said, shaking her head. And she wasn't. "But I think it's . . . important."

"We were standing in the middle of a forest at three AM. The ground was wet with dew—"

"That's not an answer!" Eliza snorted. "The first time I had sex it was in a sleeping bag in the Rockies. In January!"

"Really!" Darcy said, smiling and sounding more like the stranger she had met at the library exhibit in New York half a lifetime ago. "I'd like very much to hear that story."

"Well, you won't," she snapped, suddenly furious with him, but without quite knowing why. "You *must* be making all of this up," she went on, knowing that he wasn't. "I mean," she said, falling back on her inbred New Yorker's tendency to view everything with cynicism, "it's just *not* possible to fall into 1810 and end up in the woods with Jane Austen."

Eliza trudged away up the lane as the anger she had used to cover her other emotions dissipated.

"We kissed a little longer and then Jane left me, promising

to send a message as soon as she'd spoken with the men who found me." Darcy had resumed walking beside Eliza, continuing quietly, resolutely, with his story.

As they reached the looming front of Pemberley House Eliza stopped again and turned to face him.

"I have another question for you," she said, interrupting his narrative. "There's a line in *Pride and Prejudice*—when Darcy asks Elizabeth Bennet to marry him the first time . . ."

Darcy nodded, smiling. "Yes, I know it very well," he said, looking into her eyes. " 'You must allow me to tell you how ardently I admire and love you . . .' " As he spoke the words he realized, with some surprise, that there was a part of him that meant it, a part that he had been sure would never be touched again.

Averting her eyes from his hypnotic gaze, Eliza cleared her throat and continued. "As a longtime Jane Austen fan, I have never quite been able to bring myself to believe that those words were not written without some basis in reality," she said. "Did you say them to her, Fitz?"

"Eliza, Jane wrote *Pride and Prejudice* before she was twenty," Darcy replied. "When I knew her she was merely re-copying the book, editing it."

He shook his head, whether in amusement or regret Eliza could not tell. "I am *not* the man Jane Austen wrote about in *Pride and Prejudice*," he said. "I don't think that person ever really existed except in her imagination. As it is, I'm still amazed that she used my name and Pemberley in the book. Why she did it I still don't know."

Eliza was completely unconvinced by his denial. "Jenny says you're the best man she's ever known," she told him.

Darcy laughed aloud. "Despite her irreverent façade, Jenny is a hopeless romantic."

"Maybe. But those are the same words Jane used to describe Mr. Darcy in her book."

"Most experts agree that Jane was the *ultimate* hopeless romantic," he countered.

"No, I don't think so," Eliza replied, distracted by the thoughts that had created the conclusion. "I think maybe you *are* a truly kind, thoughtful and honorable man, Fitzwilliam Darcy."

Before he could voice another protest and taking him by surprise, she impulsively reached up, took his face in her hands and swept his hair aside, revealing the jagged white scar just below the hairline. She stared at it for several seconds, quickly kissed his lips, and then instantly released him. She turned and walked across the lawn. He watched as she hurried away. Electricity shot through his body when she kissed him; he had wanted to put his arms around her and return it but there was a feeling of . . . betrayal, so he had restrained himself. But a betrayal of whom? A woman long dead? Recovering, Fitz started out after her, catching up quickly.

Less than forty feet away, in a darkened upstairs window, Faith Harrington stood looking down on Eliza and Darcy. With her arms folded tightly across her naked chest; her beautiful features set in a rictus of barely contained rage, the tall blonde woman in the window resembled nothing so much as a pale marble statue of a vengeful angel.

Faith continued to watch in silence as the unwitting couple below linked arms and strolled slowly across the broad lawn leading down to the lake.

Following their brief, passionless kiss Eliza had somehow managed to put her roiling emotions in check. Allowing Darcy to take her arm, she had followed his lead through the inky shadows covering the grounds of Pemberley Farms.

Whatever was happening in her heart, Eliza knew, would have to be dealt with, and soon. But she was convinced that the final consequence of her tumultuous feelings for Darcy would be largely determined by the outcome of his experience. Experience—the word surprised her. Did she believe? Was it possible? Needing to get past the turmoil and having finally collected herself, Eliza calmly brought him back to his story.

"Okay, so you left Jane that night and went back to her brother's house to wait for a message from her."

And so she walked and waited with trepidation for him to go on.

"There was nothing else I could do but wait for Jane's message that she had found the men," Darcy began. "But even as I rode back to Edward's house I felt rather than knew it was getting very dangerous . . . How dangerous I had not imagined."

Passing no one on the road to Chawton Great House, Darcy rode quietly past Edward's tall brick mansion and down to the stables. Guided only by the light of a small lantern burning at the gate, he placed Lord Nelson in his paddock and turned for the house. He was silently congratulating himself on his good fortune in having returned undetected when Frank Austen startled him by suddenly stepping out of the shadows and blocking his way.

In contrast to the captain's immaculately groomed and uniformed appearance at dinner the previous evening, Darcy saw in the dim light that Austen was noticeably disheveled at this late hour. His white shirtfront was open, exposing his bare chest, his face was flushed with drink and he carried an unsheathed saber in one hand and a sloshing wine bottle in the other.

"Been out riding quite late, have you, Darcy?" Darcy could not help but notice that the statement was tinged with sarcasm in spite of the drunken man's slurred speech.

"Captain Austen! Yes, I was feeling a little restless," Darcy, replied, cursing himself for having been so easily and predictably trapped.

"Ah! Meeting with a lovely lady, no doubt!" Austen delivered a leering wink.

"Not at all," Darcy lied, eyeing the path up to the main

house, and judging that if he broke and made a run for it the drunken man would never be able to catch him in the dark.

Following Darcy's gaze with crafty, red-rimmed predator's eyes, Frank Austen slowly raised his curved saber and pointed the razor-edged tip menacingly at the other's throat. "I noticed your keen interest in my younger sister this evening," he said in a tone that was all the more menacing for its lack of inflection. Except for the slur, Austen's voice was almost conversational as he added, "Others noticed as well."

"Captain, I think perhaps you have had too much wine," Darcy said, trying his best to ignore the wickedly sharpened sword point hovering unsteadily in the lamplight six inches from his throat. "Let's walk up to the house together and I'll help you get—"

"Our Jane is like an innocent child," Austen interrupted, his tone suddenly tinged with melancholy, "ever dreaming of her lovers, poor lass, but with no hope of ever finding love."

The captain shook his head sadly, and to Darcy's amazement a glitter of a tear formed in the corner of the drunken officer's eye.

"Poor Jane's gentle heart is more easily breakable than most, I fear," her brother blearily concluded.

Horrified that the man obviously believed that he was out to seduce his favorite sister, Darcy raised both hands in a gesture of denial. "Captain, I assure you—" he began.

"I have a warrior's knowledge of the fragility of human hearts," Frank Austen loudly proclaimed in a voice that was once more devoid of emotion. "Did you know, Darcy, that a well-placed thrust can cleave a man's heart in two so cleanly that both halves will go on beating for many seconds, as though nothing at all had happened?"

"Captain Austen, I must insist—" Darcy's feeble protest ended in a croaking gasp as Austen lunged forward without warning. Missing the American's exposed neck by a fraction of an inch, the gleaming steel blade slid past him with surgical precision and was effortlessly buried to the hilt in a bale of hay.

Despite his drunken state the captain deftly retrieved the saber from the bale and raised it to his own chin in a mocking salute. "I don't know who you are, Darcy," he growled, "but know you that the killing of men is my main business and I have spent a lifetime at it. If I learn that you have meddled with my sister," he vowed, "I shall track you down like a mad dog and take your guts for garters."

His murderous declaration at an end, Frank Austen stood there, swaying drunkenly from side to side in the light of the glowing lantern.

Darcy stared at him for a long, breathless moment, then he slowly turned on his heel and walked away, fully expecting to feel at any instant the deadly kiss of cold steel sliding up between his shoulder blades.

But Frank Austen did not move. Instead, when Darcy was perhaps twenty paces from him, the other raised his sword high and screamed after him.

"You have been fairly warned, sir!"

Two miles away from Chawton Great House, Jane sat at the mirrored table in her bedroom; before her on the polished wooden surface lay a tall stack of manuscript pages.

By the light of the blazing fireplace she was furiously working on her novel, dipping her pen into the inkwell, impulsively scratching out entire passages, substituting new ones that had the unaffected ring of genuine experience to them, adding one name to the book, over and over again.

She looked up impatiently at the sound of a knock on the door and Cassandra's worried voice entreating her. "Jane, please let me in. Why have you locked your door?"

Ignoring her sister's pleading, Jane returned to her careful, crucial work, murmuring to herself as she wrote the thrilling words that she imagined her dream lover might speak when next they met: "You must allow me to tell you how ardently I admire and love you . . ."

Lifting her eyes from the page, Jane regarded herself in the mirror. Though she still found it hard to believe, he had said that she was beautiful. Her cheeks flushed with a pleasure she had never before known, she closed her eyes and imagined she was still with him in the wood.

"Yes, dear Darcy," she whispered with a contented smile, "do tell me that I am beautiful. Then kiss me once more, so I'll have another dream to sleep on."

Even as Jane was dreaming of being with him in the wood, Darcy was standing nervously behind the draperies at a second-story window in her brother's manor house.

On the drive below, Captain Francis Austen was yelling and reeling about drunkenly as two frightened servants in nightclothes attempted to help him up the steps.

"I waited for the dawn, expecting him to come for me. And that whole time all I could think about was Jane and what her brother had said about her fragile heart." Darcy raised his eyes to Eliza's. "Because, even in his drunken state, I wondered if Frank hadn't been right in wanting to protect her from me."

They were sitting at the end of the small dock on the shore of the lake at Pemberley Farms, where he had earlier found her sketching. Turning away from Eliza, Darcy looked out over the black waters while she steadily continued to gaze at him.

"So are you saying that you didn't really love her?" she asked in a tremulous voice.

"Oh I *could* have loved her with no effort." He laughed bitterly. "Maybe I even did. Then. But to what end? I couldn't stay and she couldn't leave . . ."

"How do you know that?"

Darcy snapped out of his reverie and frowned at her. "What?"

"How did you know that Jane couldn't leave?" Eliza asked. "Maybe you could have brought her back here with you." She hesitated, then added, "Maybe you *should* have."

"No," he replied with absolute certainty. "I didn't want to bring her to this world, to deprive her of her place in literature, her family and friends, everything familiar."

He stared out over the glassy obsidianlike waters of the lake and his voice again grew distant. "I determined that the best thing I could do for her was to get out of her life as quickly as possible."

Eliza laid a tentative hand against his cheek. "You really were in love with her, weren't you?" she whispered.

He slowly shook his head, denying her assessment. Eliza got to her knees and turning his face to her, she kissed him softly on the lips. This time he kissed her back. They pulled apart and looked into each other's eyes. The feeling of betrayal seized him again and he grasped her shoulders, holding her at arm's length. "Eliza, I don't . . ." he began.

Gently she placed her fingers over his lips to still his doubts. "Like Jane," she added lightly, "I just wanted to see what it would be like to be kissed by you in the moonlight."

A light breeze sprang up, whispering among the trees, riffling the smooth surface of the lake. Eliza rolled her shoulders and turned her neck, uncertain whether to feel relieved or upset by Darcy's silence.

Getting to her feet and offering him her hand, she said, "Let's go back up to the house. You can finish telling me about Jane there, where it's more comfortable."

Wordlessly he took her hand and stood, just as a beam of light lanced out from the shore and pinned them in a bright circle of illumination.

Eliza emitted a long-suffering sigh. "God, not *again*," she groaned. For she had not yet heard the whole of Darcy's tale and she knew she would not sleep that night until she had heard it all.

Shielding his eyes with his free hand, Darcy called brusquely to the dark figure hurrying down the wooden dock toward them. "Who's there? Get that light out of my eyes!"

The powerful flashlight was immediately switched off and Jenny came up to them, looking embarrassed. "I'm really sorry to break in, Fitz, Eliza, but I'm afraid we got us a little *problem* up at the house."

Chapter 28

At Jenny's insistence, Darcy and Eliza had immediately rushed up from the lake with her and entered the darkened house. Sounds of shattering glass and shrill screams had brought a few sleepy servants out into the halls and they were standing about whispering worriedly to one another as Darcy and the others hurried past.

"You all go on back to bed," Jenny ordered in a stern, nononsense tone that sent the help scurrying back to their respective rooms.

The crash of breaking glass was much louder as they reached the tall double doors of the grand Pemberley ballroom. Eliza shot Jenny a what-on-earth-is-going-on glance as Darcy halted before the ballroom doors, his gentle features set in a grim mask.

Taking Eliza's elbow, Jenny held her back a few paces while Darcy swung the heavy doors open and peered into the huge, lavishly decorated chamber. In the center of the ballroom, which was eerily lit with only a few flickering candles, Faith Harrington stood hurling cut crystal punch cups against the nearest wall.

Wearing a diaphanous white nightgown that left few details of her spectacular figure to the imagination, Faith was carefully selecting the cups from a wheeled table that was covered in stacks of priceless crystal. She held each glittering piece to the light for a moment and carefully examined its sharply faceted surfaces before suddenly screaming, "Not that one!"

Then, winding up like a professional baseball pitcher, Faith sent the cup flying and picked up another.

"Nor that one!"

SMASH!

"Or that one!"

SMASH!

"Or *this* one!"

Harv and Artemis, who had been watching helplessly from the shadows near the doors, hurried over to the newcomers as Jenny quickly filled Darcy in on the sequence of events that had led her to come searching for him.

"She's been at it for about ten minutes," Jenny concluded in a hoarse whisper. "Said she wouldn't stop till you came and personally asked her to, and then threatened to bean anybody who came close."

Jenny flinched as another exquisite lead-crystal cup exploded against the wall. "I thought I'd better go find you while you still had some crystal left."

Darcy silently nodded his understanding of the situation and stepped out onto the ballroom floor. "Faith!"

At the sound of his voice Faith turned, a fresh cup poised above her head ready to throw. With the piece of sparkling crystal dangling from one finger by its handle, she let her throwing arm fall limply to her side and smiled lopsidedly at Darcy.

"Fitz, darling, I thought I'd *never* get your attention," she gushed. "Thank you *so much* for coming."

Remaining back in the shadows with the others, Eliza was completely confused by the grotesque scene playing out on the ballroom floor. "What is going *on*?" she whispered to no one in particular.

Harv Harrington obligingly stepped up behind her and leaned disturbingly close, his vodka-tinged breath uncomfortable on her neck. "Nothing too unusual. My big sister is just pitching one of her infamous tantrums," he informed Eliza in a hushed tone that made him sound like a sports announcer at a golf tournament.

"She's also *way* drunk," Artemis added analytically.

"That's true, Artie." Harv turned to address the big doctor. "But the *really good* tantrums only ever take off that way. Otherwise Faith sticks pretty much to biting sarcasm."

Darcy, meanwhile, had moved closer to the blonde socialite and was regarding the mess of shattered crystal underfoot. "Okay, Faith," he began softly, "what's this all about? Those are very old family pieces you're destroying."

"I'm sorry, Fitz," she said, as if they were discussing where to place another flower arrangement, "but if I can't have these heirlooms, then *nobody* will." Faith stuck out her lower lip and her casual, matter-of-fact tone turned suddenly poisonous. "Certainly not some uncultured, frizzle-haired Yankee upstart."

She pointed an accusing finger, tipped with a blood-red nail, toward the little group hovering in the shadows near the doors. "I want you to *order* her off the place this minute," she demanded.

Harv grinned and affectionately squeezed Eliza's shoulder. "It appears you've won a permanent place in her heart," he said.

Darcy took another tentative step closer to the distraught woman. "Now you're just being silly, Faith," he said soothingly. "Eliza is my guest and you are embarrassing me in front of her."

He reached for the cup in Faith's hand but she swiftly eluded his grasp, raised her arm and flung it across the room. "It's not *fair*, Fitz!" she cried as the crystal burst into a cloud of sparkling shards that clattered like diamonds to the polished hardwood floor. "You were supposed to marry me," she declared. "Your mother and mine planned it when I was five."

Before she could grab another piece of crystal, Darcy deftly stepped forward and wrapped his arms tightly around her, pinning both of her flailing arms to her sides. The fight suddenly gone out of her, Faith collapsed sobbing against him.

"Now we've discussed all of this before, Faith," he told her in his soothing Southern accent. "You will *always* be my dear friend," he assured her, "but we don't love one other, either one of us. You *know* that."

Faith stubbornly tossed her head from side to side, loosening her fine hair, which shone like spun gold as it swung free in the candlelight. "It's just not *fair!*" she wailed.

With a nod Darcy signaled Jenny and Artemis. They both went out onto the ballroom floor and, each taking one of her arms, led Faith back toward the doors.

"Come on, honey," Jenny crooned in a motherly tone. "Artie and I will tuck you in."

Faith meekly allowed them to lead her off the floor, but she suddenly pulled free and jerked to a halt in front of Eliza. "I could *kill* you!" she hissed at the startled artist.

Artemis frowned. "Hush now," he told her. "You know you don't mean that nasty talk."

Faith smiled up at him like a doting child and willingly took the arm he held out. "Oh, but I do, Artie," she assured him as they walked away. "I *really* do."

Darcy watched as Faith was escorted from the room. He supposed this was just one more of the ways he would pay for his indiscretions in England. Heaving a sigh of regret for the weakness of a moment, he returned to Eliza, who was still standing with Harv. "I'm terribly sorry," Darcy told her. "I hate it when she gets this way. Are you all right?"

Eliza managed a weak smile. "Well, I guess so. Although except for my credit card companies and the occasional cab driver I don't get that many death threats in New York."

"Don't be silly, Eliza, my sister wouldn't *really* kill you,"

Harv happily assured her. "Not without an ironclad alibi at any rate."

Darcy shot him a withering glance. "Harv," he suggested without much diplomacy, "perhaps you should go to bed now."

Taking the hint, Harv stepped away from them and went toward the ballroom doors. "I think I will, Fitz."

"Sweet dreams!" he said, grinning at Eliza.

"Thanks," she said grimly. "You, too."

"Come on," Darcy said, taking her arm. "I'll walk you to your room."

Eliza was disappointed. "Does this mean I don't get to hear the rest of your story tonight?"

He arched his eyebrows in surprise. "I didn't think you'd want to after all of this. It's very late. Sure you're up for it?"

Eliza managed a nervous laugh. "Something tells me I'm not going to fall asleep that easily anyway, what with your homicidal guest roaming the corridors."

Darcy shook his head ruefully, "I'm afraid poor Faith never knows when to stop, especially when she's been drinking. But I guarantee you she won't remember a thing in the morning." He suddenly frowned and looked at Eliza with concern. "I do hope you didn't take anything she said too seriously."

"No, I guess not," Eliza reluctantly admitted. "But I wouldn't turn my back on her on a subway platform either."

Darcy laughed. "I can assure you that for all her theatrics Faith is perfectly harmless," he said. "It's just that she was raised with the unfortunate belief that she should always get her own way. The rest of us have been watching her pitch these tantrums since she was a toddler."

They walked holding hands up the spectacular main staircase.

"Did your mothers really plan on you two marrying?" Eliza asked.

Darcy nodded. "Yes, they did," he said with a smile. "But they also figured on Harv becoming president."

When they reached the Rose Bedroom Eliza paused before opening the door, unsure if he meant to come in or whether she should invite him. She considered for half a second how Jane Austen would have handled such a potentially awkward situation.

That was then, this is now, Eliza concluded. Grinning inwardly, she pushed open the door and stepped into the bedroom. Darcy followed her without hesitation, so she assumed she had made the right choice.

But to her surprise, instead of following her to the small suite of chairs and table near the bed, he walked over to examine the low-cut Regency ball gown that hung on the open wardrobe door. He pinched the heavy emerald green fabric between his thumb and forefinger, held it up to the light. "You're wearing this tomorrow night?" he asked, turning to her.

"Yes," she admitted. "Jenny more or less insisted. Do you think it's too terribly . . . Oscarish? I seem to remember you saying at the library that Jane would never have worn anything like this."

"You're not Jane," Darcy replied, dropping the fabric.

"Good point," Eliza agreed, unwilling to follow that reasoning to its logical conclusion.

Crossing to the bed, Darcy picked up her sketch pad and carefully examined her drawing of Rose Darcy. "This is beautifully done," he said, glancing up at the life-size matriarchal portrait in the alcove.

"Thank you." Eliza followed his gaze to the painting of the enchantingly beautiful Rose in her silken gown. "Now that's a dress I could picture Jane Austen having approved of," she ventured. "Though it's actually more revealing than the one that Jenny picked for me, it's also very classy, don't you think?"

Darcy nodded thoughtfully. Then he settled himself in an armchair covered with brocaded vines of wild rose.

Sensing that he was tired of conversation and anxious to resume his narrative, Eliza kicked off her shoes and sat cross-legged on the bed to listen.

"I told you about my encounter with Captain Austen in the stables," Darcy began. "Fortunately, he did not come looking for me again and I finally fell asleep."

Chapter 29

Despite the extraordinary tensions of his first day outside the secure confines of Jane's bedroom at Chawton Cottage and the unavailability of so much as an aspirin tablet to soothe his throbbing head, the exhausted Darcy had fallen almost immediately into a deep and dreamless sleep upon returning to his luxurious room at Chawton Great House.

He awoke seven hours later to the rumble of heavy wheels on the drive below his window.

As he had every morning since arriving in 1810 Hampshire, Darcy spent his first several minutes of wakefulness with his eyes tightly shut. When he opened them, he tried to convince himself he would discover that he was back in the Cliftons's rented Edwardian mansion in his own time and his vivid memories of the last four days would turn out to have been nothing more than an interesting dream.

Listening closely to the morning sounds of the household, he strained to pick up the familiar whine of a vacuum cleaner and sniffed the air for the scent of exhaust fumes from the old green Range Rover his friend Clifton kept parked in the drive.

He heard instead the clop of hooves on the drive and the impatient snorting of a horse. The sounds were inconclusive, he told himself, for the horse might have been Lord Nelson out for a morning exercise with his trainer, or one of the handful of gentle saddle nags that the property owners kept on the place for their renters to ride.

Still, he did not have much hope that he had returned.

Opening his eyes at last, Darcy blinked at a bright shaft of sunshine pouring in through the open window. He clambered stiffly out of bed and walked over to peer down onto the drive. A heavy black traveling coach pulled by a team of four horses was just disappearing beyond the gates of Chawton Great House.

It was still 1810.

He had just spent half of the previous night with a beautiful woman named Jane Austen, and part of the remainder with her murderous brother.

Grimacing at the prospect of facing the hostile Captain Austen, whose temper would doubtless not be improved this morning by what must be a monumental hangover, Darcy splashed water on his face from a pitcher on his washstand and looked distastefully at the ivory-handled straight razor that had been laid out for his use.

Picking up the deadly implement, he grimly regarded his gaunt features in the mirror. "Perhaps I should just cut my own throat now and save Frank the trouble," he murmured.

Twenty minutes later, dressed in yet another of Edward's uncomfortable suits and badly shaved, Darcy entered the dining room. Edward and several of his guests from last night were nearly finished with breakfast as Darcy was escorted to a seat near the end of the table.

Darcy looked around nervously for some sign of Frank, and decided that the captain must still be recovering abed.

"Morning, Darcy!" Edward stopped chewing long enough to wave his knife in greeting to the guest.

"Good morning, sir."

Darcy looked around, startled, as a servant leaned over his shoulder and dropped a slab of the same meat his host was enjoying onto Darcy's plate.

"Got some bad news for you, I'm afraid," Edward reported between mouthfuls.

Darcy's stomach turned over as he stared down at the purple chunk of bloody flesh, momentarily forgetting that the modern practice of tinting meat a more appetizing shade of red had yet to be invented. He closed his eyes, waiting for the bad news, which he feared involved the missing captain.

"Frank has been recalled to his squadron at Portsmouth this morning," Edward said. "I'm very sorry to say that you have just missed him."

"Oh, that's too bad." Darcy swallowed hard, feeling the tension in his stomach ease and glancing again at his plate. Actually, the slab of rare beef nested in a pool of its own juices didn't look all that bad, he thought.

Edward, however, seemed to be quite upset by the development of Frank's unanticipated departure. "Yes," he grumbled, albeit with an unmistakable note of pride in his voice, "seems my younger brother is being given the temporary rank of admiral and sent out to the West Indies to put a stop to these troublesome arms smugglers."

Picking up his fork and knife, Darcy cut off a small piece of meat and popped it into his mouth. To his surprise, it was quite good, though unlike any steak he had ever tasted. Of course, he reflected, it contained none of the preservatives, steroids, antibiotics or artificial coloring he was used to. He wondered if that made it safer or more dangerous than USDA-inspected beef and looked around, wondering where the thick slabs of toast that the others were eating had come from.

"It is a shame about Frank," Edward was saying from the head of the table. "I had hoped to take the two of you out today for some shooting, though it's not really the season at all."

Darcy tried to adopt a regretful expression as the servant magically reappeared and placed a rack of fire-singed toast before him. In fact, he was feeling better by the moment, for he couldn't imagine any enterprise more hazardous than being forced to accompany the volatile Frank on a shooting expedition.

Now, he thought, if only Jane would contact him to report that the farmers had been found and the stone wall located, everything could still be fine.

Jane. Darcy's pulse quickened as he recalled the touch of her lips on his the night before, felt the urgent trembling of her slender body pressed to his in the moonlit forest.

"Well, it cannot be helped, I suppose."

Darcy looked up to see Edward gesturing at him with his knife again. "My brother Frank sends you his compliments and begs you to recall your conversation of last night," Edward said convivially. "I am delighted that you two fellows became such fast friends."

"Oh, thanks very much." Darcy lowered his eyes and busied himself with the food. "Your brother is a fascinating man," he said, hoping they could change the subject.

Edward laughed. "Yes, a fine, brave fellow is our Frank. Bit rough around the edges, though, what?" He swung his knife over his head in imitation of a vigorous sword fight. "Comes from his having seen too much blood and guts on the high seas, I daresay."

Another servant entered the dining room carrying a small silver salver. The man bent over and whispered something in his ear. Edward smiled and pointed to Darcy.

"It seems our Jane has sent you a letter this morning, Darcy. I would say you made a good impression on her, as well as on our Frank."

The letter was brought down the table to Darcy who clumsily broke the seal and read the few lines written in Jane's neat, compact handwriting. He felt his heart thumping joyously at her message:

Sir,
  I have after some study located the passage that you and I were discussing last evening. If you will call on me

at home at 2:00 P.M. today, I shall be glad to point it out for you.

Beautiful, brilliant Jane! She had cleverly coded her note to make it sound as if she had located a passage from a book, when she was actually telling him that she had discovered the location of the stone wall, the passage back to his own time.

Glancing up at Edward, Darcy saw the expression of naked curiosity written on the other man's face. And so he did the only thing he could think of to do. Smiling at her brother, Darcy passed Jane's letter down the table to him. "Your sister is very thoughtful," he explained. "We were discussing a book last night that we had both read, but neither of us could remember exactly where a certain passage was to be found. Now she has discovered it and invited me to call on her this afternoon so she can point it out for me."

If he had expected Edward to be pleased by that revelation, Darcy was disappointed.

"Humph! That is bad news indeed," the other man complained, barely glancing at the letter before laying it next to his plate.

"I beg your pardon?" Edward's sour mood set off a new alarm bell in Darcy's head, and he wondered what he had done wrong this time.

After a moment Edward laid his knife and fork aside. "Well, I suppose there is no possibility at all of us going shooting if you will be visiting my sister this afternoon." he complained. "Damned bother, if you ask me!"

Darcy shrugged helplessly, barely able to contain the grin that was straining to spread across his features. Thanks to Jane it was just barely possible, he thought, that he might actually make it out of the nineteenth century alive.

Precisely at 2:00 P.M. that afternoon Darcy found himself in a downstairs sitting room at Chawton Cottage. From the lovingly polished piano in the corner to the small writing table placed under a north-facing window and the collection of French country prints that graced the walls, the room had Jane's mark on it.

And, indeed, she had confided to him the night before that she preferred doing most of her writing here during the day, where the light was good. For the most part, she'd said, she worked at the vanity table in her bedroom only when felt compelled to continue writing late into the night, or when it was too cold to heat the entire house.

Like Jane's bedroom, he also noted, the downstairs sitting room bore the faint, tantalizing scent of the rose water she loved so well and that she and Cassandra distilled from petals they collected all summer long from the gardens at Chawton Great House.

As befitted a proper afternoon visit, Jane and Darcy were seated stiffly on straight-backed chairs, facing one another with their knees a few feet apart. Cassandra sat beside a small table a little way across the room from the two, presiding over a china tea service decorated in an oriental-blue dragon motif. From time to time she cast disapproving looks at their guest.

"So Frank was recalled to Portsmouth this morning," Darcy told them, repeating the news from Chawton Great House. "I'm afraid that Edward was quite disappointed, as he had hoped we would all go out for some shooting today."

He saw a sparkle in Jane's eyes as she absorbed this bit of information. "And you, sir?" she playfully inquired. "Were you also unhappy at being denied a vigorous tramp through the countryside with my brothers?"

"Naturally, the prospect of calling on the two lovely ladies who restored me to health was far more pleasant than the idea of spending the whole day walking about the fields with guns and dogs," Darcy replied graciously, wondering how on earth he was going to manage to get her alone.

Cassandra looked pleased by his compliment and she actually rewarded him with a little smile.

Jane, however, pretended to be stricken by his flowery remarks. "Oh, that *is* too bad," she said. "For now that you are recovered from your injury I had myself hoped to show you some of the countryside hereabout, if you were of a mind to walk. All the loveliest spring blossoms are just coming into bloom in the far meadows," she added. "Or so I have been told."

"That is true," Cassandra said, jumping eagerly into the conversation. "And we have heard they are wonderfully colorful this year."

"Well, of course, there is nothing that I'd like better than a pastoral walking tour with an agreeable guide," Darcy quickly said, backtracking to cover his blunder and realizing at the same time from Jane's self-satisfied smirk that she had led him straight into a verbal trap just to see how he would manage to extricate himself.

"Then it is settled." Jane laughed, clapping her hands. "We shall go out to see the flowers of the fields." Turning to Cassandra she put on a hopeful look. "Oh, Cass, please say that you will join us."

"Jane, you *know* I cannot," Cass replied testily, evidently not taken in for a moment by her sister's transparent manipulations. "For I have promised the vicar to see after the altar cloths at the church today."

Jane appeared to be devastated by her reply. "Oh, poor Cass! I completely forgot," she cried.

But her dark eyes sparkled with shared mischief, and she shot Darcy a conspiratorial look, then turned back to Cassandra. "To make it up to you, dear sister, I shall gather for your bedroom the loveliest spring bouquet that has ever been seen," she promised.

Having finished their tea and exchanged pleasantries with Cassandra about the extraordinarily fine spring weather and the healthful benefits to be gained from robust exercise in the clean country air, Jane and Darcy walked side by side down a quiet country lane.

"You are so bad," Darcy told her, "deceiving your poor sister that way."

Jane laughed and skipped on ahead of him to examine a patch of delicate pink wild flowers she spied growing alongside a crude stile set into a wooden fence. "You do not know my sister at all if you think she was deceived," she laughed, waiting for him to catch up. "The two of us planned the whole intrigue together so that you and I could be alone."

She placed a finger to her lips and said in a stage whisper, "You see, sir, my sister believes that we are lovers."

Darcy wanted to reply to that, but when he caught up to Jane she immediately stepped onto the stile and, climbing to the top of the fence, pointed across the long, open meadow. "The place where you were found by the farmers should not be far. Just at the end of this field, I believe."

He climbed over the fence and helped her down to the damp, grassy sod on the other side.

"Do you think you shall be able to return to your time as easily as you arrived?" she asked, holding onto his arm just a bit longer than necessary.

"I don't know," he said as they began to walk through the damp grass. Halfway across the meadow Darcy stopped and turned to face her. "Jane, about last night . . ."

Something like pain flickered behind her dark eyes and she suddenly broke away and ran ahead of him toward a low stone wall overhung with trees. "Oh, look!" she called. "This must be the very spot."

Darcy followed her to the wall and looked up at the distinctive high arch formed by the branches. He gingerly placed his hand on the neatly stacked stones, noticing that the afternoon sun had warmed them. "Yes," he said after a moment of silence, "this is it."

Jane sat on the wall and turned her head to gaze through the arched overhang at the perfectly ordinary-appearing meadow on the other side. "How are you to return?" she asked, knitting her brows as if she were at her piano contemplating a difficult musical composition.

He looked over the wall into the adjoining meadow and his hopes for a simple return to his own world withered. "I haven't the faintest idea," he admitted.

Stooping, he picked up a twig fallen from one of the trees and experimentally tossed it over the wall. It landed on the other side with a soft plop and lay there in the grass, exactly as one might expect a piece of thrown wood to lay. He could detect nothing at all out of the ordinary.

"Perhaps if you actually went across to the other side," Jane suggested.

Darcy thought about that for a moment, and then he stepped up and across the wall. But once again nothing extraordinary happened. He was simply standing on the other side. He looked at her and shook his head. "Nope!"

"Nope!" Jane laughed. "I must remember that word. For it matches perfectly your expression at this moment."

Feeling foolish, Darcy quickly clambered back over to her side. As he stood in the other field it occurred to him that if he had somehow managed to step back into his own time at that instant he would never have seen her again.

"Anyway, I can't go back without Lord Nelson ... my horse," he added, anxious to cover his dismay at the near blunder.

"Sir, I did not think you were referring to Lord Nelson, the hero of Trafalgar," Jane teased. She gave him a dazzling smile, obviously not at all displeased that he was safely back with her, for the moment at least. "I remember how shocked I was when you told me that your horse was named after my England's greatest naval hero," she said, "especially with poor Lord Nelson not long dead from a French soldier's bullet."

She paused then and her tone turned more serious. "I am sorry to say that was my first impression of you, Mr. Darcy.

Such arrogance, I thought. But, then, what else was one to expect from an uncivilized American?"

Darcy winced at his dimly recalled memory of their painful first encounter. "I must have been quite a shock to you," he said. "Brought dirty and bleeding into your house with my strange clothes, demanding to use your phone . . ."

He slowly placed his hand on hers. "Jane, I do hope I've managed to undo at least some of the unfavorable impressions you formed of me those first days."

"Oh, yes, Mr. Darcy," she replied, smiling. "You have managed quite well. In fact, I confess that I shall not be at all happy to see you go. For Chawton has never before been so exciting a place—"

Jane's voice broke and she turned away to prevent him from seeing the tear glistening on her cheek.

He raised his hand to her shoulder and gently turned her until they were again facing. "Jane . . . I wish we had met under different circumstances," he breathed. "Knowing you has been the most wonderful experience of my life."

"And of mine." She sniffled bravely, smiling and brushing away the tear with the back of her hand. "For now I know at least a little of those tender passions and emotions which I have so often and yet so poorly attempted to describe in prose."

Touched by the depth of feeling in her words, Darcy slipped his arms around her and held her close to him. "Has it really meant that much to you?" he asked. "The few hours we spent together last night?"

Jane looked up at him with an enigmatic smile. "Last night and the three days and nights before that, as you lay in my bed, watching my every move and listening to me speaking my heart."

He pulled back, surprised. "You knew?"

"I cannot say I knew absolutely that you were not always asleep or in the deep swoon you pretended," she told him. "But there were many times when I imagined that I felt eyes

upon me when no one else was present. And poor Mr. Hudson's perplexity over your failure to awaken had at last led me to suspect that you might not be so grievously wounded as you seemed."

At the mention of the bumbling old doctor's name Darcy laughed. "Let's not forget that it was *poor* old Mr. Hudson who finally convinced me I had better awaken soon, or be treated to a visit from his pack of stinging wasps. Is that really a standard medical treatment for people in coma?"

Jane broke into a grin. "Actually, no," she laughed. "Mr. Hudson confided to me his suspicion that you were perhaps more alert than you pretended and the dear old man assured me that in his long experience the mere mention of stinging wasps often worked miracles in restoring disingenuous patients to health."

Darcy's face turned red. "So I even underestimated him," he said with chagrin. "You were absolutely right when you called me arrogant. For I stupidly assumed that the changed social customs and advanced technology of my time somehow made me superior in yours. I forgot all about wisdom and intelligence. Can you ever forgive me, Jane?"

She replied by lifting her face to his and softly kissing his lips. "I *have* forgiven you, dear Mr. Darcy, for I do not know of another man in this world who would admit such imperfections in himself to a mere woman. Nor can I think of one who, knowing the terrible and dangerous secrets of the future as you must, would not be tempted to exploit them to his own advantage."

She kissed him again, then stepped back and, glancing. the arch of trees above the wall, asked brightly, "When you think you shall leave?"

Darcy shook his head, for although he was not ready admit the possibility, even to himself, he was not at all cer that he *could* leave. "I'm not sure," he replied evasively. ' portal, or whatever it is, doesn't seem to be working a moment."

He closed his eyes, trying to remember every detail of the moments leading up to his leap through the arch. "I remember the sunrise was filling the space between the wall and the trees with blinding light," he said, "so maybe that had something to do with it. I'll try at dawn tomorrow."

They sat on the wall in silence. Darcy fingered the medallion he'd worn since his mother had given it to him for his sixteenth birthday. He reached around and unhooked the clasp. Putting the medallion in the watch pocket of his waistcoat, he took Jane's hand in his and turning it up placed the chain into her palm. Jane picked up the beautifully wrought necklace and looked at him questioningly.

"I heard you and Cassandra talking about the cross your brother sent and how you didn't want to wear it on a ribbon," he confessed.

Jane was overwhelmed, "Oh, Mr. Darcy, it is beautiful."

He took the chain and draped it around her throat, bestowing small, gentle kisses to the back of her neck. Jane turned to face him again. She gently touched the necklace. "So near my heart, as you shall always be."

Darcy leaned over and kissed her. They lingered on the wall in the warm afternoon sun of that long-ago year, exchanging secrets neither of them had ever revealed to another living soul. Exchanging kisses as well. For both were acutely aware that their miraculous but cruelly brief allotment of time together was nearly spent.

Chapter 30

The lengthening shadows of late afternoon were creeping across the narrow country lane as Jane and Darcy walked side by side to Chawton Cottage. They stopped by the front gate, where Lord Nelson had stood patiently plucking bits of greenery from around the gateposts while awaiting his master's return.

"Will you stay another night at my brother's house?" Jane was looking at him quizzically, though they had not again discussed his leaving during the entirety of the afternoon or the long walk back to the cottage.

"No, I think that's unwise," he replied. "I'll thank Edward at supper for his hospitality and tell him I'm off to London. Then I'll find a place to wait for the sunrise."

Jane suddenly turned and scrutinized the cottage to be certain that Cassandra hadn't come out, then she stepped closer and entreated him in a breathless whisper. "Let me wait with you."

"Jane, are you sure you—"

"Know what I am doing?" she impatiently interrupted. "Yes, I know precisely what I am doing." She smiled and he saw the familiar mischievous sparkle come into her eyes. "I am greedy for dreams, sir . . . If you will share a few more with me."

Resisting the temptation to take her in his arms in full

view of the entire sleepy village and her taciturn sister, whom he suspected was peeking out from behind the lace curtains that graced the cottage's upper windows, Darcy bowed formally. "The same place as last night, then?" he intoned, his voice barely audible above the clucking of an unseen hen.

Returning his formal bow with a slight inclination of her head, "The same place," she whispered. "Come again at twelve, so I do not have to explain to Cass." A secret smile touched the corners of her mouth. "A little way into the wood there is a small summer house where we can go to be out of the damp. Perhaps there, in comfort, we shall play again at being lovers, and you may show me more of what I wish to know."

"Jane," he whispered, remembering what Frank had said to him the night before, about her fragile heart, "you do realize that we will likely never see one another again after tonight?"

"Tonight is all I ask," she replied, her gaze unwavering.

"Until midnight, then."

The sun was fast sinking toward the horizon as Darcy rode Lord Nelson back through the gates of Chawton Great House and down to the stables. He had scarcely dismounted and led the horse inside when a rough hand darted out of the shadows and unceremoniously jerked him into a stall. For a heart-stopping moment Darcy feared that Captain Francis Austen had heard of his visit to Jane and had returned to keep his murderous promise.

Then, as his eyes gradually adjusted to the dim light, Darcy saw the frightened face of Simmons anxiously regarding him. "Simmons! What the hell—" he exclaimed angrily.

The young groom's nervous eyes darted to the open stable door at their backs. "Thank God I caught you, sir," he said in a tremulous voice. "You mustn't go up to the house again."

"Why? What's happened?"

"An express come for Master Edward this afternoon," Simmons breathlessly reported, "from Mr. Henry, his brother, the banker in London," he said by way of explanation. "He'd been making some inquiries about you and wrote back to say it's a well known fact that the American horse breeder Mr. Fitzwilliam Darcy of Pemberley Farms has never set foot in England."

Simmons paused for breath and Darcy could see that the poor fellow was genuinely terrified by this unexpected turn of events. "They know you ain't the gentleman from Virginia, sir," he concluded.

"Damn!"

"That ain't the worst of it," Simmons continued. "Mr. Edward has sent word to the captain in Portsmouth, asking him to return here straightaway with a squad of his marines. I think they mean to arrest you for a spy, sir."

Simmons's eyes again darted anxiously to the open stable doors behind them. "You must leave here now," he warned. "They could come for you at any moment."

"Yes," Darcy quickly agreed. "But there's something I need first, Simmons. Do you have a pen and paper?"

Simmons stared at him and slowly shook his head, as if the American was mad to be requesting writing materials at a time like this. "Them things is kept mostly up at the big house, sir," he answered. "You'd better go on now. Or it'll be the worst for both of us if they catch you here."

Darcy struggled with his conscience for a moment. Of course, he did not want to implicate the affable young groom in his now-dangerous troubles with the vengeful Captain Austen. But neither could he simply flee without sending some word to Jane, letting her know what had happened. Removing the gold medallion from his waistcoat pocket, Darcy pressed it into Simmons's hand.

"You have my solemn word of honor that my name is Fitzwilliam Darcy and that I'm no spy," he assured the frightened young man, "but I need your help."

"This must be worth fifty pounds!" Simmons gasped, feeling the weight of the gold in his hand.

"It's yours if you'll help me," Darcy said. "I only need to write a note. Then I want you to deliver it for me and hide me until nightfall."

Simmons slowly nodded and pocketed the medallion. "This is a matter of the heart, then, is it, sir?" he asked in a tone that made it clear he believed that he understood completely what was going on. "I warned you that the captain had a fearful temper. He's a dangerous man, sir. If he thinks you've been making free with his sister, there's no telling what he'll do."

Darcy nodded, more than willing to let Simmons assume naively that the entire matter was simply a case of brotherly revenge and had nothing whatever to do with spying.

At Chawton Cottage Jane was sitting before the dressing table in her bedroom, gazing thoughtfully into the depths of the silvery mirror.

The moment after Darcy had left her at the gate, Cassandra, who had indeed been watching them from an upstairs window, had rushed out of the cottage, demanding to know what they had discussed and what had happened during their long trek through the fields. Jane had evaded her sister's pointed questions and injured looks by pleading a headache and retiring immediately to her room. Though as she had watched the tall American riding out of sight it was her heart and not her head that ached, and she had sought solitude to analyze the unfamiliar sensation in private.

Her only consolation since parting from Darcy was his promise to share with her the night ahead. But when that was over, Jane wondered, what would then become of her and her poor aching heart?

At first she had allowed herself to indulge the wild fantasy of traveling forward into his time with him. It was in fact something they had jokingly discussed this very afternoon, after he had tried and failed to return by crossing the stone wall.

"Perhaps you should hold my hand and we'll jump together," he had said. "Then you can see for yourself what a terrible place the future will be."

She had laughed along with him, not daring to voice the thought that had been in her heart at that moment, that no future could be so terrible with him in it.

But she was never quick enough to say the things that were in her heart at the most important moments. Instead she waited until minutes or even days later, when the moment was past and there was no longer anyone there to hear them.

"Then, when it is far too late," she confided to her reflection in the mirror, "but loathe to waste my sage replies and witty repartee, I transfer them to the mouths of my always-brilliant Miss Elizabeth Bennet and her sisters."

Even though Jane imagined herself making a speech from which Darcy would easily have divined that she would gladly travel with him into the future, she was not really certain that she could actually survive in the fast, exotic new world he had described.

For, although the concept of rocketing about the earth at indescribable speeds while being served microwaved dinners and cocktails—whatever those things might be—was endlessly thrilling to her, the idea that most romantic relationships were fleeting, that ordinary women often appeared naked, or nearly so, in public places, that they openly approached desirable men with invitations to intimate dinners, swore like sea cooks if they felt like it, demanded sexual satisfaction and prevented unwanted pregnancies by the simple expedient of swallowing tiny tablets were all anathema to Jane's quiet, romantic spirit.

"I fear that I could never fully adapt myself to such a life," she sadly confessed to her wan mirror image. "How much nicer it would be," she mused, "if dear Darcy was unable to return to his own time and forced instead to remain here in mine with me."

The moment she spoke those words, however, Jane realized what she was asking of the fates. "Oh, no," she exclaimed, shocked at her own selfishness, "I did not mean that. For there is no more a place for him in this world—much of which I can see in his expressions he finds loathsome and barbaric—than there is for me in that jangling, noisy, electric place that he calls home."

She sat and stared morosely at her reflection a while longer, concentrating on remembering the taste of Darcy's kisses. Fingering the gold chain he'd draped around her neck only an hour earlier, she thought of the rare gentleness she had discovered in him, and worrying that by imposing her wishes upon him on this final night—a night during which she would dare to become his lover in the flesh as well as in spirit—she might be setting them both upon an emotional course from which there would be no turning back, a course that she knew he feared.

And because she could never speak the words that would let him know why she was willing to expose them both to that monumental risk, Jane turned, as she always had in times of strife, to her pen; for she had determined to send another message to Darcy at Chawton Great House before their midnight meeting. And she prayed that he would read it and understand.

Taking a pristine sheet of vellum from the drawer of her vanity table, she spread it on the polished wood and began to write.

My Dearest Darcy,
    Though you agreed that I might wait with you tonight, your expression told me you feared I might be breaking my heart for a love that can never be . . .

At that very moment Darcy was in the saddle, leaning over Lord Nelson's neck to duck under the low-hanging limbs of passing trees. He was following Simmons through a stand of thick forest, along an overgrown path that was just barely discernible among the weeds.

Presently the path opened into a small, sunny clearing. Simmons reined his horse to a halt before the ruins of a dilapidated thatched structure and jumped lightly to the ground.

"This is the old gamekeeper's hut," the groom told Darcy. "Nobody's lived in it since Chawton Cottage was built, back in the times before I was born. You should be safe enough out here till night comes, sir."

Darcy dismounted and quickly surveyed the tumbledown hut. Half of the graying thatched roof had fallen in from neglect, and he could see through the open doorway that the interior was jumbled with piles of leaves and a few sticks of broken furniture scattered around a blackened stone hearth.

Glad that he would not be spending more than a few hours in the dismal place, he looked about the tiny yard for someplace to write. He spotted a huge silvered tree stump a few yards from the door, and on its flat surface he laid out the paper and other writing implements that Simmons had procured for him from Chawton Great House. He wrote:

Dearest Jane,
    The Captain has found me out. I am being forced to go into hiding immediately. But if I am able, I shall still be waiting at the same spot tonight. Then you will know everything you wish to know.
                                                    F. Darcy

He blew on the ink to dry it, then folded the hastily composed note and sealed it with a blob of hot wax dribbled from the end of a small red candle that the increasingly nervous groom had impatiently lit for him.

When he was finished, Darcy addressed the letter to Jane at Chawton Cottage and thrust it into Simmons's hands. "Deliver this to Miss Austen," he instructed the groom, "but under no circumstances are you to tell her where I am. I will not risk her being caught with me. If she wishes to write a reply you may bring it back here. But only if you consider the way to be safe."

The younger man nodded his understanding and vaulted up into his saddle. He wheeled his horse about to go, then stopped, seeming to remember something. "Here's a bit of bread and cheese I nicked off Cook as I passed through the kitchen," he said, withdrawing a bulging linen napkin from his coat and passing it down to the American.

Darcy smiled gratefully and took the food. "Thank you, Simmons." He reached up to clasp the groom's strong, work-hardened hand in his own. "You're a good man."

Simmons grinned and looked at their clasped hands. "You be a good man yourself, sir, I'll affirm," he replied, "and the only proper gentleman what ever thought he wasn't too high and mighty to shake with the likes of Harry Simmons."

Withdrawing his hand from Darcy's grip the youngster touched the brim of his tall hat in a jaunty salute. "Good luck to you, then, sir. I'll be back with a message from the lady, soon as I can."

With that, Simmons ducked low in the saddle and rode away at a fast trot, quickly disappearing beneath the drooping trees.

For a long time after the groom had departed Darcy sat on the stump before the hut, watching the deep green woods fill with shadows. Though food was the last thing on his mind, his grumbling stomach reminded him that he'd eaten nothing since breakfast but one of the tiny barley cakes that Cassandra had served with tea.

Now, mostly out of curiosity, he unfolded the napkin that Simmons had given him, discovering inside a large chunk of coarse dark bread and a palm-sized wedge of hard cheese the color of sunflower petals. Biting into the bread, which tasted something like Jewish rye, Darcy realized that he was ravenously hungry and he quickly devoured it, alternating with bites of the savory cheese.

Chapter 31

Jane had just sealed her letter when she heard the sounds of a rider ringing the bell at the gate below. Downstairs, she could hear Maggie muttering and then her clumping footsteps as the irritated housekeeper hurried, fussing, to the door.

"Letter for Miss Austen," came the breathless voice of the rider.

"*Which* Miss Austen?" Maggie inquired imperiously. "There's two of them here, you know."

Laying down her letter, Jane went downstairs to the front door and saw the housekeeper glaring at the flushed face of young Harry Simmons, whom she recognized as a groom from her brother's stables. "All right, Maggie," she interjected. "Leave it to me."

Huffing at the outlandish idea of a lady taking her own letter, much less engaging in conversation with a sweating stableman, Maggie shrugged and stomped away. Jane took the letter, tore it open and quickly read the short message. Alarmed at the news that Darcy had gone into hiding, she looked directly into Simmons's honest blue eyes.

"Simmons, do you know where Mr. Darcy has gone?" she quietly asked him.

The nervous young servant lowered his gaze to the ground and shuffled his feet on the doorstep. "I'm, uh, not sure, miss," he replied evasively. "That is, he made me promise I would not say, for he feared you would try to go there."

Jane scrutinized the man's face, searching for some sign of guile. But she succeeded only in making young Harry Simmons look even more uncomfortable than he already was. "Wait here!" she commanded, then turned without another word and went into the cottage. A moment later she was back with her newly written letter.

"Please see that Mr. Darcy gets this letter," she said. "It is very important."

"Yes, miss. I'll try my best." Simmons climbed up onto his horse and was on the point of leaving when a troop of a dozen mounted Royal Marines thundered by on the road to Chawton Great House. The dust of their passage had not yet settled when a heavy coach went past, traveling in the same direction. Inside, the two astonished watchers glimpsed the flushed face of Captain Francis Austen.

"Oh Lord!" Simmons breathed. "They're coming for him."

"Go to Mr. Darcy now and warn him that my brother has returned," Jane ordered. "Hurry, Simmons! Please hurry. And tell him that I shall be waiting at midnight in the wood behind the cottage."

Simmons dug his heels into the ribs of his horse and rode off at a fast gallop across the fields.

Still stunned by the unexpected and potentially deadly development of her brother's return Jane stood trembling by the gate until Cass, who had heard the commotion of the passing troop, came out and touched her shoulder. "Jane, what is it?" she asked.

"Oh, Cass," she cried, turning to look at her sister with tear-filled eyes, "I think I have killed him with my foolish meddling."

Sitting in the lonely forest clearing with Lord Nelson grazing nearby, Darcy had nothing to do but anxiously wait for Simmons to return with a message from Jane. For there was little doubt in his mind that she would respond to his urgent note with one of her own.

Darcy pictured her reading his scrawled words, then dashing off a few hurried lines of her own, reaffirming her desire to meet him at midnight in the quiet wood. The only question in his mind was whether he should actually go to the appointed place, assuming, of course, that Frank and his squad of marines did not find him in the meantime.

In fact, Darcy actually believed that the possibility of his being captured by Jane's brother was fairly remote. Instead, he guessed, that when he didn't return to Chawton Great House by nightfall, Edward and Frank would simply assume that he had done the logical thing and fled to nearby London, where he could easily lose himself among the masses of the great teeming city that Jane had described in detail for him that afternoon.

Somehow the American doubted seriously that her two aristocratic brothers would waste very much time searching for him in the dark among the scattered fields and hedgerows surrounding the estate.

If all went well, then, he decided, and no sign of an organized pursuit had developed by midnight he would still go to Jane. Of course, he told himself, he would approach the appointed meeting place with the greatest possible caution. And only after he had ruled out the possibility that her brothers were lying in wait for him would he go to spend the few precious hours until dawn with her.

Though Darcy still worried about the possible physical dangers that their meeting posed to Jane, as well as the emotional effect that his leaving might have, especially should their relationship become more intimate than it already had, he was determined to carry out her wishes and go to her.

Far too often since he had entered her world, Darcy reminded himself, he had been guilty of making false and arrogant presumptions.

He was determined not to repeat that same error again.

For Jane Austen had made it crystal clear that she wanted to be with him, if only for a little while. And God knew he wanted to be with her one last time as well.

He allowed himself a grim smile. Because, of course, he was assuming—had to assume—that, come the dawn, he would ride Lord Nelson to the arched tree limbs above the stone wall where, by the same unknown process that had brought him to the year 1810, he would magically leap back into his own time.

And if he could not return?

If his trip into the past had been a one-way ticket?

Darcy's conscious mind refused to seriously contemplate the unthinkable answers to those questions. Although he realized that it was recklessly irresponsible of him not to have made some basic plan for the very real possibility that he might be permanently locked into this world, he could not in fact even bear to consider the reality of such a fate.

If he was doomed to remain here, he knew, he would not dare to approach Jane Austen again. For he would be an outlaw, a marked fugitive relentlessly hunted by her vengeful brothers, forced to run to the farthest outposts of civilization merely to survive.

Darcy could imagine only one fate worse than returning to his own chaotic and frenzied time without Jane Austen, and that was to be trapped in this one, where she still lived and breathed, unable to be with her.

He was shaken from his grim reverie as Lord Nelson abruptly stopped nibbling at the shoots of tender spring grass growing around the wall of the ruined hut and raised his magnificent head, snorting softly in the breeze.

Alarmed, Darcy looked up at the agitated horse. Then he, too, heard the sounds that had startled the animal. From somewhere in the distance came the faint drumming of hoofbeats and the cries of shouting men. Feeling his blood suddenly run cold, the American got to his feet and, pushing aside drooping branches and tangled brambles of undergrowth, he walked a little ways through the trees. At the edge of the wood he stopped and cautiously peered out into an open meadow.

To his horror Darcy saw a line abreast of perhaps a dozen armed-and-uniformed men riding directly toward his hideaway, their sabers extended, the polished blades flashing brightly in the orange rays of the setting sun.

Without a moment's hesitation Darcy retreated back through the wood, making his way in seconds to the collapsed hut. Leaping onto Lord Nelson's back, he shouted to the great black stallion, urging him into a full gallop.

Branches and small limbs lashed his face and arms as he drove the powerful horse crashing through the trees. Breaking out into the meadow, Darcy angled sharply away from the approaching horsemen, praying they would not see him in the dying light. Before he had gone ten yards, however, he heard a new shout raised behind him.

Turning in his saddle, Darcy recognized the flushed features of Frank Austen at the head of the military formation. The captain was pointing his saber directly at him, rallying his men to follow. The line of horsemen wheeled about, urging their mounts to the chase. From the corner of his eye the fleeing American saw two of the mounted soldiers unslinging long flintlock rifles from their shoulders.

Without waiting to see any more Darcy aimed Lord Nelson toward a low hedgerow and prepared to jump. A shot rang out, then another, as the horse leaped and landed awkwardly in the next field.

Crouching low in the saddle Darcy pushed the speeding stallion onward, pressing his face hard against the animal's muscular neck. "Come on, Nelson, old boy," he shouted into the wind, "give it everything you've got!"

The magnificent creature increased his stride, swiftly pulling away from their pursuers until he splashed through a muddy ditch and into another meadow and was suddenly slowed by the softer ground.

Looking ahead Darcy saw the fiery ball of the setting sun blazing through the distinctive arch formed by the pair of tall trees overhanging the low stone wall. "There it is, boy!" he shouted as a full volley of shots rang out behind them, tearing muddy gouts in the turf to either side. Turning back to look over his shoulder he saw Frank Austen at the head of the pack not fifty paces behind him and quickly closing the gap. The captain's face was contorted with rage and he was screaming an epithet that was lost in the thunder of hooves.

Darcy raced across the emerald green turf to the very verge of the field bounded by the low stone wall, riding hell-bent into the sun. Though he assumed it was impossible to leap back into his own time before sunrise, he prayed that a jump through the narrow arch might at least intimidate and slow his pursuers, who would have to follow in single file.

The wall was approaching fast. At the last possible instant and with no more time to think, Darcy leaned forward, forced to squeeze his eyelids shut to avoid being blinded by the dazzling light.

He braced himself as he felt Lord Nelson's hooves leave the ground.

They were airborne for several instants, during which he clearly heard the thumping of his own heart over Frank Austen's screamed warning for him to stop or be shot dead.

The sound of Austen's voice died away, as if someone had quickly dialed down the volume on a too-loud radio. Lord Nelson's front feet hit the ground with a bone-jarring jolt and Darcy opened his eyes. Reining the huffing horse to a halt he turned and looked back over the wall that they had just cleared. In the final rays of the dying sun he saw nothing but dissolving shadows filling an empty meadow.

In the distance he heard the rumble of an engine and turned to see a yellow-painted farm tractor coming toward him, its lights turned on against the gathering gloom. He waved and waited until the vehicle reached him and a red-faced man yelled over the top of the black steering wheel.

"Here now! What're you doing in my field? I haven't sp
all day planting this seed for you to be tramping on it w
your bloody great horse."

Barely trusting himself to reply, Darcy opened his mou
to ask for directions to his friends' rented country house.

The shriek of a low-flying fighter jet from the near
NATO base obliterated his eager words.

Chapter 32

" And so I had returned."

Darcy was standing at the open French doors in the Rose Bedroom, looking out at the first golden rays of the sun rising over Pemberley Farms. Eliza got softly to her feet and went to stand beside him.

Almost whispering, she gently said, "So you lost her."

Quizzically, "I beg your pardon?"

Her heart went out to him. "Your last meeting with Jane never took place?"

He shook his head, still looking into the distance. "No. I never saw her again. And, as far as I can tell, the entire incident was never spoken of by anyone in the Austen family. There's no mention of Jane Austen having ever met anyone remotely resembling me, at least not that I've been able to find in any family archive or historical record."

He paused, and then turned to Eliza. "The only hint that something might have happened is that, according to several of her biographers, Jane left Chawton for several months immediately after May 12, 1810. But until her first letter to me turned up in an estate sale two years ago I was unable to find any documentation that anything I have told you really happened."

Smiling he added, "So now you see why I said that I spent a very long time doubting my own sanity. When that first letter turned up in London in a huge collection of unrelated documents it had already passed through several hands. So although it couldn't be traced to a specific source, it gave me hope because it proved I had actually been there."

Darcy smiled again. "Then you turned up with more substantial proof that it was all completely true, just as I'd remembered it."

"Well, at least you know that she got the letter you sent Simmons to deliver," Eliza said.

"Yes, and the unopened letter must be her reply. Do you understand now why I said that letter was meant for me?"

Eliza walked out onto the balcony, considering all that he had told her. She slowly nodded her head and gazed into the sunrise. "So it is really possible to travel back in time." Her voice sounded small and full of wonder.

Darcy joined her at the hand-carved railing and shrugged. "Theoretically, yes. As I explained to Jane, time travel is possible; at least if you're willing to believe Einstein, Hawking and a few thousand other eminent thinkers. "*How* it's done is still the big question," Darcy said. "The only reported incidents I was able to discover in my research have been like mine—accidents."

"Unbelievable!" Eliza yawned and felt her eyelids suddenly growing heavy, the cumulative result of her emotional turmoil and nearly twenty-four hours without sleep.

"I really do believe you, Fitz," she explained dreamily. "But you have to admit it all seems so incredible. My mind is reeling."

Darcy nodded, then unexpectedly leaned over and kissed the top of her head. "You must be exhausted," he said quietly. "Try to get some sleep now. We can talk more about all of this tomorrow."

"Tomorrow is already here," she reminded him, pointing to the glowing ball of the rising sun. "I think you'd better try to get some sleep yourself. Your big day is beginning."

"God yes! I almost forgot the ball!" He reached down and

touched her hand, then walked through the bedroom to the door and opened it to leave. She spun around.

"Fitz!"

Darcy stopped and looked back at her.

"Thank you for trusting me with this," Eliza said, raising her fingers and blowing him a kiss.

He smiled and mimed catching it, pressing it to his lips. Then he closed the door and was gone.

Pausing only long enough to drop her clothes in an untidy heap on the floor, Eliza collapsed across the rose-colored satin coverlet and closed her eyes.

But sleep would not come. Seconds later, she opened her burning eyes again and gazed across the dimly lit room to the alcove. The haunting portrait of Rose Darcy seemed to be questioning her from the shadows.

"Yes, of course I'm falling in love with him," Eliza said defiantly. "Who in their right mind wouldn't? And, if it makes any difference, I'd gladly fill that stupid bathtub of yours with rose petals or whipped cream or whatever else turns him on and hurl myself naked into it this second. But do you really think that would be enough to make him fall in love with me?"

As she expected, the enigmatic beauty in the portrait offered no answers to that one.

Flopping angrily onto her stomach, Eliza buried her face in the soft, soft fabric and wondered miserably what she was supposed to do now.

How was she—or anyone, for that matter—supposed to compete with Jane Austen?

Alone for the first time that day, Darcy lay on the bed staring at the vaulted ceiling of his bedroom. When he had begun the story of his meeting with Jane Austen it had been for strictly mercenary reasons: he wanted the letters. He had anticipated that it would be very painful to reveal the details of his experience; but as he lay there trying to rest he was surprised that it was actually a relief to have shared it, and luckily with someone who had not dismissed it out of hand. Eliza believed.

Eliza. He saw her face behind his closed eyelids, remembering the way her hair fell softly to her shoulders. He chuckled to himself; she made him feel good. In fact he had been having sensations since they met that he had been sure would be reserved only for Jane. Sighing, he remembered the thrill and warmth of Eliza's kiss. It had taken a great effort not to envelop her in his arms and smother her with kisses, burying his face in her beautiful hair.

What had stopped him? Was it the feeling of betrayal, as he was trying to convince himself, or was it the fear of loss? The fear of loving and losing again had made him keep his emotions in check for most of his adult life; Jane had been the only one to unlock his heart, until now. And as with Jane he seemed to have little or no control over his roiling emotions with Eliza and it scared him.

In spite of the tumultuous state of his mind, Darcy drifted into a contented sleep with thoughts of Eliza's sweet kiss and gentle touch.

Chapter 33

Eliza awoke beneath the satin coverlet in the huge antique bed, with the sunlit portrait of Rose Darcy gazing down at her from its alcove above the copper tub. Glancing over at the small travel clock on her bedside table she discovered that she had slept through the entire morning and well into the afternoon. "Don't look at me like that," she told Rose Darcy. "I bet you never got up before noon in your life."

Drawn by the sounds of voices and hurrying footsteps from the drive below, Eliza arose and went out onto the balcony. Looking down she saw dozens of workers and volunteers, many of them already attired in period costumes, scurrying in and out of the house with armloads of flowers, baskets and chairs.

Farther out on the lawn the luncheon tables and a buffet were set up as they had been the previous day. "Well, it looks like everything's under control," Eliza muttered. Feeling helpless and disconnected from reality she went off to the luxuriously appointed bathroom where she deliberately took her time showering and washing her hair.

An hour later Eliza passed through the busy house unnoticed by the small army of servants and helpers making last-minute preparations for the ball. Pausing at the closed doors to the grand ballroom, she pushed them open a crack, hoping to catch a glimpse of Darcy. Instead she saw men standing on tall ladders affixing hundreds of candles to sockets in the chandeliers and wall sconces while others polished the parquet floors or draped snowy linen on dozens of small tables set around the perimeter of the room.

When similar inquisitive forays—into the kitchens and the flower-bedecked gallery where arriving guests would be welcomed upon entering the house—turned up no sign of Darcy, Eliza found the front doors and stepped out into the bright summer sunshine.

She had already crossed the lawn to the buffet table when she realized that the only other diners still at lunch were Harv and Faith Harrington. Brother and sister were sitting together at a table, eating and chatting.

"Wonderful!" she murmured, looking frantically for some other direction to take.

Before Eliza could retreat, though, Harv spotted her and cheerfully waved her down. "Aha! Another of the undead has risen at last. Hi, Eliza."

"Hi," she replied, cautiously approaching the pair.

Looking like a cartoon vampire in a way-too-flouncy yellow sundress, Faith pushed her dark wraparound sunglasses up onto her pale forehead and squinted at Eliza through seriously bloodshot eyes.

"*Oh, there* you are, Eliza!" Faith exclaimed, managing to sound as if she'd just discovered a particularly beloved sorority sister. "Harv was telling me I threatened to murder you in your bed last night, you poor thing."

"Well, you didn't specify the exact place . . ." Letting her hunger overcome her sense of self-preservation, Eliza sidled over to the buffet table and began heaping a plate from a marvelous-looking platter of seafood salad and fresh fruit.

Faith rose stiffly from her seat and walked by, pausing to affectionately squeeze the arm of her archrival. "I don't remember a *thing* about last night," she said, smiling. "Isn't that awful?"

Eliza made a sour face. "Positively tragic," she muttered through clenched teeth.

"Well, I absolutely must run now," Faith exclaimed, ignoring the caustic reply. "The caterer is having another nervous breakdown."

"Why don't you give him some of your Prozac?" Eliza suggested under her breath as the blonde flounced away across the lawn in a cloud of filmy petticoats.

Actually, Eliza had briefly considered yelling out the Prozac remark to the loathsome Faith. She was restrained by the ominous sight of a heavy carving knife sticking out of a plump Virginia ham on the table, and had a quick mental flash of the erratic Faith returning to slice up something besides ham.

Turning with her plate Eliza saw that Harv had gotten up and was gallantly pulling out a chair for her. She stomped over to where he stood, slammed her plate onto the table and flopped sullenly into the chair.

"Goodness, you seem a tad overwrought today, Eliza." Harv's big blue eyes were twinkling like a department-store Santa Claus.

"Don't start with me today, Harv," she warned.

"Let me get you some refreshing tea." Harv smiled, backing slowly away from her with his hands in the air. He went over to the beverage table and returned with a tall, frosty glass of iced tea for her and a fresh Bloody Mary for himself.

"Where's Fitz?" she asked, scanning the endless procession of people in and out of the house.

"Off running around somewhere." Harv waved his hand vaguely in the direction of the stables and lowered himself into the chair beside hers. "I doubt if you'll see much of him before this evening. He and his committee of helpers will be all over the place all day long, working like the proverbial pack of beavers."

Eliza began consuming her salad, delicious chunks of cold

lobster and avocado steeped in a wonderful vinaigrette dressing. "Should we be doing something to help them?" she asked, looking toward the busy workforce up at the house.

"Us?" Harv was aghast at the mere suggestion that they join in the work. "Good Lord, no! You are an honored guest and I a mere helpless bungler," he explained. "Our job is to stay out of the way and admire the industry of the others, so they'll all feel properly appreciated."

"Harv, I like you." Eliza found herself laughing in spite of her foul mood.

"Why, thank you, Eliza. I like me, too."

At that moment a pretty young woman in a long blue gown came walking across the lawn toward them. She was carrying a matte-black high-tech portable phone in one hand.

Harv grinned at the newcomer. "Amanda, my love, you are the perfect vision of antebellum splendor," he exclaimed. "However, I must tell you that the telephone spoils the effect entirely."

Amanda, who had obviously weathered previous encounters with Harv, smiled tolerantly at him and addressed Eliza. "Are you Miss Knight?"

Eliza nodded and the pretty young woman handed her the phone. "You have an urgent call," she said, "from your Aunt Ellen in New York."

Harv and Amanda looked on with interest as Eliza frowned and put the phone to her ear, unable to imagine who might have tracked her down at Pemberley Farms. For she had deliberately left her mobile phone turned off in her luggage and, as far as she knew, nobody in New York had Darcy's unlisted number. And she did not have an Aunt Ellen.

"Hello?"

Thelma Klein's graveled voice rasped harshly in her ear. "Eliza, what the hell's going on down there?" the gruff researcher demanded. "You said you were going to call me as soon as you'd talked to Darcy. What did he say?"

Eliza rolled her eyes and glanced over at Harv, who was

busily engaged in examining Amanda's rather ample cleavage. "Oh, hi, Aunt Ellen!" Eliza said brightly. "We're still talking about . . . that business," she told Thelma evasively. "Can I call you back on Monday?"

"Monday? Are you out of your mind?" Thelma's screech was loud enough to make the couple look up from their foolishness. "We're doing the press conference on Monday. Remember?" Thelma hollered. "The people from Sotheby's will be there."

"Right, Aunt Ellen! Okay. I'll see you then," Eliza said in the I-really-can't-talk-now voice she reserved for ending inconvenient telephone conversations.

There was a brief silence on the line, followed by a plaintive meow. Thelma's voice when she came back on was ominous. "Eliza, you're forgetting that you left your damned cat in my apartment. If you hang up on me now I will put Wickham down the garbage disposal. Talk to me."

"I can't really talk now, Aunt Ellen," Eliza said with a grin. "Be sure to give Wickham a big kiss for me. And don't forget his tuna."

Thelma Klein, a lifelong cat fancier, sighed, defeated. "All right, Eliza. I don't know what's going on down there, but I'm willing to guess the handsome Mr. Darcy has been working on your head. I just want you to think about *one thing* before you do anything too stupid," Thelma continued. "Sotheby's called late yesterday to say they're estimating that your unopened Jane Austen letter could go for up to a million and a half dollars."

There was a long pause on the line, then the cranky researcher added, "As long as it *stays* unopened."

"One and a half?" Eliza's voice was a mouselike squeak.

"Yes! And that's straight from Aunt Ellen. So get your butt back up here by Monday," Thelma ordered. "I'll keep the cat alive until then, but that's it."

In her New York apartment Thelma Klein slammed down the phone and scowled at Wickham who was stretched comfortably across the end of her sofa. "What the hell are *you* looking at?" she asked the gray tabby.

When the cat did not immediately answer, Thelma resignedly got to her feet and padded barefoot to the kitchen. "Come on," she said grumpily. "Let's go get some damned tuna. Aunt Ellen's buying."

On the lawn at Pemberley Farms Eliza still sat holding the dead phone, looking slightly stunned.

"I once saw an expression like yours on a ballet dancer who had just wandered into a biker bar," Harv wryly remarked over the salt-encrusted rim of his Bloody Mary.

"Your Aunt Ellen sounds like a real piece of work!" Amanda observed.

The rest of the afternoon Eliza spent alone at the end of the small dock on the lakeshore. Her pad was in her lap and she idly sketched as she considered the astounding news that Thelma had imparted.

A million and a half dollars! A lot of money, she thought. No. Correction: a *whole* lot of money! More money in fact than Eliza Knight or anyone in her family had ever made, or even seen at one time in their entire lives. Combined.

One and a half million dollars for a letter, Eliza marveled, the letter that was now tucked into a pocket of the portfolio she'd casually left lying on the blanket chest in the Rose Bedroom.

Looking down at the sketch she'd been making she studied Fitz Darcy's sea green eyes. His eyes told her everything and nothing at the same time and she hoped by looking into the competent image she had crafted of him she might divine what she was to do next.

He had offered to buy the unopened letter from her at whatever price she named. But would he pay one and a half million dollars? Would Jane's last letter really mean that much to him? And if it did . . . If Fitzwilliam Darcy was willing to pay that much, what did that say about the depth of his attachment to a woman who had been dead for two centuries? More importantly, she wondered, what would it say about his feelings for a slightly addled Manhattan artist?

Putting aside her sketch pad, Eliza closed her eyes and tried to drive away the haunting image of Darcy's face and the faraway, almost reverential quality of his voice as he had related to her the details of his journey into that other time, and of his romantic encounter with Jane Austen.

She opened her eyes and saw a small gray bird sitting on a wooden post beside her. The bird cocked its head to one side and trained a bright eye on her, as though anxiously awaiting her thoughts on the matter of Darcy.

Ignoring the inquisitive creature, Eliza again closed her eyes and was rewarded with a quick mental flash of Jerry encouraging her to be rational for a change, reminding her to think of her personal financial situation, her taxes . . . her own self-interest.

She opened her eyes to find the bird still regarding her. Eliza suddenly laughed aloud at the absolute absurdity of her predicament. The bird chirped and fluffed its wings as the sound of her laughter rolled across the still surface of the lake, echoing back to mock her for her silliness.

Because Eliza knew that Darcy wouldn't fall in love with her, *couldn't* love her, not any more than he loved or could have loved the beautiful but supremely irritating and neurotic Faith Harrington.

Maybe, Eliza miserably reflected, she might have had a chance with him if she hadn't started their relationship by being so deliberately horrible on the Internet—an offense she since had compounded, first by deceit, when she had bluffed her way through the gates of Pemberley Farms, then by ridiculing Darcy's first halting attempts to explain to her why he had to have her letters.

"He can't fall in love with me because I have given him nothing to love," she told the little gray bird, which cocked its head to the other side and appeared to be intensely interested in what she was saying. "And even if I had shown myself to be kind or understanding," Eliza told the bird, "I doubt that it would have made any difference. Because Fitzwilliam Darcy is in love with Jane Austen, and he'll probably always be in love with her.

"Let's face it," she told her small listener, "I don't stand a chance with *my* Mr. Darcy."

She scoffed at herself because of course he was still *Jane Austen's* Mr. Darcy and if he wanted her letter so badly there was nothing to stop him from going to the Sotheby's auction and bidding for it, just like any other love-struck millionaire.

"Besides," she rationalized bitterly, "even if he doesn't buy the letter it's not like the contents are going to stay a secret for very long. Ten minutes after the bidding ends, it will be opened and the whole world will know what it says anyway... maybe."

Obviously dissatisfied with Eliza's reasoning—reasoning that Jerry with his accountant's soul would not have been able to fault—the small bird angrily chirped at her and then flew away into the trees.

Feeling a sudden chill Eliza hastily gathered up her sketch pad and started back toward the house, which in the deepening twilight was beginning to come alive with the glow of candles. As she walked she briefly considered packing up her things and leaving Pemberley Farms immediately. In the frenzy of activity surrounding the opening of the Rose Ball, her departure was hardly likely to be noticed.

It was the coward's way. The easy out. But it would be quick and painless, for her at least.

But in her heart Eliza knew that she didn't have the capacity to be that cruel. Darcy had bared his soul to her, trusted in her wit and imagination to listen and, against all odds and logic, to ultimately believe in his mad, impossible tale.

The very least she could do in return was to face him and inform him of her decision.

Chapter 34

Returning to the candlelit house Eliza slipped past the busy main rooms and made it back to the eerily dark second floor without seeing anyone she knew. When she was safe inside the Rose Bedroom she closed the door behind her and leaned heavily against it with the sinking realization that she had deliberately sneaked upstairs hoping to avoid Darcy.

Facing him was not going to be as easy as she had thought, and again she considered simply packing her things and leaving. It would be simple enough for her to hitch a ride down to the gates in one of the empty carriages that were constantly shuttling back and forth to pick up and deliver arriving guests.

Eliza stood by the door for a minute, thinking it over, forming a clear image of Darcy in her mind.

"No!" she said resolutely. "I will not run from this good and decent man. I will go to his damned ball and I will tell him face-to-face that he can't have my letters. I'm awfully sorry but Jane Austen is his problem, not mine, and he will just have to deal with it."

Her resolve set, Eliza walked to the wardrobe where the green Regency gown that Jenny had helped her choose for the evening had been hanging on the outside of the door.

To her surprise, the emerald gown was not there. She opened the tall wardrobe and looked inside. But, except for the few pairs of jeans and shirts she had brought with her, the wardrobe was empty.

Frowning, Eliza looked around the room. That was when she saw another gown lying across the bed, a flowing, low-cut gown of rose-colored silk so close to the shade of the satin bed coverlet that she had not noticed it before.

Eliza went to the bed and stared down at the exquisite garment. Then, slowly, her eyes lifted to the painting in the alcove. Though the portrait had not changed, Rose Darcy's enigmatic smile now seemed to be directed exclusively at Eliza Knight.

"Oh my God!" she whispered as she continued to gaze at the life-sized likeness of the beautiful Rose in her silken rose-colored gown.

A gown identical to the one that now lay spread on the bed before her.

Eliza whirled about as the bedroom door suddenly opened and Jenny Brown stuck her head into the room. "May I come in?"

Eliza nodded dumbly, then pointed a trembling finger at the bed. "Jenny, look!"

"Yeah." Jenny nodded, smiling. She stepped into the room wearing a spectacularly beaded dress of golden satin that lent a magical glow to her shining ebony skin. "Fitz said he'd like you to wear that one tonight," she said, indicating the gown on the bed.

"Oh, I couldn't!" Eliza gasped.

Jenny shrugged. "Well, then I guess you're going to the ball in your blue jeans, 'cause I went ahead and gave that green dress to one of the hostesses."

Still not understanding, Eliza cautiously lifted the yards of delicate rose-colored silk from the bed. Beneath the gown lay a pair of matching slippers and a petticoat embroidered with wild rose vines. Turning back to Jenny with the dress, she held it up in front of her.

Jenny glanced from Eliza to the painting of Rose Darcy in the alcove and nodded approvingly. "Isn't that something?"

she marveled. "I told Fitz it would probably need to be altered but he said he knew it would fit you."

Eliza looked down and saw that the spectacular gown did indeed seem to have been tailor-made for the contours of her own slender body.

"Pretty amazing when you consider that dress hasn't been worn for almost two hundred years," Jenny continued.

Eliza, who had been only half-listening until that point, stared at her new friend in horror. "This is Rose Darcy's *actual* dress, not a reproduction?"

"Yep, Fitz sent Artie and me up to the museum in Richmond this morning to get it." She laughed at the memory. "I thought we were gonna have to arm wrestle 'em for it. Some stuffy old curator told us it was a priceless historical artifact and that it would be on our heads if anything happened to it."

"Jenny, why would Fitz *do* a thing like this?" she asked, dropping the filmy gown back onto the bed as if her hands had been burned.

Jenny Brown placed her hands on her hips, closed one eye and focused appraisingly on the distraught artist with the other. "Now why do *you* think he did it, Eliza?"

Eliza shook her head helplessly, not daring to confront the only possible explanation that popped into her mind. She looked again at the delicate froth of precious silk and tentatively picked it up. It was so soft that the folds fluttered like feathers falling from her hands. "What if something happens to it?" she whispered.

"What if it does?" Jenny said matter-of-factly. "It's just a dress."

"But . . . you said the museum people told you it was priceless . . ." Eliza stammered.

"Sure," Jenny snorted, "and they also had it draped on some damned dummy in a glass case, like one of their stuffed birds. It was a dead thing up there, Eliza."

Jenny smiled then, her lovely features filling with warmth.

"When you put on that gorgeous gown tonight it will be alive again for the first time in two hundred years." Her eyes flicked up to the face of Rose Darcy silently watching them from the safety of her gilded frame. "Like it was meant to be," Jenny added softly.

Wavering, Eliza continued to hold the nearly weightless gown in her hands, which she noticed were shaking. Her brain was reeling with doubts and all of her carefully reasoned logic had again turned topsy-turvy. The sheer enormity of Darcy's gesture was so overwhelming that she could hardly breathe.

"Why?" she whispered for the second time. "I really don't understand why he would do this, Jenny." Eliza lowered her eyes and her voice fell to a barely audible whisper as she confessed, mostly to herself, "I've been pretty awful to him." She held the shimmering gown before her. "So why would he . . ."

Eliza left the sentence hanging, afraid to give voice to the unreasonable surge of hope that she felt building within her heart.

The other woman simply shook her head and sighed. "Eliza," she said, "let me tell you something about Fitz Darcy. He may be a cautious person when it comes to parceling out his goodness, regard and love, but when he does it's not in small spoonfuls or halfheartedly. And you can believe me when I say that Fitz never does anything with ulterior motives, there is nothing devious about him, everything is open and aboveboard. And there's no stingy little accountant standing by to keep tabs on what he does either. Do you understand what I'm telling you?"

Eliza nodded, a disturbing image of Jerry chastising her for her fiscally unsound impulsiveness and her unbridled flights of fancy surfacing in her mind for just a fraction of a moment.

Several seconds of silence ensued before Eliza could trust herself to speak again. "Jenny, are you saying that you think Fitz likes me?" she asked in a small, tremulous voice.

Jenny's deep, rich laughter echoed off the richly decorated walls of the Rose Bedroom. "*Likes* you! Honey, you are the only woman the man has bothered to even look at for three whole years." She lowered her voice an octave and gave Eliza a knowing wink. "And I have to tell you that I *never* saw him look at *anyone* the way he looks at you," Jenny declared. "Hell, even dumb old Faith can see that. Why do you think she threw that incredible temper tantrum last night?"

Eliza stared at her newfound friend, wishing it could be true. But Jenny had no way of knowing that Fitz was deeply in love with someone else, someone who was dead and gone, but who would live forever in his heart.

"You'd better get dressed now," Jenny said quietly. "I'll be back in half an hour to see if you need any help."

Eliza slowly nodded and watched her go out and close the door. Then she walked over to the floor-length mirror on the wardrobe and again pressed the magical gown to her body.

She returned to the bed, carefully laid out the dress and sat down. Fingering the delicate fabric, Eliza again questioned why Fitz had gone to the trouble of arranging for her to wear it. Jenny's theory notwithstanding, was he simply trying to secure the letters for himself with a bribe? Thinking back over the two days she'd been here, he had done nothing sneaky or underhanded, which was more than she could say about herself. No, from what she could tell he was an honorable man. And in spite of his admission that Jane Austen had initially thought him arrogant, she had seen nothing of it. In fact he was very down-to-earth with no pretensions at all and except for a flare-up of temper, triggered by her own deception, he had been a perfect gentleman, in the truest sense of the word. Everything pointed to its being simply a gracious gesture on his part.

The clock in the hall chimed the quarter hour and roused her from her reverie. Glancing at the clock on the bedside table she went into the bathroom to get ready . . . for whatever the evening might bring.

Chapter 35

Dressed in the antique silk gown, her shining black hair arranged in a loose, flowing style that flattered her long neck and almost-bare shoulders, Eliza stood on the balcony of the Rose Bedroom, gazing down at the torch-lit drive.

From her vantage point she saw a stately procession of horse-drawn carriages, their side lamps glowing like moving jewels in the darkness, wending its way toward the front of the house where costumed attendants awaited.

Somewhere an orchestra was playing a lively tune she had never heard before, flutes and strings predominating.

As each carriage reached the steps of Pemberley House its occupants were assisted out by liveried footmen, and then guided to the entrance by a gowned hostess carrying a silver candelabrum before her.

"Pretty spectacular, wouldn't you say?"

Eliza hadn't heard the bedroom door opening. Now she turned to see Jenny standing at her shoulder.

"It's breathtaking," Eliza agreed, returning her attention to the scene below. "Do you think this was really what Pemberley looked like once upon a time?"

"Once upon a time," Jenny replied, smiling at the timeworn phrase, "Pemberley House looked exactly like this. Thanks to Rose Darcy's diary, which describes the very first Rose Ball down to the smallest detail, everything you see down there has been faithfully reconstructed according to her description, and then repeated every year since."

Eliza stared at her. "They've been holding this ball at Pemberley Farms for more than two hundred years?"

"Except in wartime. During the Civil War the Union Army rode through here and during the Second World War they were rationing food and gas. Every other year there's been a Rose Ball at Pemberley Farms. It's only been a charity event since Fitz started hosting it; before that it was just a society party." Turning back to the room, Jenny said, "We'd better get going now. Don't want you to be late."

Eliza laughed. "How can I be late, when I'm already here?"

Jenny flashed a mysterious smile. "As long as we went to all the trouble to get that dress out of the museum for you, Artie and I figured we ought to put it to good use. So we made a little suggestion to Fitz and he agreed. And now you have an important role to play at tonight's ball."

Eliza felt her knees go suddenly weak. "What role?" she asked suspiciously.

Jenny's smile broadened and she took Eliza by the arm. "Don't you worry about a thing," she said, propelling her smoothly across the room and out into the candlelit corridor. "You don't have any lines to remember. It's what they call in the theater a walk-on part."

"Jenny!" Eliza, suddenly very nervous, stopped dead in her tracks. "What are you talking about? Playing what part?"

"Relax, we're doing it for Fitz."

Terror gripping her, "Doing what? I don't want to do anything but show up at the ball."

Jenny's disappointment was evident. "Didn't you say that you treated him badly?"

Eliza dropped her head, saying grudgingly with some embarrassment, "Yeah."

"Well, this is a chance for you to make it up to him," Jenny said. "It's just a small thing and it will make him happy."

Jenny's tone softened and she looked into Eliza's eyes. "Can't you just trust me on this one and do it because Fitz would like it?"

"Jenny, I'm sorry," Eliza replied, her heart suddenly filled with gratitude for this lovely and intelligent woman's kindness to her, an outsider. With her voice trembling slightly, "What do I have to do?"

"Just do what I tell you," Jenny said with a mysterious smile. "I promise you it will be completely painless." She took Eliza's arm and led her down the corridor and around a corner. They followed another, narrower, corridor—one that Eliza had not noticed before—to a brightly lit landing atop a staircase.

"Where does it go?" Eliza asked, squinting in the sudden glare at the ornate carved railings before her.

"See for yourself." Jenny nudged her to the top of the landing.

Eliza moved forward and found herself looking down into the grand ballroom. The night before, the huge, high-ceilinged room had been lit by only a few flickering candles and so she had not noticed the staircase in the shadows at the far end. And today, when she had peeked briefly into the ballroom through a crack in the door, the stairs had been shielded from her view. Now she saw that they curved gracefully down to the end of the great chamber opposite the double doors.

Tonight Pemberley's ballroom was illuminated by hundreds of candles glittering through the crystals of three large chandeliers that cast a magical glow on the glittering assembly below. As Eliza gazed down into the storybook scene an orchestra in a gallery at the opposite end of the room began to play and the shining floor was filled with the swirl of colorful gowns, elegant tailcoats and dazzling uniforms as the guests of the Rose Ball began to dance.

Enchanted by the marvelous spectacle Eliza could merely stand and watch, unable to imagine what role she could possibly be expected to play in this grand display. She turned and looked back to Jenny for reassurance, but the corridor behind her was empty.

Suddenly, someone down on the dance floor looked up and pointed at her. Following that cue, others began to look up, too. Eliza felt herself verging on panic as the dancing slowly came to a halt and an electric murmur ran through the crowded room. The orchestra fell silent.

Then a familiar figure dressed in gleaming boots and a coat of hunter green stepped out of the crowd and came to the bottom of the staircase.

Like a hero out of a dream, Fitzwilliam Darcy smiled up at Eliza and extended his hand to her.

At the same moment, Artemis Brown stepped onto a small balcony directly across from the landing where Eliza stood. The crowd fell silent as he began to speak in his deep, resonant baritone.

"Ladies and gentlemen," Artie announced, "it is our great honor to present to you Miss Eliza Knight, who this evening is portraying Rose Darcy, the inspiration for the first Rose Ball and the first mistress of Pemberley Farms."

The guests began to applaud and the orchestra softly played a dramatic fanfare as Eliza tentatively placed one satin-slippered foot on the topmost step and slowly descended the stairs toward Darcy.

"In 1795 it was love at first sight for an adventurous Virginia horse breeder named Fitzwilliam Darcy when Miss Rose Elliot, the daughter of a socially prominent Baltimore banker, accompanied her father to the Shenandoah to bargain for several of Pemberley Farms' renowned steeds," Artemis continued. "But when the prosperous young Darcy proposed marriage the beautiful Rose rejected him, citing his rural farm as a poor substitute for the glittering pleasures of the Baltimore society she loved so well."

Halfway down the stairs Eliza paused to gaze regally over the awestruck crowd, inclining her head and rewarding them with a smile. For, as she had begun her descent the turbulent emotions she had struggled with all day seemed to miraculously crystalize and she no longer feared what she must say to Darcy.

Artemis was still speaking as Eliza continued her slow, deliberate progress toward her waiting host. Nearing the foot of the staircase, she raised her hand in anticipation of receiving his touch.

"Determined to win her hand at any price," Artemis read, "young Darcy immediately hired the most prominent architect in the United States and had him set about constructing this fine house. Other trusted individuals were sent off to scour the design salons and art galleries of Europe and the Americas, charged with furnishing the mansion with the finest of everything. And when next Miss Rose Elliot was scheduled to visit Pemberley Farms with her father, Darcy invited the cream of American society to attend a grand ball that he had named in her honor.

"So overwhelmed by her dashing swain's gesture was the lovely Rose that she accepted his proposal of marriage that very evening. And ever after there has been a Rose Ball held at Pemberley Farms."

Reaching the bottom of the stairs at the exact moment that Artie's introduction concluded, Eliza looked directly into Darcy's eyes and smiled. A thrill shot through him as he took her hand in his. As the assembly erupted into applause, he bent and kissed her hand, and then led her to the dance floor.

"Why didn't you tell me about this before?" she asked in a voice so soft that only he could hear.

Darcy grinned happily. "You might've said no."

"I hope you're not expecting me to perform some obscure nineteenth-century line dance now," she replied, smiling for the benefit of his guests. "Because I don't know any."

"The one element of authenticity that we've let slide over the years at the Rose Ball is the dancing," he said as the orchestra began to play. "Everybody seems to want to do the ones they already know, which is why the musicians are now playing a waltz that wasn't even written until the mid-1800s."

"Shocking!" Eliza relaxed and laughed as he took her into his arms and twirled her gracefully around the floor. Dozens of other smiling couples joined in, until the two of them were part of a large and joyous multitude of dancers.

"Fitz, why did you do this, the gown?" Eliza asked, looking up into his smiling eyes.

"You said you liked it," he replied. She smiled to herself and her attempts to rationalize the gesture. She had said she liked it; it was as simple as that.

"Thank you for allowing me to wear it. I'm honored."

"Eliza . . ." he began.

"Before you say anything," she interrupted, "I want you to know that I've come to a decision, about the letters." Eliza slowed and looked around the crowded floor. "I think I'd like you to hear what I have to say in private," she told him.

Darcy nodded and led her off the floor and out through the ballroom doors. "We can go to my study," he suggested.

Eliza shook her head, suddenly feeling slightly dizzy and overwhelmed by all that had happened. "No. I'd like to have some air. Please can we go outside, Fitz?"

Chapter 36

An open carriage was just depositing a quartet of late arrivals at the entrance as Darcy and Eliza stepped onto the torch-lit porch. Lucas, the elderly gatekeeper, stood next to the carriage. He was wearing a red coat and an elegant top hat. "Lovely evening, isn't it Fitz?" Lucas greeted him.

Darcy nodded. "It is, Lucas. Have you got time to take us for a little drive around the property?"

"Why yes, I think we can arrange that," Lucas replied, winking. Smiling at Darcy, he helped Eliza up into the soft leather seat. Darcy got into the carriage and sat opposite Eliza.

Lucas climbed into the driver's seat and clucked softly to the horses, a beautiful pair of matched grays in a gleaming harness rig trimmed in silver, and started them moving down the drive.

Darcy leaned toward Eliza and took her hand, "You must allow me to tell you how lovely you look tonight," he said. "Thanks for indulging Jenny and Artie and making that wonderful entrance to the ball. Rose Darcy herself couldn't have made a better impression on our guests."

Eliza flushed. "Somehow I doubt that," she replied, "but I'll be eternally grateful for the compliment." Darcy released her hand and sat back in the seat, his eyes never leaving hers.

The carriage entered the green tunnel of trees beyond the house. Eliza took a deep breath. "I want you to know that

I've thought this through very thoroughly," she began, "and I won't change my mind."

Eliza searched Darcy's face, unable to read his eyes in the dim glow of the carriage lamps. "Though we hardly know one another at all, I feel that I've come to understand you, Fitz," she continued. "And I know that the reason you wanted my letters so desperately was to learn what Jane thought of you, what she was feeling and, perhaps, to confirm absolutely in your own mind that what happened to you in England three years ago was really true."

Darcy nodded but said nothing.

"But those aren't good enough reasons for me to give the letters to you," Eliza hurried on with her explanation, "because the letters would probably become public anyway and you'd still have what you want."

"Eliza . . ."

She saw the pain registering in Darcy's face as the carriage moved out of the trees and into the light of the rising moon.

"Please," she said gently, "let me finish."

Darcy fell silent and they moved along through a rolling meadow filled with glimmering fireflies.

"Over the past two days I have gradually come to realize a very real truth about you. Sometimes it takes an outsider to see what you cannot see yourself."

He turned his head toward her, his expression grim. "And what is the truth about me, Eliza?"

"Even if there were *no* letters," she told him, "there would be no doubt in my mind that the story you told me actually happened." She paused, watching his brow furrow in confusion. "And there should be no doubt in your mind as to how Jane Austen regarded you after you were gone," she concluded.

"I don't understand," he murmured.

Eliza smiled. "Do not you, sir?" she asked, playfully mimicking the formal aristocratic language of Jane Austen's Regency period. "Fitz, you *are* the essence of Jane Austen's Mr. Darcy in every way. She wrote—or perhaps rewrote—*Pride and Prejudice* to make that character you. And in doing that she created the most romantic character in English literature— only you were real, and she made you real to anyone who's ever read the book."

Darcy fell back against his seat, speechless.

"Now," said Eliza, "for my decision."

"Your decision?" he breathed. "Didn't you just tell me that it was your decision to keep the letters?"

"No, Fitz," Eliza said, reaching into the silk bag she was carrying and removing the sealed letter from Jane Austen. "I only expressed the opinion that you didn't need this," displaying the unopened document, "to confirm anything."

Smiling, she pressed the unopened letter into his hand. "But this is your letter. Jane wrote it to you, and whether it ever becomes public should be your decision alone, not mine."

"Eliza, I . . . I don't know what to say."

"Don't say anything," she said with a smile. Eliza looked around, suddenly aware that the carriage had come to a halt at the far end of the moonlit lake. Lucas was standing up front with the horses, lighting his pipe and gazing off into the distance.

She looked up at the huge, glowing orb of the moon. "I think it's bright enough out here and you've waited a long time, read it . . . now."

Darcy looked up, as if noticing the moon for the first time. "Yes," he said, "I believe it is light enough to read by. And I would like to read the letter now."

He stepped out of the carriage. Then he reached in and took her hand. "We'll read it together," he said. "It belongs to both of us."

Moments later, standing at a spot where a glittering path of moonlight across the water touched the shore, Darcy held up the letter and looked at Eliza. "You're sure you want me to do this?" he asked.

She nodded and he broke the wax seal with a small snap, then unfolded the yellowing paper and began to silently read.

Something fell to the ground at Eliza's feet and lay sparkling in the moonlight. Gathering up the folds of her gown, Eliza bent to retrieve the shiny object.

And then she began to laugh. "Well, I guess it's a good thing I decided not to let Sotheby's auction off this letter after all," she said, holding up Darcy's high-tech plastic business card.

Darcy stared at the holographic Darcy crest gleaming on the surface of the card, and then he, too, began to laugh. The sound of their voices melded, echoing merrily across the lake.

After a moment, Eliza grew serious again. Her mouth had suddenly gone dry and she felt the blood pounding in her temples as she lightly touched the fold of vellum in his hand. "What did Jane say, Fitz?"

"This letter was also written on the day I left," he replied. Holding it up in the moonlight, he began to read aloud.

12 May, 1810

> *My Dearest Darcy,*
> *Though you agreed that I should wait with you tonight, your expression told me you feared I might be breaking my heart for a love that can never be . . .*

Darcy's voice broke and he paused to clear his throat. He began again, his voice stronger now.

> *Oh how wrong you are to think like that. Do you not know that I of all women would gladly trade a single moment of love for a lifetime of wondering what such a moment might have been?*
> *And though you have concerned yourself with my heart, let me now concern myself with yours. For some-where in that faraway world of yours, I know there*

awaits your one true love. Find her, dearest! Find her whatever else you may do . . .

Darcy paused.

"Is that the end?" Eliza asked.

Darcy slowly shook his head. "No, she wrote one more thing," he said.

And when she is found, you must tell her she is your dearest and loveliest desire. Be happy, my love.

Yours forever,
Jane

Eliza watched in stunned silence as Darcy carefully re-folded the letter and slipped it into his coat pocket. Then he looked down at her and moved closer.

An eternity passed there in the moonlight as she waited for him to speak.

At length Darcy smiled and there were tears in his eyes as he lowered his face to hers and whispered, "Dearest, loveliest Eliza . . ."

Eliza smiled and closed her eyes, wondering if this was all just a marvelous dream.